FIRE
WATER

BLACK MAGIC OUTLAW
BOOK FIVE

Domino Finn

Published by Blood & Treasure, Los Angeles
First Edition

Cover Design by James T. Egan of Bookfly Design LLC.

ISBN: 978-1-946-00805-3

DominoFinn.com

FIRE WATER

BLACK MAGIC OUTLAW

BOOK FIVE

Chapter 1

Burning alive's no fun. Of all the ways to go, it sits firmly in my top three never to experience, right between being gutted in a zombification ritual and going for a midnight swim with a mermaid. Bad ideas, all around.

I know from personal experience. The other two are old hat, but fire... fire was new to me. Flames blanketing my flesh, pain flaring through every synapse, brain overloading, giving in to panic and gutless screaming.

Wait, wait, wait. Let me back up. Just a smidge—I promise. We'll get to the burning real soon. After all, you don't know who Cisco Suarez is yet. If I haven't introduced myself, if you aren't privy to all my hopes and dreams— well, you're not really invested in the catching-on-fire part, are you?

So introductions are in order. Thing is, that's easier said than done. My story's not simple, but I can give it the old college try. Here goes:

I'm just your average ex-zombie, ex-hit man shadow charmer on the run.

Okay, that's a mouthful. But it's the plain truth. Even plainer would be if I told you I know magic and have a host of associated problems.

Case in point: I was currently hiding out in the Fontainebleau in Miami Beach. Granted, Millionaire's Row is a pretty swanky place to lie low in, but I'm pretty much rich now. How I came about that cash isn't important. It's enough to say it's more than I can spend. Of course, that didn't stop me from trying. Spend it I did, living in a three-thousand-dollars-a-night luxury vacation suite.

"You're ridiculous," said Evan, who was supposed to be my best friend. He had close-cropped blond hair and was about as straight-edge as they came. He wore a summer shirt, loose pants, and white loafers without socks. Apparently he wasn't going swimming.

"What's ridiculous?" I asked. Our eyes were on my daughter, splashing in the fancy pool with a stupid grin on her face.

"Drink tabs, room service, daily massages? You went soft."

I shrugged and killed my bottle of beer. "Would you prefer I continued as a homeless vagrant? You know my safe house is blown now. The Fontainebleau is as good a place as any."

He chuckled. "So you're a new Cisco Suarez. Footloose and fancy free."

"That's right, bro." I stood up from the lounge chair. "And if you don't mind, I'm going to enjoy Fran's tenth birthday. I'll be back."

I still sported jeans and a tank top, but not for long. I headed into the air-conditioned lobby and rode the elevator up eight floors. A brand-new pair of trunks and flip-flops waited for me on my bed. Even more important was the little gift-wrapped box I'd left on the wet bar. Fran didn't know I was her biological father, but damn if that was gonna stop me from spoiling her.

I swiped the keycard and opened my hotel door. Sunlight flooded through the glass balcony windows. I didn't remember leaving the curtains open. I shuffled toward the glass, saw the black cat perched on the high-rise balcony railing, and froze.

"Living it up, I see," said a familiar voice, sitting in a corner chair.

I spun around. He looked the same as always. A mane and beard of wavy red hair. A blue polo and sports coat covering a burgeoning belly on an otherwise lean frame. His attitude, especially, was familiar. Casual, calm, collected.

Remember how I said it wasn't important where my money had come from? Well, Connor Hatch would disagree because it was his. Not only was he a Caribbean drug kingpin, he was a jinn too. Mean stuff.

My body tensed. It was Connor who had opened the curtains. In direct sunlight, my shadow magic was weak. I took in my surroundings, noting the bow-tied gift on the counter. "You said you'd leave my family and friends out of this."

"And so they are," he remarked, flipping through blown-up photographs I'd left on the nightstand. "Dr. Trinidad's work?" he asked.

I clenched my jaw. I'd taken pictures of a conquistador artifact, once in my possession, now in Connor's. The doctor at the Historical Museum hadn't been able to decipher the Taíno pictographs. There wasn't much in the way of notes with them.

"This is useless," grumbled Connor, flinging the stack of

papers in the air. They fanned out and rained down between us.

I waited, alert, watching him, ready for him to make his move. My eyes drifted to the belt pouch resting on my bed. The one with all my spellcraft tokens.

"Life is funny," he mused. "Human and jinn alike, we spend so much time working toward an end goal, thinking all our problems will magically be solved when we succeed. But you and I both know that kind of magic doesn't exist."

He was talking about the Horn of Subjugation. The artifact.

"Take your riches," he said. "This hotel. Are you a happy man, Cisco?"

"Money was never what I wanted," I squeezed out.

"Ah, that's right. You wanted me dead."

I shrugged and took a step closer to my belt pouch. "You telling me you're disappointed in the power of a five-hundred-year-old wraith?"

"Disappointed?" His eyes lit up. "Hardly. The Spaniard wields formidable spellcraft. It's the Horn itself that beguiles me. Unlocking its mysteries is taking considerable effort. More than I imagined. Just when I think I have it, you see, I find something anew to hold me back."

Connor sighed and looked inward, allowing me to creep closer to my spell tokens.

"Perhaps it's human magic," he said. "Using spirits as a go-between to channel the Intrinsics is foreign to me."

"Don't tell me you're here for advice." I moved toward my bed. Connor stood and I stopped.

"You know, Cisco, I'm happy that I'm bound against hurting your family. I've grown fond of the little girl, and her mother once served me well. But you're a problem, aren't you? Lying low, but for how long?" He paused thoughtfully, mouth twitching into a wicked grin. "You once dared me to set you on fire."

I dove to my bed and scooped up the belt pouch. At the same time, I thrust my left hand between us, willing the enchanted tattoo on my palm to life. Turquoise energy exploded into a semi-spherical two-foot barrier.

The jinn's hands were outstretched too. Flames lanced from them and engulfed me. The fire danced around my shield as I ducked. Too much of it. The Nordic barrier of protection was too small. The heat was too great. I jerked as the flames spread around me—overtaking the carpet, the bed, my clothes.

"Vacation's over," said Connor as the fire consumed me.

Chapter 2

Fire retardant or not, the luxury hotel suite was an inferno before I knew it. The pain forced me to my knees. I dropped my shield. Flames roared over me as Connor bellowed in joy.

Shadow. I needed shadow to dive into. But it was too late. Between the sunlight and the raging fire, sinking into darkness would only stave off the inevitable. And there was no guarantee I could hide from Connor's magic.

I twitched as my arms blistered. Even my enchanted skin was giving in to the heat.

The cat. The curious image on the balcony flashed through my frantic mind. I knew that cat.

A firecracker next to me popped. No, a shotgun shell. My belt pouch was on fire. It was filled with sacraments and bullets. And spark powder.

I flung the belt pouch at Connor as hard as I could. The leather bag beamed him in the chest and barely bounced to the floor before violently exploding. Without sticking around to see what had become of the ifrit, I reached under the bed. Still some shadow there. I thrust my hand into it and came away with my single-barrel shotgun.

I fought the pain and charged the balcony window. I

fired the birdshot into the glass. Cracks spiderwebbed across my view. Still on fire and at top speed, I barreled into the fractured safety glass, put a cowboy boot on the top rail of the balcony, and leaped away from the building.

I swear, Olympic judges would've given me gold for my launch form. The landing? Not so much. By the time I plummeted eight floors and splashed into the pool below, I pulled off the mother of all belly flops.

Air slammed from my lungs. Charred skin screamed in pain as it slapped the water. That was pain, but it paled in comparison to actually being on fire. I kicked to the surface and grabbed the sidewall, hungrily gasping for air.

Standing where I'd left him was Evan Cross, protectively clutching a towel around Fran. Both of them were slack-jawed, watching me like I was Evel Knievel.

"Why are you looking at me like that?" I asked desperately. "Oh, God. Please tell me I still have eyebrows."

Glass sprinkled onto the patio. I looked up. My hotel room was the red glow of a dying sun. Smoke billowed from the missing window. Flittering pieces of flaming paper drifted down like snow.

"Meow!" came a sharp cry. The black cat stood by the pool now, canting his head at me. He wasn't even wet. Holy shit. I guess cats do always land on their feet.

I dragged myself out of the pool and stumbled forward, grabbing the mangy thing before it could dart away.

It *was* the same cat. A piece of former roadkill I'd animated a few months ago. But not just another zombie. This cat was special. Besides having a knack for disappearing on me, it seemed to have a life of its own.

I had to admit, despite months of puzzling it out, I still

had no idea what the black cat's deal was. The best I'd come up with so far was that it served some inscrutable higher purpose, like fate.

The cat bit me.

"Son of a bitch!" I yelled as I dropped him. He bounded away to the street. Thanks a lot, Fate.

Screaming vacationers scurried away from the pool, some running into the lobby, others prescient enough not to charge into a burning building. Evan approached me cautiously.

"It's Connor, isn't it?"

I nodded wordlessly, looking into his face, then Fran's. This had been why I'd stayed away from them. And here I thought I could make an exception for her birthday. "That's why you can't get involved," I told him.

"Cisco—"

"You can't get involved."

I looked up again. No sign of Connor, but it was highly doubtful the explosion hurt him at all. He was a jinn. He could disappear and blink around at will. It's why I hadn't been able to wring his neck yet. He was pretty much invincible.

"So much for a happy birthday," I said, mussing Fran's wet hair. I turned to Evan. "You'll just need to settle for the gift of peace, then. Take her home. Keep your family safe and let me deal with Connor. It's what we agreed."

He worked his jaw but knew I was right. Especially with Fran right here.

As I skirted the pool, a burning shred of paper landed on the surface of the water. It was a close-up photograph of the Horn of Subjugation. Pictographs on Taíno gold. It was one of the few symbol groupings Dr. Trinidad had been confident of deciphering. A man in the middle, stuck between a sun and a bat. Life and death.

That was me right now. And it wouldn't be over until Connor Hatch was dead. So much for footloose and fancy free.

Chapter 3

I beat out to the street as fast as I could. I didn't have a plan except getting away from Connor and the authorities who would show up asking questions about my hotel room. I had no real ID so they'd never find me (given I didn't stick around and announce myself).

Despite my lengthy downtime, a calm fell over me. The quiet confidence of a practiced soldier. I was used to the streets. Besides, the cat had skittered this way. Not that I'd see him again. He frustrated me with enigmatic cameos in my life, for better or worse. Mostly better, I thought. That beats most cats.

No such luck this time. After I crossed the street and rounded the corner of the block, I ran headfirst into a white guy with dreads. He had a nose ring with a tiny skull charm on it. That was either code for on-his-way-to-a-goth-club or he was a necromancer, like me.

In a flash of movement, he flung a handful of powder at my face. I was in the sun so I spun away from it, avoiding a direct hit to my eyes and nose. The puff of smoke was airborne, though, and impossible to avoid inhaling. Even as my eyes misted with water, I rolled away and coughed.

Seeing me distracted, the necromancer came at me with

a knife. His poison was child's play. Little more than pepper spray. His blade came down on my tattooed forearm. A quick spark of blue light bounced the knife off my flesh and from his grip. I punched him in the face and acquainted him with the sidewalk.

I tried to brush past him but he tossed some bones on the concrete like dice. They tumbled and popped beneath me. Three scorpions grew from the pieces of ivory. Small but obviously poisonous, and I didn't have my usual bag of tricks.

Hell, why fix something that ain't broke?

Instead of retreating, I brought a red cowboy boot down on the nearest insect. It crunched satisfyingly under my sole. Another struck at my foot but failed to breach the alligator hide. It squelched under my other foot.

The third scorpion was a bit quicker than the others. It avoided my stomps and, instead of striking, jumped onto my boot and crawled up my jeans. I don't like things with more than four legs—scorpions are practically spiders in my book—but there was no time to scream like a sissy. Before it could strike, I clapped my hand against it and crushed it like a fly.

Amateur spellcraft. The wannabe necromancer was still reeling from my punch. He managed to regain his feet but just stood there dumbfounded as his last pet dropped to the floor. I took a step toward him. His eyes widened and he reached for more powder. My fingers clamped around the skull on his nose and ripped it free. He convulsed. I shoved him to the ground and tossed the spellcraft fetish across the street. An animist of his meager caliber would have a hard time casting anything without that.

I turned to go and noticed another onlooker approaching. A Cuban woman with a dead chicken in her hand, and not a fake one made out of rubber. A santera. Another animist coming for me.

All of a sudden my streets didn't feel so cozy.

I cut between the buildings into an alley, walking casually. As soon as I was out of sight, I snapped into a run. I was supposed to be on vacation, damn it. Relaxing poolside with a brew. I really didn't want to get into a scrap on the streets today.

I hopped a stone wall and crossed through a construction site. Some workers on their lunch break shot me funny looks but I kept my head down and made my way to the next street. As I crossed it a gang of Haitians screamed in alarm.

What the crap? These kids had white skulls painted on their faces. Bone Saints from Little Haiti. What were they doing after me?

A delivery truck honked as it slowed in front of me. I scrambled out of the street and down another alley, getting serious vibes of déjà vu. Chased through South Beach by a voodoo gang. Where had I seen that before?

I turned the corner onto an empty side street. No one around. A dumpster against the brick building.

"Oh, what the hell," I muttered and jumped in.

In the fetid darkness of sour garbage, I finally realized what this reminded me of. This was my new life, all over again, back where it started: on the run and in a dumpster. Was my story gonna end the same way it began?

No, I assured myself. I was in control now. More powerful, even without my pouch of spell tokens. And the gangs didn't have a way of tracking me this time.

I kept quiet as shoes skittered past on the asphalt. At least three people, no doubt the Bone Saints. Last I'd seen the Haitians, we'd made a great deal of money together. That was right before I pissed them off by trading the Horn to Connor. They'd warned me of the danger of doing so, but it happened anyway.

It wasn't something I'd planned. I did it to keep my friends and family safe. To make sure Fran lived to see this next birthday. Even now, I knew it was worth it.

Several yards away, a foot twisted in gravel. I stiffened. Feet stomped closer and men muttered in creole.

Damn. I didn't have to understand them to know they'd found me. Deciding to go for broke, I waited in silence, wishing I'd buried myself deeper in garbage. Too late now.

After several long moments, I heard a familiar voice. Not Connor this time. It was the voice of a friend.

"Suarez," announced Chevalier flatly.

The head of the Bone Saints was here in person. Maybe I could talk some sense into him. I meekly pressed the dumpster lid open.

Four bokors surrounded me. Two kids, initiates I'd worked with before. Another man I didn't know. And Jean-Louis Chevalier, decked out with a sash around his chest, silver gauntlets and hanging earrings, and white skull paint. He sneered when he saw me, the painted teeth showing double against his real ivories.

These guys had always gone for creepy. Intricate props and horror movie makeup that seasoned animists like myself learned to ignore. But something was genuinely creepy about my friend this time. Chevalier's countenance had changed. The measured strategist I'd expected didn't stand before me. Instead he seemed more like a rabid dog. Careless, rushed, more prone to hate. Maybe I'd just never seen him this pissed off before.

His silver eyes blended with his makeup, hard to read in the bright light. I stayed in the shadow of the dumpster, wary of my supposed friend's intentions.

Chapter 4

"What is this?" I growled. "Corralling me in the street?" One by one, my eyes locked on Chevalier's three soldiers. Their dark eyes were fogged over with a milky glaze.

What had he done to them?

"Your time has come," said Chevalier in a measured Haitian accent.

"You kidding? Where's the rest of your army?"

The bokors gritted their teeth. One of the kids pulled a burlap sack from his waist. I jerked my hand. A twine of shadow extended from beneath the dumpster and lashed his wrist. He dropped the sack and spilled frog legs on the street.

"Nobody think about making fast moves," I warned. "Or even slow, stupid ones."

The young gangbanger stared at me blankly, ignoring the pain from the shadow whip. He'd grown a lot in the two months since I'd seen him. Something had emboldened him.

I turned to my friend again. "I know you're pissed about the Horn, Chevalier, but I'll get it back."

He cocked his head. "The Horn."

The other full-grown bokor grabbed a cross around his

neck. I sent the shadow at him but he rolled away. He backed out of range and let his hands fall to his side. For a second I thought I'd warned him off his spell. Then I heard rustling in the garbage underneath me.

"Oh, screw this," I said. I hopped out of the dumpster before whatever animated vermin was in there could snap at me. My boots clapped on the blacktop. Only Chevalier tensed at my approach.

"Back off," I warned.

The bokors rushed me. I stepped back against the dumpster and slipped into the shadow beneath it. In my ethereal form, I slid to the side of the obstacle and rematerialized at the flank of the converging gang members. I grabbed the back of the closest head and slammed it into the steel wall. He went down without a fight. Yup, still human.

With my foot still in a bit of shadow, I drew some around my fist and punched the older man in the chest. He tumbled to the ground. The third swiped me with a blade, slashing my right forearm, the one without the protective tattoo.

"Ah!" I recoiled away from the knife, into the sunlight.

A bright red line opened on my arm. Sizzling fluid escaped the cut. I instinctively reached for a neutralization powder in my belt pouch before remembering it was gone. When the kid came at me again, I fended him off with my left forearm. My Nordic protection flared to life. I caught him with a vanilla punch to the jaw. He fell away, rubbing his chin.

Curiously, Chevalier hadn't made a move yet. And he was the one I was most worried about.

"What is this about?" I asked. "We're supposed to be friends."

"Friends," said Chevalier flatly, without recognition. If he wasn't standing right before me I would've sworn it wasn't him. It was like he didn't know me anymore.

The kid who kissed the dumpster was still out cold, but the man had regained his feet. The other kid slashed his knife menacingly in the air.

I was in the sun now. I could still pull some tricks with the shadow, but I couldn't draw it to me. I grimaced at the wound that continued sizzling on my arm, blackening the flesh around it. I had no choice but to draw my own knife from my belt.

This wasn't a Crocodile Dundee number by any means. It was a small, ceremonial thing. Bronze with a curved blade. Perfect for cutting yourself like a moody teenager but not much else. Still, it was all I had.

"Stop this, Chevalier, before somebody gets hurt." I didn't want to cut them, but they were coming at me pretty hard.

My friend's eyes flashed when he saw the knife. He raised a hand and his men paused in unison, waiting for his order.

That's when I saw it. Chevalier's eyes are silver so I hadn't noticed at first, but his right eye was glazed over just like the others.

They were thralls of some sort. Slaves, like I had been. Not quite dead but devoid of the best parts of life. Only Chevalier wasn't completely gone yet. He still had one good eye and tried to speak. He recognized the bronze knife.

"You know this?" I said carefully, presenting the

ceremonial voodoo blade. "It was yours once. You gave it to me. Remember?"

"Mine," he said.

I nodded. The bubbling on my arm had mostly stopped. "We're friends."

A quick intake of air and then, "Friends," he repeated.

By now the kid on the floor was groggily shaking his head. His now-brown eyes took in his surroundings with confusion. "Jean-Louis," he said. "Jean-Louis."

The head of the Bone Saints turned to him sharply. The startled initiate froze under his glare. "Kill the shadow charmer," grunted Chevalier. "Kill Cisco Suarez."

The kid swiveled to me slowly and, right before my eyes, his brown irises went white.

This was some Borg-level shit right here.

Chevalier sneered and his men mimicked the expression. Together they brandished weapons of spellcraft. Things were about to get dirty.

The second they stepped toward me, someone kicked the alley door in the brick wall open. The bokors spun around. The man with the cross necklace took to the air like a kite and landed twenty feet behind me.

Out of the door stepped a small girl with a bob of bright red hair. She wore ripped skinny jeans, a Fugazi T-shirt, and gummy bracelets. Just a teenager, but one of the most powerful telekinetic witches I'd ever met. She waved a statuette of Hecate, the Greek witch god, to the side. Another bokor flung in that direction.

"Get inside!" she screamed.

I kicked the back of Chevalier's knee, forcing him to buckle to the ground without breaking anything. Then I elbowed him in the face to force him lower. I rushed past the Haitian and went inside without thinking it over. Darcy hopped in behind me and bolted the door shut.

"Follow me," she said firmly, marching down the hall. She stopped when she noticed I wasn't complying. Gummy bracelets went to her hips. "What is it?"

I tickled the shadow on the floor, ready for her to make a move. "The last time I saw you, I was chained to a wall for hours."

She held her fetish at her side. "I didn't do that."

"You sure helped."

She shrugged. "Look, you're not in shackles now. I can't keep you out of the shadows. And in case you're not paying attention, you're either with me or you're with them." She nodded to the door, which the Bone Saints started banging on.

"I'm not so sure you're better," I said. "They're the devil I know."

She scoffed. "You don't know them. Not anymore." She stormed to the front of the building.

I waited alone in what would have been silence were it not for the incessant attempts to break in. The door rumbled on its hinges. The bokors were getting more creative.

I sighed and caught up to Darcy. "Where are you going?"

She weaved past cubicles with stoic determination. "All I know is I'm getting out of here. You should too until you understand what's going on."

"What *is* going on?"

She cracked the front door and peeked both ways down

the sidewalk. Satisfied, she threw it open and led me to a VW Bus painted bright orange. The roof and window trim were white. "Get in and I'll tell you."

The driver was a heavyset woman I didn't recognize. All business, from the short black hair to the functional yet drab clothing. She barely glanced at me before starting the van.

I turned to Darcy. "Get into that hippie wagon? With you?"

"I helped you once before. Let me help you again."

The teenage witch climbed in the back, leaving the door open for me.

Since no one else was listening, I grumbled to myself. Darcy was just a kid, but she was powerful. Her spellcraft had been vital in imprisoning me two months prior. I didn't blame her for too much of that, though. She worked for a secret society I'd butted heads with a few times. For her part she was just a kid in training.

But what she said was true. She had helped me before, in a way. She'd been unsettled at my capture and at Connor's attack on my family. And while she didn't exactly help me escape, she saw it happening and didn't intervene.

I grumbled one last time to get it out of my system and jumped in the bright orange van.

Chapter 5

Of all my stupid moves, this had to rank among the most desperate. Accepting a ride from *this* crowd? It wasn't that I didn't know who they were. Quite the opposite. The problem was I knew exactly who they were.

The Society of Free Thinkers, if memory served me right. The Society for short. They're an American business collective from frontier times, if you can believe that. Apparently "free thinker" is code for animist in this context. Which is fair enough. Spellcraft has been vilified for as long as it has existed. I can understand the need for secrets.

The Society is every bit as mysterious as it sounds. One part political lobbying machine, one part wizard's guild. I used to liken them to a cartel before I had a legit drug cartel on my ass. Now I saw them as independent actors, tied to Connor Hatch's business dealings, but not part of the drug trade.

That hadn't stopped me from making enemies. Rotten memories flooded my head. Simon the lightning animist, their ruthless enforcer. Shen the illusionist. Even Darcy the telekinetic.

These animists were no friends of mine. They'd wanted the Horn just like Connor. By now they knew I didn't have it.

So what the hell did they want from me?

I kept my head low as we drove through the crowded street and had to admit the win here. Uncomfortable conversations were cake compared to fighting every two-bit street necromancer in South Beach.

"So what's going on?" I asked Darcy. "Why are they chasing me?"

She shook her head. "Are you serious? This is your fault. You gave Connor the Horn. What did you think would happen?"

I grimaced. I'd surrendered the artifact to keep my family safe. I'd do it a hundred times over. The trick was getting it back. I promised myself I would. Promised others. The weeks had passed without any headway and, in the absence of consequences, I maybe kinda got a little lax.

I rubbed ashes from my hair. No consequences. Yeah, right.

The driver silently took us toward North Miami Beach.

"Where are we going?"

Darcy yawned. "A safe house."

"Safe how?"

She stared at me in annoyance. "Safely away from Connor and his men."

"He's a jinn," I explained. "Connor can teleport at will. It's kind of his thing. Physical distance doesn't help."

"That means he doesn't know where you are. If he did, he would have attacked you by now." She glanced behind us. "Besides, physical distance from that ambush of necromancers helps. Berna won't let anyone follow us. The safe house is warded. Connor and his thralls won't be able to get in."

"Excuse me if I remain a tad jumpy."

Sorry, but I didn't trust the cool confidence of a teenager. That attitude came from the movies, not experience. At the same time, if anyone knew what they were doing, it was the Society. And I wasn't stupid enough to think Darcy and Berna were running this show by themselves. The last time they had me, I'd been introduced to Margo Gray, an enigmatic woman who everyone obeyed without question. I winced at the thought of seeing the old lady again.

We pulled into the underground parking garage of a high-rise condo.

"Just drop us here, Berna," said Darcy. The driver wordlessly slowed to a stop by the elevator. I hopped out.

"Going down?" I said in an ominous voice.

"Keep your dad jokes to yourself," she replied. She pushed the up button and stepped inside.

She was right. I had better material. We rode to the top floor in silence.

The building was new and modestly fancy. Two units on top. We entered the north one and were greeted with a panoramic view of Biscayne Bay on one wall and the Atlantic on the other. I'd expected a crack team of animists. All I got was a white guy in flip-flops eating cheese puffs.

"Hey man," he said, not bothering to get up from his lounger. He had long hair and a beer belly and was well into his sixties. He wore a loud, multi-colored shirt and a tan handkerchief rolled into a headband. As we measured each other, his hand dug into a family-size bag of cheese puffs. The unmistakable scent of marijuana hung in the air.

"This explains the VW van," I said.

"A timeless classic," he beamed.

"Who are you?"

"Your best friend, Cisco."

I glanced around the serene penthouse. Darcy stepped to the panoramic window and stared at the ocean. I waited for Margo to stroll in but no one else was here. Granted, this was an improvement from the junky warehouse I'd last met the Society in, but it was still unexpected.

"Are you kidding me?" I asked Darcy. "What is this guy, your weed hookup?"

He laughed and licked cheese dust off his fingertips. "I haven't heard that one before. You should make fun of my long hair and jean shorts next. I find those to be popular targets."

"I was actually gonna go with the Jim Morrison necklace."

He laughed and stood up. My face darkened. Hard to get at a guy who didn't take himself seriously.

"You should see what you're wearing," he said before stepping out of the room.

I checked my clothes. The jeans were scorched from Connor's fire but had held up okay. The white tank top... not so much. It was blackened and full of holes. The old man returned and tossed a T-shirt my way. I caught it and unfolded it as he sat down.

"This is a bright-orange Phish T-shirt," I noted. "It matches the van."

He shrugged. "It's a less conspicuous look than burn victim."

I scowled and put it on. "Why am I here?"

He held his hands up in peace. "Cool it, man. I just said I was your friend."

"Friend? I know who you guys are. You're working with a psychopathic drug kingpin who's trying to kill me." I tossed my scorched shirt on the floor to emphasize the point.

He nodded. "The Society tolerates Connor, yes. Were he to be deposed, we would just be forced to connect with whatever neighboring power assumed his place. It's simple macro-politics, man. A security measure. Make allies with those with whom you share borders."

"Tell me why I give a shit about your motivations again?"

He smiled. "Let's just say we *both* give a shit about Connor's."

I narrowed my eyes. By any legitimate measure, this man was the jinn's business partner. That didn't mean they were buddies, necessarily. I knew that much. And this guy was old enough to be a real player in the Society, like Margo Gray. Someone who could clue me in. Except unlike the Gray Lady, he hadn't put me in handcuffs for the sit-down.

"I'm listening," I conceded.

He crinkled the bag of chips closed. "Connor Hatch owns the Caribbean. You know that. Strange hobby for a jinn. His fascination with the New World has grown with his time here. He's particularly interested in the area's legends. The Fountain of Youth, the Bermuda Triangle. You've seen his collection of artifacts on his private island. You've recently added to it. That was a grievous mistake, Cisco. It's what turned those men on the streets against you."

Subjugation. The Horn's true power and one I hadn't tapped. In the hands of a psychopath, it could prove a deadly weapon. Chevalier had known that.

"You're his partner," I said. "Can't you do something about that?"

"It doesn't work like that, Cisco. He's a participating member of the Society, but it's mainly a partnership to protect our coastal interests. We have more sway in the Northeast and the South. South Florida's a whole different beast. An international beast. Without his influence, the gate to Latin America would be unguarded."

"From what?"

"Everything and anything that concerns us, man. 'What' isn't important. The 'why' is all you need to understand. People think we're the Illuminati but we're just territorial businessmen and women. Nothing more."

"Who all use spellcraft."

"Granted, but it isn't magic that makes a man. Wouldn't you agree?" He uncrinkled the bag in his lap and snuck in another cheese puff. "I swear, these things are more addictive than the powder he pushes."

I paced to the window. "I already got the necessary-evil lecture from Margo. Is she a part of this too?"

"Margo?" My host tossed the bag of chips on the end table and wiped his hands on his jean shorts. "The Gray Lady's a bit overzealous in her fanaticism, don't you think? Or is that fanatical in her zeal? I mean, anybody who has a contingent of royal guards takes themselves too seriously."

"So what is this then? What is she to you?"

"Board members," he said. "We get equal votes but don't always have equal say. That's how business works."

"A happy-go-lucky bunch of free thinkers, huh?"

He shrugged, amused. "You really do hate the Society. Eh, I hate them too. More than you, I bet."

"Yet you rose to power in their ranks?"

"What better way to keep them off your back? Listen, man. We all have our own moral compasses. Our own goals to drive us forward. We're not Hydra. I want to strip Connor of his power too. Take away the violence he brings to the streets. Trust me, that business with the gang war wasn't on my radar. I'm afraid Connor's more plugged in to South Florida than we are. That's why you need to understand what's going on here. You'll never catch him otherwise."

I took a slow breath and licked my lips. There was no way I trusted the old hippie, but so far he wasn't torturing me. And Darcy was all right. I stretched my neck and leaned over the back of the couch opposite him, still standing.

"So what's Connor up to?"

"That's the magic question, isn't it?" The man leaned forward in the chair and steepled his fingers. "I believe Connor's looking for a lost city of gold."

I crossed my arms and stood there blinking. "You can't be serious."

"Why not?"

My eyes flashed to Darcy and back to him. "Come on. Those are new-world myths."

"Like artifacts that raise the dead? Like magic?"

"I get the point. But just because some of the supernatural is real doesn't make every whisper of legend authentic. Otherwise we'd have unicorns shitting rainbows everywhere we looked."

The old hippie leaned back again, taking my skepticism in stride. He wasn't put off by it. He'd expected it. "What's unbelievable, exactly? That gold exists in the New World? That the Spanish Crown funded their naval empire on what they reaped from the Americas? That there might still be some left?"

I frowned. "So Connor's scouring South America for a gold depot?"

"Could be. He has obvious business interests on the continent and the Society's eyes don't see in those shadows. But Connor's recent behavior suggests he's looking for a coastal settlement or even an island."

"An island." I stepped around the sofa and sat down. "I have an idea. You wanna find a golden island? Check Google Maps."

He shrugged. I didn't know what was stranger. That I was talking to a guy who probably hadn't shampooed his hair since Woodstock or what he believed Connor was up to. The ghost of the Spanish conquistador had certainly never mentioned a city of gold to me before. Then again, I'd never asked.

"Okay," I contended. "Say I buy this city-of-gold business, just for the sake of argument. What's the problem? Connor's your associate. Why not help him out? Share the wealth."

His brow furrowed. "Connor's gone dark. He's skipping the usual appointments. He's all but abandoned his private island. For the past two months he's been leading his *Agua Fuego* cartel from his new submarine." He paused and looked inward with a chuckle. "Huh, an ifrit in a submarine. Fire Water. I never thought about that before." He shook the thought away. "Anyway, combined with his newfound lore in pre-conquest history, Connor's becoming worrisome."

I finally got it. "He's cutting you out."

My host cocked his head. "He's also flooding Miami with an army of death animists. And going for your head."

"So you want me to do your dirty work for you."

He let out a long sigh, then stood up from his lounger and joined me on the couch. "That's one way to put it, but it ignores the bigger picture. Look, man, the Society can't officially break the alliance with Connor. Not until it's too late. And if I openly move against him, Margo will have me killed. I'm powerful, but I don't have the resources to survive in the shadows like you do."

I smiled at the penthouse. "Got used to the glamour, did you?" In truth, I'd gotten used to it over the last two months as well. "I don't even know your name."

"G. R. Winthrop," he said, offering his hand. After a second he realized his fingers were orange and withdrew them. "Better not."

I shook my head. Winthrop was just about the last name I would've pegged on the old man. Winthrop sounded like old money. This dude looked like peace and free love. But appearances were deceiving, especially with animists.

I twisted my lips and looked over my shoulder. "And the kid?"

"Darcy's one of the good ones. She has a conscience hidden beneath that spunky shell. I think you know that or you wouldn't have stepped into my van."

He watched me expectantly. When I still didn't budge, he said, "Bottom line is, you're going after Connor anyway.

Unless you wanna be chargrilled every other week, you need to get him more than I do. But his ability to blink keeps him one step ahead. You're not gonna catch him with a butterfly net."

"And you know where to find him?"

"Something like that," he said. "But I was inspired by your recent strategy to go after the cartel. Don't attack the jinn, attack his interests. Keep playing Marco Polo until you collide."

I hissed. "If I start hitting the *Agua Fuego* cartel again, it could be months before he responds. I don't have a better line on him anymore."

He smiled. "And that, my man, is why you need me. The drugs are old news. His lieutenants are running that end for him now. To go where he'll be, you need to focus on his latest pursuit."

I squeezed my jaw and frowned. "The city of gold."

"Bingo."

Chapter 6

Soon enough, Darcy was sitting on the couch with us, three ice-cold cans of Mountain Dew on the coffee table and me having a go at the cheese puffs. Hey, I didn't trust this guy but I was only human.

The junk food wasn't the only thing on the table. Winthrop laid out satellite images of an island.

"Connor's island compound," I noted between crunches. "I checked it out once when I was hitting the cartel. It's cleaned out, like you said. What good is it to us now?"

The elder animist shook his head. "You don't just forgo an asset like this, man."

"Why not? He owns tons of land in the Caribbean. If he doesn't want to be found, he won't be there. We know about the place. You said it yourself. He's in hiding."

"I didn't say he's in hiding. I said he went dark. He's around but he's throwing shade on his movements. Keeping his trail secret. Keeping his head down. Connor isn't officially hiding because we're not officially looking for him. *Comprende?* Take a look at these pictures." Winthrop arranged them in a row. "Notice anything?"

I wasn't sure what would stand out from a series of satellite images. The interior of the mansion wasn't visible and the grainy photos didn't have the definition to show individuals on the ground.

The island was shaped like a crescent, nearly a full circle with the majority of the land mass on one wide half. An inlet broke the edge and led to a pool in the center. That half of the island was wooded—a far cry from the manicured lawn and picturesque beach beside the compound. A long dock extended from behind the building, much of it hidden by the greenery.

"Connor's overseen a little construction project over the last two months," said Winthrop. "He retrofitted his dock to better facilitate his submarine. You can clearly see the extension here. In the last shot you can even catch the surfaced vessel under the tree cover."

I stared at the photo. "So he's back out in the open?"

"Not exactly," he said. "Connor doesn't stay at the compound much at all. He's living in his sub, but he uses the port to refuel and keep a supply line open."

"It's still an easy place to hit him. Lie in wait until he makes a pit stop."

Winthrop laughed and leaned back. "My God, we're not assassins. Anyway, you're forgetting his private army. Getting there unannounced isn't easy."

I chewed my lip. I knew a secret way to the island that utilized the magical underworld of the Nether, but I wasn't about to spill.

"Besides," continued Winthrop, "leaving the country isn't safe. An action like that would announce our intentions on his turf. It's suicide."

Darcy sat next to me watching videos on her phone. She was only half listening. But then, she already knew where this conversation was going.

"You have a job for me," I said. "But if Connor's running *Agua Fuego* on autopilot, and only using his compound for resupply, and hiding his movements from everyone, how do you know where he'll be?"

Winthrop smiled. "That's the strength of not declaring war. You see, just like us, Connor needs to keep up appearances. He won't enter Miami without giving us a heads up. Professional courtesy."

My face darkened. "You knew he was gonna hit me this morning."

Winthrop offered nothing in his defense.

"You could have given me a warning. My"—I caught myself and changed my wording—"*friends* were there."

Nobody but a select few knew Fran was my daughter. Not even her. It didn't hurt to keep it that way. As it stood, she was off-limits to Connor. The Society had no such restrictions.

"We got to you as discreetly as we could," he assured. "This is the big play. The big secret. If we're to help each other, that's the only way it can be. On paper, Cisco Suarez remains a problem for the Society and *Agua Fuego* alike."

I huffed angrily. Friendly intentions and calculated strategy didn't go hand in hand. "So what's your plan? Leave me out as bait until we kill each other?"

"Too late for that," laughed Winthrop. "Connor missed you. I doubt he's coming back. He has bigger and better things to worry about. That's why you were able to enjoy some R&R in the first place. He's too calculated to waste time with you."

"Easy for you to say. He didn't set you on fire."

The old man shrugged. "I know it hurts your ego, Cisco, but you were just his cover story. Appearances, remember? Connor's really in Miami for something else. Something time sensitive that he didn't want to tell us about. Something he needs."

I stood up from the couch and walked to the window, keeping my back to them. Winthrop's assertion made sense. Connor had left me alone for two months. Two whole months. With the newly acquired Horn of Subjugation, an artifact he'd tracked down over decades, it stood to reason he'd ultimately switch his focus from me to his prize. What had the jinn said in my hotel room? Unlocking the Horn's mysteries was taking considerable effort.

No doubt Connor had been studying my photographs in hopes of discovering more about the Horn. Finding out what I knew. Burning Cisco alive was just a two-for-one bonus. Connor Hatch was crafty, all right. And Winthrop was right. It hurt to hear I was little more than a cover story.

At the same time, there was no way in hell Winthrop was giving me a clean line. He was part of the Society, an organization that—by its nature—is manipulative and covert. Winthrop might not be as bad as Margo, but there was no doubt he was using me.

I took a long, reflective breath. "If Connor's not in Miami for me," I said, "then what is he here for?"

Winthrop twisted around in the couch to look at me, but I kept my gaze on the window. "That's what we want you to find out, Cisco. I think it has to do with the city of gold. All I can offer you is a starting point. A house on the Intracoastal where Connor's submarine is docked. That's where he started. If you go there, maybe you can follow his trail."

I grunted. With half the necromancers in Miami hunting me, that was easier said than done.

Chapter 7

The major beaches in Miami lie along barrier islands that protect the coast. That's why you need bridges to get to them. In the city proper, those bridges span Biscayne Bay, a large body of water that has islands of its own, including the shipping hub that is the Port of Miami.

Back in the VW Bus beside Darcy, Berna at the wheel, we headed up Ocean Drive, out of North Miami Beach, hopping from one barrier island to the next until we were close to Hallandale Beach. Up here, the water between the islands and the coast collapsed into a thin snake that twisted along like a river: the Intracoastal Waterway, a channel all the way up to Boston, used freely by commercial shippers and recreational boaters alike.

Our destination was much closer: the upscale mansion Connor had claimed as a base of operations on the border of Miami-Dade County. He'd taken his Soviet submarine right into the Bay and up the Intracoastal. We followed that same path from the road.

"Wow," I said, gawking at the wide inlets, large houses, and accompanying yachts. "Really opens your eyes to how the other half lives." I turned to Darcy. It surprised me that she wasn't on her cell phone but she still wasn't especially talkative. I leaned forward. "What do you think, Berna? You gonna retire out here one day?"

The woman's meaty cheeks stiffened, but that was the only reaction I got out of her. Not even a glance in the rearview mirror. Tough crowd.

I sighed and kept quiet until Darcy announced, "That's it. The yellow house with the fountain in the driveway. See it?"

I cleared my throat. "It's kinda hard to miss."

Berna didn't slow until we were a few blocks past it. She pulled into the outskirts of a mall and parked.

"We can't go with you," said Darcy. "You heard Winthrop. We can't risk exposing ourselves. We'll wait for you here." She jerked the side door open and stepped out ahead of me.

My cowboy boots landed on the pavement. I stretched. "That's it? No, 'Go get him, stud' or any words of luck?"

Darcy rolled her eyes. "Make sure you're not followed back to us."

"Sure thing," I said about as earnestly as a McDonald's cashier wishes you to have a nice day. "I'll also do my best not to get killed, in case that's a concern."

She flashed a resentful smirk. "I don't like this any more than you do, okay? I'm just trying to get by, same as you."

I returned a skeptical nod. "Who are you working for, Darcy? Winthrop or Margo?"

"Younger talents like me and Shen get traded around as needed." She collapsed the gummy bracelets on her arm to her wrist. "You too. Congratulations. You're on the Society's radar now."

I snorted. "Doesn't really sound like I won much."

"I know what you mean."

I backed away and turned down the road, eager to get a lead on my nemesis.

"Oh," called back Darcy. "And don't die."

I nodded.

The yellow house with the fountain was big enough that I spotted it from two blocks out, but it wasn't a snap to get to. The path was circuitous. I had to cross an inlet and circle around on my approach. Hiking in the Miami sun worked up a bit of a sweat.

Two pickup trucks were parked in the front driveway. Same make and model, probably rentals. It was hard to tell now because the rental agencies had stopped putting giant stickers announcing tourists on vacation after several high-profile muggings. The last thing South Florida wanted to do was scare tourists, so rentals were disguised.

Still, that was my guess. I figured a couple guards were sitting on the property while Connor was off doing his thing. Not a problem for me.

I was running dry on spell tokens. No belt pouch of powders and candles. No shells for my shotty. My only weapon was a bronze knife.

Once again I wasn't concerned. Unlike some of the amateurs on the street, I didn't need sacraments for casting. I had my dog-collar fetish on my wrist. My skull-and-pentacle belt buckle. And my tattoos weren't going anywhere. I didn't need a loaded gun, because I was one.

At the same time, I wasn't an invincible tank. I opted to go in quietly, from as near the back of the property as possible without swimming.

The Intracoastal has countless offshoots springing out

along its length, giving waterside property to thousands in South Florida alone. This particular house was no exception, but the waterway was more private than most. Wide and deep, it followed a bend into a dead end, making Connor's house special. A good place to surface a submarine out of sight, even if no such vessel was docked now. I wondered if it was underwater right there, barely hidden, its staff keeping Connor's secret safe while he was away. Maybe that meant nobody was inside the house.

I scanned the yard. No empty beer cans, spent cigarettes, or other signs of recent use. The dock was abandoned. I couldn't see anything underwater.

I crept to the brickwork patio, using gazebo curtains for cover against the large windows spanning the back wall. I closed in against the glass and peeked inside. Lights off. No movement. So far, so good.

I tried the handle of the sliding glass door. Not only was it unlocked, but it glided open silently along its frame. Look at that. Money really did make everything better.

I entered but stopped short when I realized there was a guy on the couch. He was lying along its length. Impossible to see from the window, but there he was. Lucky for me, he was snoring like a coffee grinder. An Uzi rested on the shaggy carpet beside him. I stepped lightly to the mercenary shirking his guard duties, picked up the weapon, and tucked it into my jeans in the small of my back.

The guy? Well, he wasn't hurting anyone for the moment. I left him to his beauty sleep and checked around.

The good news was he was the only one in the house. The bad news was the place was cleaner than I'd hoped. I supposed if Connor had only been in town a day or two, he wouldn't have time to really use the place. That was too bad because it was gonna make tracking him down harder. The thought occurred to me that I didn't need to play Winthrop's game at all. I could just kick back here and wait for the jinn to return. Surely, when he was done in Miami, Connor would exit the city from the same private dock he'd used to enter. Of course, that plan didn't sate my curiosity.

With nothing jumping out at me on the ground floor, I went straight for the master bedroom upstairs. A large balcony overlooked the patio. The bed was used. I checked the closets for spare bags but didn't find anything. When you're a jinn, wearing real clothes was pointless. The second Connor blinked into thin air he'd lose them. So he did what many magical beings do: clothe themselves with innate magic. Not spellcraft but a part of his being. It meant he traveled light.

A large coffee-table book on the nightstand caught my eye. *An Illustrated Re-creation of Arawak Life*. The Arawak were a collection of indigenous nations along the Caribbean, the Taíno being one. They were the first natives encountered by Spanish explorers when Columbus sailed to the New World.

I flipped through the pages. The book was a combination of high-resolution photographs of tribal artifacts and full-color illustrations of what everyday life for the natives would've looked like. Food prep, fishing, construction, agriculture, funeral rites. Not your usual light reading but nothing arcane.

A folded page of newspaper slipped out from between the front cover and the first page. It was an article about public school funding from the *Herald*. Some bureaucrat was appealing for a review of expenditures in Miami-Dade County. I flipped the page over and skimmed half an article about cultural milestones in South Florida setting the stage for the rest of the country. My quick read didn't get the whole story and I was kind of lost, but I was pretty sure Connor didn't care about this article either. At the bottom corner of the page was an advertisement for History Miami Museum.

The hairs on the back of my neck stood on end.

"Attend a Taíno Funeral," it read. Then in small print: "Experience a lost culture through the eyes of those honoring their dead." The picture showed a distinctive U-shaped artifact with a protruding head in the middle that I recognized as Maquetaurie Guayaba, the Taíno god of the dead and their underworld, Coaybay. He was senior to my patron, Opiyel, the Shadow Dog.

Chills ran up my spine. I wasn't sure why. Some instinct inside me dreaded this new information. It was bad enough Connor had the Horn, but now he was digging deeper. Closer. To answers, maybe, but to me as well. It felt like a violation. He was too close to my Taíno power line.

The date of the exhibit ran across the bottom of the ad in bold print. A three-month display, opening today.

"Connor's gonna be there," I said aloud. I strode to the door and stopped, realizing that it wouldn't just be the jinn. The Spaniard would be there as well, the conquistador bound to the Horn and a great ancestor of mine.

I quietly slipped past Sleeping Beauty and made my way back to the van.

Chapter 8

Darcy pulled her attention away from her cell phone. "That was fast."

I climbed in and slid the door shut. "We need to get to Downtown Miami as soon as possible. There's a Taíno display at the History Museum that he's interested in."

"Interested how?" she asked.

"I don't know."

She furrowed her brow. "Well, what does he want?"

"I don't know," I said a bit more forcefully.

She sighed loudly. My eyes flitted to Berna for sympathy but Berna was Berna. She didn't say a word. She just pulled onto the street and drove where she was supposed to go. I appreciated that much at least. We had a lot of ground to cover. This time she took us back to the mainland and merged onto I-95.

"He was looking at Dr. Trinidad's notes," I said to myself.

Darcy crossed her arms over her chest. "What are you going on about?" She was clearly annoyed by my lack of explanation so I made sure to act clearly annoyed by her lack of participation. Kids today. It was all results without wanting to do the work. My father used to say that all the time and I finally understood where he was coming from.

I grumbled and decided there was no reason not to be straight with her. "This is about the Horn of Subjugation, right? I had a curator at the museum studying it for me."

Darcy stared at me blankly for a moment. Then she shrugged and mumbled, "I don't get all the fuss over a stupid horn."

I looked at her like she was crazy. And finally, for once, Berna agreed with me. It was just a quick exchange in the rearview mirror, but her eyes said it all.

"You've been helping the Society chase this thing down and you don't even know what it is?" I asked.

"Of course I know!" she said defiantly. "It has... necromantic powers."

I took a long breath. "Darcy, you need to wrap your head around all of it. The whole thing. The Horn is a cage for a Spanish necromancer who died in the sixteenth century. He was overcome by the natives and trapped by Taíno spellcraft etched in gold. He's a powerful wraith now, and whoever holds the Horn commands the Spaniard. That means power over the dead. It means power over the living who converse with the dead. It means a bunch of things nobody even knows yet because the Spaniard isn't happy about freely giving away his power."

The teenager took in the information with a grim face. "But he recovered it two months ago."

"And he's been researching it. But he's not done. Winthrop said he was in Miami for a reason besides me. Well, this is it. The museum exhibit of a Taíno funeral."

"More artifacts?"

"Maybe," I said. "But I think it's more information.

Answers he's been looking for."

Berna surprised us by speaking up. "It's gonna take us half an hour to get there." Her voice was deep and sure. Something about it said she knew how important this was. It also said we wouldn't be fast enough.

I paid her no mind. Whatever intricate plans Connor had lined up, I could skip them completely. All I needed to do was make a beeline for the jinn. It was like a car chase. The onus was on the driver scrambling to get away. He was the one that needed to choose the path, avoid traffic and obstacles, and push the limits to escape capture. All the police cruisers needed to do was keep up and trail along a path that was already blazed. Capture was almost inevitable.

I pulled out my phone and considered calling to give Dr. Trinidad a head's up. It was a burner, though, and didn't have any numbers saved in it. I didn't remember her number by heart. Besides, there was nothing she could do to stop him. I could call the police but was afraid that would only get a bunch of people killed. And I definitely couldn't pull Evan into this. So I settled for silent anxiety. Amped to confront Connor Hatch on my terms. Nervous to see my old ally, the Spaniard.

The drive took closer to forty minutes despite my attempts to get Berna to go faster. When she pulled alongside the wide plaza of red and white brick, I pulled the stolen gun from my jeans and checked the action.

"What is that?" asked Berna.

"Don't you watch action movies?"

"You can't go in there with that," she said. "That's not the plan. You need to follow Connor. Find out what he knows."

"First thing I need to do is stop him," I countered. "If that means killing him, all the better. I'll let Winthrop worry about the lost city of gold."

Berna's eyes hardened. Darcy tensed.

Then the unmistakable reports of gunfire erupted inside the museum. The front doors were kicked open by fleeing visitors.

"Guess that settles it," I said. I jumped from the van and turned to Darcy. "You coming?"

She froze mid breath and then looked away. "You know I can't."

"You can do anything you want, kid."

Instead of answering with words, she closed the door behind me. She didn't look happy about it but she wasn't helping.

Fine with me. Since when did I need help anyway?

I weaved through the panicking crowd and stormed into the open doors. Pistol shots echoed through the halls. It was impossible to determine where they came from. A terrified mother clutching her son darted around the corner toward me. The fear in her eyes was plain. I charged that way, running past permanent displays of transportation and farming in old Miami.

I moved into a room with dark green and gray walls. I immediately knew I was in the right place. The sober color scheme was offset by dramatic lighting. A clean, polished floor was lined with rows of natural dirt and plant life. Symbols of Taíno worship lined reconstructed dioramas. Like the illustrations in Connor's book, real life mannequins in Taíno dress were set into scenes of the past.

Another report pierced the emptying museum. A

mercenary, like the one I'd caught sleeping, fired his pistol into the ceiling. He wasn't going for any kills, just scaring people away with a bullish grin on his face. When he saw me moving toward him with my gun, he rethought his strategy and trained his pistol on me.

Before he could fire, I slid into the shadow. The mood lighting in the room ensured there was plenty to go around, so I disappeared into the floor and rematerialized a few yards to my right, behind a freestanding display of. a funerary urn. I dipped into the ground and slid along the floor again as the mercenary frantically sprayed the area with lead. When I came up for air, my Uzi let loose. Pimples of blood burst across the man's body and he collapsed.

Another mercenary fired at me before retreating down a back hall. That was the last of them. South American guns for hire. The *Agua Fuego* cartel. Connor was gone. I dashed forward, using the zigzagging wall as cover. A few of the display cases were shattered, whether from gunfire or blunt instruments. Loose artifacts were knocked over or dropped here and there but, again, I couldn't make a snap-second judgment as to their importance.

At the next twist in the wall I caught sight of the cause of the gunfire. A security guard with an empty holster lay dead. His body was riddled with bullets from both sides. The poor guy never had a chance.

I stomped past him to the main display. A diorama depicting several Taíno natives conducting a funeral rite. Beyond them was a cave-like recess. Hidden spotlights in the rock highlighted a large dip in the ground. It was empty.

I moved to the edge of the room and took a calming

breath. I didn't want to get my head blown off. I peeked around the corner the mercenary had disappeared around. The hallway was empty. I burst into a run and covered ground until the next intersection. This time when I peeked, I saw the back of the mercenary running away. He glanced at me over his shoulder and accidentally bowled over a woman hunched down in terror. His pistol slid free as he tumbled to the floor.

I made a break for them but was too far away. The South American easily recovered. Instead of going for his gun, he whipped a knife from his ankle and hauled the horrified woman to her feet.

"Put down the gun!" he screamed.

My boots skidded on the tile. I didn't have a clean shot at him. Instead of stopping completely, I settled into a slow approach.

"Put it down," he repeated.

I tossed the Uzi aside and continued walking toward him. "Now let the lady go free," I said. There were still ten yards between us.

He backed her away confidently. Looked behind him, further down the hallway. No doubt Connor and the others were escaping right at this moment, but I couldn't do anything for that.

"Let her go," I said. "She's not a part of this."

"You're right," he said.

Standing beside his pistol, he shoved her to the floor and reached for it. I thrust my hand forward and channeled Opiyel. The shadow surged through me. A tentacle reached up from the floor and snagged the man's ankle. Before he could grab the gun, it yanked him away. The mercenary slid toward me in shock. I dodged a wild slash of his knife before bringing my boot down. Two blows bounced his skull on the floor and he stopped moving.

The lady screamed. I helped her up and she shook away from me. "Get out of here," I told her. "That way." She was scared of what was around the next corner but did as instructed. No doubt she was more scared of me.

I backtracked, scooped up my automatic, and continued the chase, boots sliding on slick floors. I steadied myself against the wooden hull of a boat display and looped to a back hallway. Someone else was on the ground.

No. Not someone. The Taíno body from the exhibit. It was hunched in a fetal position, knees to head. The mercs had lugged it this far but ditched it. They knew I was close.

I sprinted past the remains. An emergency exit door was open, blinding sunlight screaming inside. I couldn't see anything but a rectangle of white. I slowed and squinted, not wanting to run headlong into a bullet. My eyes adjusted and I stepped out. A man yelling. A woman flailing her limbs in panic. Otherwise not much activity. Certainly no drug mercenaries.

I stepped toward the plaza to check the street. Two police officers rounded the corner. I turned to the side to hide my Uzi. I stepped back into the doorway and tossed the piece.

"Help!" I said. "They have guns!" I pointed into the museum.

They flashed hardened glances within. Instead of moving past, one of them spun me around, checking me. I didn't have anything incriminating. The scorched jeans were a red flag but the orange T-shirt was more noticeable.

More officers rounded the corner.

"Go with them, sir," the first one told me. They forced me away from the building. A police officer from the new team escorted me to the street while the others headed inside. I scanned the block but saw no sign of *Agua Fuego*. I bitterly complied as the police rounded me up with two other museum-goers. Apparently, they weren't letting us leave.

Chapter 9

The city police were careful. They cleared the museum with squad tactics, moving in before the SWAT team arrived. Evan had told me they had new procedures in light of recent publicized school shootings. Breaching quickly didn't allow suspects to hunker down.

Unfortunately, there were no suspects to speak of. Connor and his men were long gone, and the police had only served to interfere with my chase. Even worse, they were holding anyone they'd caught on the grounds. At best we were witnesses. At worst, suspects. They made us sit in a roped-off section of the open plaza, surrounded by men. No one told us what was going on, but I heard the word hostage thrown around.

I was gonna complain but bit my lip when police escorted the woman I had saved outside. I turned away and snapped my head down. She was the only one who had seen me with a gun. If she mentioned what happened, I'd be taken into custody.

I considered calling Evan. He was a police lieutenant. This was a jam he could get me out of. But I was concerned about getting him involved. Here I was, directly on Connor's trail. That was forbidden ground for Evan. He couldn't join the hunt without opening himself up as a target to the jinn. And I'd sacrificed so much to get him that protection. I wasn't gonna give that up.

The wait dragged on for a couple hours. We were hastily interviewed several times. Name, business, stuff like that. I didn't have ID and I wasn't exactly legally alive anymore, but luckily it didn't get to that. The woman I'd rescued locked eyes with me but saw me loudly protesting any involvement and kept quiet about me. I thanked her with a nod.

The police slowly and carefully came to realize what I'd concluded as soon as I saw them: the heist was over. I began counting the minutes till they let us go. Still, things moved slower than I anticipated.

Then I saw Dr. Trinidad with the police. Dark-skinned, hair wrapped in a bun—she appeared more concerned than shaken up by the whole affair, like a seasoned professional wanting to fix bad news rather than pout about it. Impressive temperament for a museum curator.

"Doctor," I called. I stepped against the cordoned police tape and waved. "Dr. Trinidad."

She turned and studied me quizzically. Despite our mutual research into the Horn, it had been a while since we'd spoken. A thief had tried to get to me through her and the doctor experienced a brush with the supernatural. I laid off after that, but maybe she finally understood the stakes.

"Sit back down," said one of the cops watching the crowd.

"He's with me," said Dr. Trinidad, breaking away from the officers. "He's my friend."

The cop turned to the officer she was talking to and he

shrugged. They let me out. The doctor and I strolled down the sidewalk for some privacy. We approached the museum but didn't enter.

"What happened?" I asked.

"Don't you know?" Her mauve lashes blinked expectantly at me. Of course she knew I was involved.

"All I know is someone wanted the Taíno exhibit. I came here to stop him." I bit down. "I was too late."

"Who killed that man inside?"

"The security guard? They did. He must've tried to stop them."

"I mean the dead gunman," she said tersely.

"Only one of them's dead?" I shrugged. "Look, I just defended myself." I glanced inside the open back door and saw the curled up Taíno body. "It doesn't make sense. I thought they were here to steal something."

"They did," said the doctor. "A Taíno holy item. A zemi. A dog statue of—"

"Opiyelguobiran." I pressed my fingers to my temples.

"You know the one?"

"Intimately. Opiyel's not the main god of the dead, but he serves as a guide to spirits on their final journey. Is that all he stole?"

"It appears that way." Dr. Trinidad crossed her arms. Her expression was pleasantly surprised but her body language was demanding. "Why would somebody do that?"

I stared at the dog collar on my wrist. Opiyel was my patron. That didn't prevent others from tapping his power if the parties were so inclined. But I didn't see what that gained them. Besides, merely swiping an object of reverence isn't enough to channel spirits. It didn't work like that.

"I don't know," I finally answered. "It initially seemed like he wanted the Taíno body. Remains of the dead. That kind of thing has sacramental significance." I noticed the curious look she was giving me. "Theoretically," I added.

She pursed her lips and turned to the body. "That might explain why they took Dr. Gaines."

I remembered what I had overheard the police say. "So they have a hostage?"

"No," she answered grimly. "The police found his body a block away." She paused a moment, revealing a flash of anger and something else. Pain. "Dr. Gaines was on the floor when the gunfire started. We thought he just got caught up in it, but no one else was taken."

"Why would they do it?"

"Because of what he knows," she said. "If what they want is the body of a genuine native Taíno, then what was on display wouldn't work for them."

I again looked at the funeral body in a fetal position. "Why not?"

"Because that one's a fake. Most of the artifacts we display are real, of course, but the funeral exhibit is in open air. It feels more immersive but it exposes the relics to damage. We couldn't take a risk with the preserved bodies."

I licked my lips. "The real bodies are somewhere else."

She nodded. "Three of them. In our archives. It's an offsite facility; part warehouse, part examination room."

"And Dr. Gaines knew about that location."

She nodded.

"Shit," I said. "I need that address now."

Dr. Trinidad didn't argue. She didn't question my motives or whether the police needed to be involved.

Something about the growing mystique over Taíno artifacts had won her over. Despite not having seen direct evidence of spellcraft, she was a student of history. Her reverence and respect for the subject told me all I needed to know. She gave me the address.

"Dr. Gaines was a friend," she said. "He didn't deserve this."

She stopped short of saying anything else. I knew what she wanted. It was the same thing I did. Revenge. I thought it best not to mix her up in the details, though. The problem with revenge is it cuts both ways. They say to serve it cold but that just means it boils in your heart for longer. I didn't want that for her. I thanked her for the help and walked around to the front of the plaza.

With the increased police presence and the incoming reporters, the orange VW was gone. I hit the sidewalk and checked up and down the busy downtown street. There it was, two blocks up. Pretty much nothing more than a limo service. I crossed the street and headed over.

Someone else crossed the street too. A young Cuban kid with wavy hair. He was between me and the van. Didn't even try to hide the fact that he was clocking me.

I kept the same pace, boots calmly rapping the cement like nothing was up. I casually glanced behind as I passed the last cross street before the van. No one on my tail.

I stepped onto the curb, fifty feet from the approaching kid. He was maybe twenty. Scrawny but lean, like a scrapper. Bathed in the storefront shadows, I hardened a mass of darkness over my fist. Forty feet to go.

Rap. Rap. Rap. Rap. Thirty feet. The kid didn't change course. It would be a simple matter to swat him down and sprint for the van.

Twenty feet.

Rushed footsteps shuffled right behind me. I spun just in time. It was the older santera I'd glimpsed on the streets of South Beach earlier. She lifted a necklace of green and black beads to her lips and kissed them. I thrust my hand out, converted the shadow to a wall between us. The woman lashed the necklace at me like a whip. It grew in size, skirted my wall of shadow, and squeezed around my hand like a snake. The beads crunched tight and the wall disappeared.

I gritted my teeth and tried to yank my arm from the old lady's grip. It barely budged. I know, she was just a little old lady. But it was the power of her orisha I was fighting, not her.

The kid charged me from behind now. He swung an aluminum bat in a horizontal arc, straight at my midsection. I put my left arm in the way. Turquoise flashed as the metal bounced. With my right hand still bound, I grabbed his collar with my left and jerked his head into mine. He stumbled to the floor, dazed.

The santera tugged on the necklace. I tried to pull away, but it had me good. Even worse, it was interfering with my ability to tap into shadow. People started yelling around us. The commotion was growing. I had to hurry before the police down the street joined in. The kid on the floor tried to get up but I kicked him in the stomach. He doubled over in pain. His bat rolled over the curb.

Somewhere in my struggle, I realized it was just me and the old lady. Instead of pulling against the necklace, I charged into her. And screw spellcraft. My free hand grabbed the santera's wrist and twisted. Her frail fingers released the necklace. It shrank down to size and went loose. I gripped it in two hands and snapped it. Green and black beads bounced on the concrete. I took a menacing step toward the lady and she fell backward in fear. Then I shook my head and darted for the van.

Berna was already pulling out before I opened the door. I jumped in and she pushed into light traffic.

"What happened?" she asked.

"We need to get to South Miami," I said. "There's a warehouse that has something Connor needs."

"This is bad," said Darcy. She pointed to a police car that pulled in behind us. We were still stuck in traffic.

"They didn't see us," I said. My cell phone rang. Evan's house. I picked it up. "Yeah?"

"Cisco?" came my daughter's hesitant voice.

My body froze. "Uh, Fran? Hi, little one."

Berna swerved around a car to get to the open road. The Cuban kid from the street was up again. Before we could get out of there, he sprinted to the van and jumped onto the back bumper, grabbing a roof flare for support. Berna accelerated.

"What the crap!" cried Darcy.

I lowered in the seat and covered my ear. "What's up, Fran?"

Her voice came back careful. Unsure. She'd never called me before. "I... I just wanted to ask if you were okay. I mean, I know you're helping protect us from bad people but the way you left us this morning—"

"I'm fine. Jumping eight stories into a pool is dangerous, but I know what I'm doing."

The santero kid banged on the back window.

"Are you serious right now?" asked Darcy. She waved her Hecate statue and the boy tumbled to the street.

"I know," answered Fran. "It's just that, Dad says you're always getting yourself into crazy situations and I don't know what to think about that."

"I'm fine, little one. Nothing crazy here."

The police siren sounded behind us. Quick chirps, on and off.

"You sure?" asked Fran.

A voice came over the loudspeaker. "Pull over!"

I cupped my hand around the phone to dull the noise. "Yup," I said. "Everything's good. Just another normal day in Miami." Berna turned down a side street and punched the gas. "Listen, I gotta go. I promise I'll call you later, okay?"

She waited a moment. "Okay."

"And Fran... Happy birthday. I'm sorry I had to run."

The siren chirped again and I ended the call.

"Look what you did," accused Berna.

"I can handle it," said Darcy.

Even though Berna had been talking to me, the girl took it upon herself to fix it. As the officer turned onto the street behind us, she squeezed both hands around her fetish and growled. The police cruiser gained on us until its front left wheel crumpled inward. It jerked to the side and spun into a parked car. Darcy collapsed into the seat and I caught her.

"Holy hell," I said.

Darcy's eyes fluttered. I rubbed the back of my hand against her face. Wet. Warm.

"She's burning up."

"She'll recover," said Berna, twisting down another road.

"She just needs time."

I checked behind us but didn't see police following. "You know," I said, "a bright orange VW Bus isn't the most inconspicuous vehicle out there."

"It's warded," she said. "It shouldn't stand out or be especially memorable."

I snorted. Wards were useful but they weren't bulletproof. Especially against the type of people you really needed protection against. But true to her word no one else picked up the chase. For now, at least, we were clear.

Chapter 10

We pulled up to the address. A block away, of course. That was as far as the Society was willing to help. I couldn't complain this time. Darcy had gotten the cops off our tail and was still recovering. I turned my attention to the museum archives.

It was a boring tan block of a building. Few windows. Iron gate that was probably always open during business hours. A small parking lot with two cars. It looked just as normal as anywhere else. Except three Taíno bodies were inside.

"You look better," I said to Darcy. She was sitting up now. Smiling but obviously lightheaded.

"I can't go in there with you," she said firmly.

"I know. You can't intervene." I winked at her.

"Street thugs are different. I can shake them off you, but I can't go after Connor. He'd recognize me. Us."

I eyed Berna and wondered if she was more than just a driver. Knowing Winthrop, probably. She relaxed in the seat, happy to see I didn't have an Uzi this time.

Darcy's lower lip was thrust out. It was obvious she didn't like being an errand girl. She let her red bangs fall over her face. I sighed. She was just a kid.

"Hey," I said. "Don't sweat it."

She shrugged.

I wondered when she'd come into her considerable power. Who had prospered from her strength. I doubted it was her.

My daughter might've been in a similar boat. I knew for a fact Connor had begun teaching her the workings of spellcraft, without even her mother's knowledge. That was over now. I put a stop to that, but at some point I needed to face facts and ask Fran what she could do. I wondered if spellcraft was a road I wished for anybody.

Darcy turned to me with hard eyes. "What?"

I shook my head. "Nothing."

I exited the van and approached the side of the building. South Miami wasn't as dense as Downtown. Nobody was really in a position to see or care what I was up to. I went right through the front door. A reception desk sat empty. The computer was in the middle of a game of solitaire. I wished I hadn't lost my gun at the museum. The sawed off was still with me, of course. It always was. It followed me wherever there was shadow. Too bad it was useless without a pack of twenty-gauge shells.

Past the small waiting room was a door that led down a long hallway with various walk-in closets storing catalogued boxes of history. Double doors opened up to an Indiana-Jones-style warehouse. Rows of shelves taller than me. Loading doors in the back. This was where I should've seen someone, but the place was empty.

There were a couple of... examination rooms is the best way I could put it. Fluorescent overheads, tables surrounded by lights and instruments and cameras, tiled floors. It almost looked like surgery was performed here. This was where precious relics were studied. So far, so good. This place was exactly what Dr. Trinidad had explained. A research space and offsite storage facility for their rotating collections. Zip on the Taíno bodies, though.

I checked through a window. Back alley. Quiet. The window at the other corner revealed another wing of the warehouse, a separate building connected by an indoor walkway. A steady stream of gray smoke billowed from the chimney. Finally some activity.

I traced the outer wall to the walkway and cautiously moved toward the new building. Double doors entered a library of sorts. It was smoky in here. Dark, with light flickering faintly on academic volumes that filled the shelves. The carpet was a tight fiber that silenced my steps.

I stretched my fingers, feeling the play of the darkness. I flanked around a center pillar of stone and what ended up being a grand fireplace in a private study. It looked like the kind of place Gandalf would've kicked back in, except it was a mess. Victorian couches had been hastily shoved against shelves to clear space. Ash littered the shag rug. Before the smoldering fireplace were three open crates. Their delicately packed contents were smeared with painted symbols. The genuine Taíno corpses, desecrated by spellcraft.

Damn. Connor had already come and gone. I'd been right on his tail but the police had given him all the time he needed.

I circled the site of the ritual carefully. In the fireplace was a blackened husk. Not a body part. I grabbed the fire poker and carefully rolled it out. A four-legged statue bounced on the carpet. My face darkened.

Opiyelguobiran, the Shadow Dog. This was the zemi that was stolen from the museum. My patron, burnt to a crisp. I wondered if it was a message or something more.

Connor had worked something here. I frowned and studied the bodies. They looked very much like the fake recreation in the museum. Fetal position. Worn by the elements and mud and time. Delicately handled, if not skillfully.

I blinked. My irises cracked. The green gave way to the black of my pupils, filling my eyes. The darkness of the room opened to me. As long as I didn't look directly at the remains of the fire, it was dark enough to see the magic. I examined the zemi and the bodies for signs of spellcraft. Glows, enchantments, workings of any sort. This site was an hour old at the most, but I didn't get much of a read on anything.

What had Connor accomplished here? I paced around the room in thought. No. What had he *failed* to accomplish? This was a test run for the Horn of Subjugation. The real reason Connor was in town. He had made a very public show to acquire these relics, only to abandon them. My guess was the jinn was trying to raise the dead himself. It would be impossible with bodies this far gone.

But something nagged at me. Shadow magic. Taíno natives. This was about more than just raising a few zombie lackeys. I eyed the smoking fireplace, wondering just what was going on.

A creak of wood announced a presence at the doorway. I turned, clenching my jaw. A black man in a clean white suit entered. His chest was puffed out and his eyes had an aggressive tinge.

I knew this man. Besides Emily, he was the only other living member of Connor's shattered Covey. But Tyson Roderick, the man standing in the room with me, wasn't a man at all. Not human. Not even close.

Chapter 11

Tyson Roderick had exaggerated features. Large nose, plump lips, puffy cheeks. His hairline was sharp. In another life he'd worked security for a corrupt politician. Now his face was different. Still a fullback of a man, but another form. His true form maybe. Or maybe he had no true human form.

Like the smoldering logs in the fire, his shimmering red eyes hinted at what was just beneath the surface. Tyson was a being of magic. Violent energy ran through his veins, searing and pure. A volcanic elemental, once summoned to the Earthly Steppe for service. The question was, why was he still here?

"Who are you working for, Tyson?" I asked. "Really?"

His voice came out like a jet engine, deep and rumbling. "You have it wrong, human. For the first time, I'm working alone."

"But you're still working?"

I let the question hang in the air. The man had been my enemy once. Twice killed on this steppe, instead of meeting oblivion he'd only been desummoned back to the Aether. At Connor's behest, no doubt, he'd returned. But I'd destroyed the Covey. Tyson no longer had ties here.

"I'm here for vengeance," he said, plain and direct. He balled his fists.

"Kita," I whispered, eyes narrowed. Elementals weren't supposed to concern themselves with human affairs.

Emily's half sister, Kita Mariko, had been Connor's soldier. As part of my effort to defeat the Covey, I'd killed her, only to later discover she was a thrall, just like the others. An innocent woman, dead at my hands.

Tyson moved into the room. I took a step back, keeping ten feet between us.

"Relax, shadow witch. It's not your head I want." The big man's face went somber. He'd worked alongside Kita for ten years, at least. Among humans the connection was clear, but I didn't know what that meant for an elemental.

"You're here for Connor," I concluded. "But how did you know he was here?"

He stepped closer again. This time I didn't back away.

"We share a connection," he said.

"You know where he is?"

"Not exactly." His red eyes traced over the Taíno corpses.

"Connor's working on something big," I explained. "He has the Horn. He's recruited the street. And now he's trying to raise the dead."

Tyson nodded once. "Flexing newfound muscles. Testing his power."

"He has a submarine now. I have some intel saying he's looking for a lost city of gold. If we can work out what he needs exactly—where he's going to be—we can ambush him together."

The elemental shook his head and searched me with his

eyes. Disappointed. "You're thinking like a human. He is a jinn. You need to understand: his operations, his money, his people—they're all expendable. He'll burn it all before he lets you catch him."

I shrugged. "It's worth it if I get the Horn back."

He grunted. "That won't be easy. Connor's hunted the Horn for decades. He's crafted elaborate plots to secure it. He owns it now. You'll never get it back."

I worked my jaw. I was staring at the glowing logs in the fireplace. Watching the fingers of smoke curl in on themselves.

"He's not invincible," I asserted. "I'll find a way to take him down."

Tyson squared himself with me. I was an inch over six feet and he was an imposing figure. "How far are you willing to go to get him?"

I met his eyes. "All the way, Tyson. I have nothing to lose anymore. Emily and the others are protected. I made a deal with Connor for their safety."

"While at the same time opening yourself to attack."

I shrugged.

A deep grunt rumbled through the elemental's chest. "Maybe you've outmaneuvered him."

"I wouldn't go that far, but I got what I wanted."

He nodded. "That's more than Connor usually gives."

I studied the bodies again. Connor didn't like compromise. He didn't like setbacks and failures. At the same time, his long lifespan ensured he could be patient. He was anxious only because his ends were close at hand but, if I managed to get in the way, it would only mean a minor delay on his end.

"What about you?" I asked. "Can you get to him?"

Tyson rolled his lips in frustration. "I'm an elemental. I cannot enter into combat with a jinn."

I wasn't sure what that meant. They were both primal beings, from the Aether. "You can't do anything?" I asked.

"It has to be you."

I hissed, unsure what Tyson was offering me. What he was doing here. "Why me?" I asked. "I was trapped in service to him, same as you. We were all slaves."

"Maybe," he countered, "but you're the only one who outsmarted him."

He jerked his head to the side, seemingly looking straight through the wall. In a few seconds, I heard it. Police sirens. They must've gotten a line on the storage facility. This smoky library was on a side lot, but it wouldn't take them long to find it.

"Okay," I said. "So how do we get to Connor?"

Tyson smiled. "You need to stop thinking like a human."

"Easy for you to say."

Tyson put his arm around my shoulder and pulled me to the fireplace. "Connor's untouchable on the Earthly Steppe, so we need to confront him on another. Attack his power base. We need to go to the Aether."

I froze. "That's *also* easy for you to say. The Aether's made out of fire and air. Mankind can't go there."

He faced me head on and chuckled. "It can be done. It has been done before. You simply need a host. Someone to protect you and lead the way."

I arched a skeptical eyebrow.

"Take my hands, Cisco. Let's hit Connor at his knees."

The elemental held both his mitts out, palm up, rough

calluses waiting on me. In the background the police announced their presence, shouting their intentions, barking sharply as they cleared each room. They were fast and efficient.

Tyson took a measured breath. In and out. Then he narrowed his eyes. "How much do you want this, Cisco? How far are you willing to go for your vengeance?"

My face twisted into a growl. I clasped his hands in mine and he nodded. His eyes flashed brighter. The skin on his face cracked. Thin lines of light widened into gulfs of molten red as his flesh flaked away and hardened into rock. I'd seen this before. Tyson was transforming into his elemental form, a jagged being of rock and magma.

Except this time the lava dripped over my hands. I jerked away from the searing heat but my arms were encased in rock. The igneous layer ran over my body. I twisted and screamed. Twice in one day I was burning alive.

Tyson dragged my struggling body toward the fireplace. The lava trickled up my face. I shook, feeling all the life flee from my blackened body. I screamed again and blazing fire poured down my open throat right before my vision went black.

The sounds of the police were muffled. I was quiet. My twisting panic had ceased. But I felt the rock working through me. Had a dull sense of folding over the warm logs in the fireplace. My knee fractured against brick. Flaking soot that used to be my flesh crumbled. I rocked forward and shattered into pieces. Then whatever was left of my form disintegrated. Ashes to ashes, dust to dust.

I had the vague feeling of rising through the chimney on the wind.

Chapter 12

I jolted awake. A huge, body-spanning convulsion racked all my joints. Except I was never asleep. It was like I jerked free of a waking dream, a level of consciousness I could barely place anymore. The more I concentrated on remembering, the more I forgot.

My eyelids fluttered against intense brilliance. My lashes blinked dust away. I sat up and a sheet of ash flaked off me like dried mud. My skin was raw and pink underneath. My hands weren't burning anymore. I spent a good minute just staring at my palms and the perfect inky snowflake tattoo.

A sound like settling earth broke my focus. I turned to find Tyson's rock form intently eyeing me.

I huffed and shook ash from my hair. "You know, you could've warned me about the whole being-coated-in-lava thing."

The elemental shrugged. "I didn't wanna scare you."

"Fear's healthy," I countered. "It's what keeps us from doing stupid things like..."

I looked around. We were in a wide open scrubland of sand and olive grass. Hillsides hemmed us in from all directions. The sun blazed in the wide-open sky, hot but dry. A rolling breeze swept the browning grass, cool against my face. Tyson and I were alone as far as the eye could see.

"Toto, I've a feeling we're not in Miami anymore."

The elemental arched an eyebrow. "Who's Toto?"

"*The Wizard of Oz*," I chided. "You could learn a lot from that movie, you know. It's clear you have courage. I just can't figure out if it's brains or heart you're lacking."

He grumbled but didn't press the issue. Not a movie buff, then. I didn't mind the silence. It gave me time to take in our new surroundings.

The Aether Steppe. The land above the earth, where jinns and elementals come from. Of course, the Aether's not just really high in the sky. It's not like any chump with a pilot license can make a pit stop here. Just as with the Nether below, spellcraft's required to make the journey.

I crawled to my feet and clapped my hands on my jeans, slowly working the cricks from my bones. That's when I noticed I was wearing a spotless white tank top. No burn marks anywhere. And no orange tee.

"Please tell me I don't need to go all Human Torch again to get out of here."

Tyson stared into the distance. His molten eyes were hard to read. Rivers of magma flowed between the crags of his rockskin, playing a rainbow of reds and yellows over his body. If he was an imposing figure in human form, he was doubly so now. Besides weighing the better side of a VW bug, his stone fingers sharpened to horny points.

"Tyson," I pried, "what aren't you telling me?"

Seeing the large beast squirm under my admonishment would've been amusing if I wasn't so afraid of his answer. "I haven't figured out how to get you out of here yet."

"Out of where?" I asked. "This field? The Aether? Can't

we just hop back out of the fireplace like Santa? Eat some milk and cookies?"

He turned his head to shake it before thinking better of it. "Elementals are not free to leave the Aether on their own. If I had permission I could take you back. Otherwise it's beyond my power. And without a host..."

"You're trapped here so I'm trapped here," I summed up. My little elemental adventure was off to a rocky start, pun intended.

Tyson was quiet and brooding, telling me just enough to take the bait while hoping I didn't notice the hook in my cheek. I narrowed my eyes.

"You died twice," I said.

A bedrock eyebrow shifted up an inch.

"Since I came back from the dead," I explained. "I've seen you die twice. The first time was at City Hall. You were still a slave to the heartstone then. Still Connor's puppet. We mixed it up and I shoved you into the warm waters of Biscayne Bay until you dissolved."

Tyson's jaw ground together like a miniature earthquake. He was prideful and didn't like the thought of getting his ass kicked by a human.

"Second time was the next day. When you and Kita fought me and the Spaniard in the commissioner's yard."

The lava flowing under his skin darkened at the mention of Kita. Tyson was suddenly no longer proud and angry. I couldn't tell what he was.

"I was trying to unsummon you," I continued, "but that revenant attacked us and pile-drived you into the pond."

"I remember, shadow witch," he said morosely.

"That's twice you died," I repeated. "And both times,

your magical energies reformed in the Aether and you were free to once again return to the Earthly Steppe. So why is it that now all of a sudden you're trapped here?"

The elemental released a long sigh. "Politics."

He turned and began hiking to a distant hill. I did a full three-sixty and couldn't tell east from west so I wondered how he knew where he was going. At this point I wouldn't put anything past him. I stood in place, clapping black dust off me, stubbornly refusing to follow. I crossed my arms and waited but Tyson never looked back. He didn't seem overly concerned about me at all. I waited till he was at the foot of the hill.

A shadow rolled over the valley. A sharp cry split the air above. A single enormous bird glided overhead. Its wingspan must've beat fifty feet, and every inch of its plumage rippled with flame. The bird—it could only be a phoenix—veered sharply and disappeared into a cloud system.

I checked Tyson again, halfway up a distant hill. I hurried to catch up.

He marched ahead forcefully, like an automaton. His large stride carried his mass forward with machine-like grace until he stopped at the hilltop and surveyed the ground below. He didn't turn to me when I stopped at his side, but he spoke.

"Before you understand my methods, you need to understand the Aether." He pointed at a dirt road below. A caravan was passing through. Two shaggy elephant beasts at the head and the foot of the line, each with a man riding atop. A string of four humanoids walked single file in between. All four were water elementals. Sloshing, rounded forms flowing blue and white. They marched mindlessly with their heads lowered.

"Prisoners," I said.

Tyson shook his head. "They're in service to the company of jinn. Water's hard to come by in the Aether without a wellspring, so water elementals are extremely valuable and rare. They'll fetch a great price from the lords in the city."

"But they're not chained up," I said. "I don't see magical bindings. Why don't they just run?"

"Politics, human. They're bound to service. Aether law is different from earthly law."

"Bullshit," I said. "Strength is the same no matter where you go. Those elementals can do some damage, can't they?"

"Those jinn aren't pushovers. But that misses the point. The two races share a harmonious relationship that's defined by much more than strength."

I frowned, recalling my encounters with Connor Hatch. Our conversations. He said the jinn were above material wealth. They treasured things that couldn't be held with physical hands. The intangible: Trust. Service. Duty. Information.

I watched the duty-bound elementals, serving in stubborn silence. "Doesn't look so harmonious to me."

Tyson took a long breath. "Your steppe refers to my kind as elementals, but in the Aether we're called aspects. We are resonances of energy. Nothing more."

"The Intrinsics," I said. "The building blocks of spellcraft and the rest of the world. The way I understand it, all beings from the Aether are magic incarnate."

"In some ways, maybe. But even the jinn cannot claim

the purity that aspects personify. My form is molten earth. Without the jinn, I would be little more. They shape us into sentient beings. Shape us for their utility. It's no different than humans harnessing the power of spirits."

I blinked slowly as I took in the new information. "Elementals are the source of jinn magic," I whispered.

Tyson nodded.

Energy inherent. Molded. I suddenly understood what Tyson meant by harmonious. Jinns and elementals needed each other. Jinns for their power, elementals for their being.

"Does your kind have no autonomy in this world?" I asked.

Tyson watched the caravan disappear around a bend. "True autonomy means going inert. Dispersing our energies until we fade into oblivion. What we have is enough."

Now that no one was in sight, the elemental tromped down the hill.

"We go this way."

I followed without the melodrama this time. My cowboy boots slipped on loose rocks a couple times, but mostly the terrain was easy going. It reminded me of those seventies TV westerns. The whole thing made me wanna saddle up a horse, grab a six shooter, and rob a train. But this land was more exotic than my nostalgic imagination. The literal bird on fire showed that much. I would need to keep my eyes open in what was essentially an alien planet.

Sticking close to a walking volcano didn't hurt.

"So you're a rogue aspect," I reasoned. "Free of Connor's control now. That have something to do with why you can't leave the Aether?"

"Yes," he answered. "The only way for us to exit willingly is at the behest of a jinn master."

I noticed he used the word "willingly" and immediately thought of elemental summoning. That might've been an option with some planning on the Earthly Steppe but it was too late for that now.

Chapter 13

We walked in silence for a while after that. Tyson because that was his way. Me because I was content to take in my surroundings. We followed the road but didn't walk directly on it. We merely kept it in sight and moved along the same path. That told me the journey was at least a little dangerous.

Tyson was right about the scarcity of water too. The sun beat down through mixed cloud cover in an azure sky. The land below was semi-arid. In fact, the further we walked, the more patchy the scrubland grew. The hills more desertlike. I was beginning to worry as the temperature peaked. (I may have lodged an idle complaint or two to the heavens.)

Tyson crested the next hill and nodded. "This way."

When I came up behind him, I was stunned. The vista that opened before us looked like the cover of a fantasy novel. The land descended steeply over a rocky ledge that jutted into a sea of fog. And that's exactly what it was. Not just a marine layer of mist hugging the water, but a dense swirl of atmosphere that washed against the land. The clouds ran to the horizon, breaking only when a giant whale breached the surface in the distance before crashing back into the mist.

Tyson descended into the ravine and scaled the edge. His molten eyes darted from one green plant hugging the cliff wall to another. He climbed below the surface of the fog as an updraft caught us like a gentle geyser. A column of fog gave way to open air.

I looked through the vertical tunnel in the fog and recoiled. Nearly crapped my pants, really. There was absolutely nothing below us but a sky diver's dream. Miles and miles of deep sky, with no land in sight. Only problem was, I wasn't wearing a parachute.

"What the hell?" I asked sharply.

Tyson silently took advantage of the temporary visibility gained from the updraft. He scaled deeper another step and plucked two shiny gourds from the tanglework of stems. Then he pulled himself up and out of the flooding fog and sat beside me twelve feet from the edge.

"These will tide you over," he said, dropping the fruit beside me.

I took them dutifully, partially in shock but ravenous all the same. I eyed the strange fruit. Looked kinda like a squash but smooth and plump. I reached for my bronze knife to slice it open. Patted my belt.

"My knife," I said.

Tyson gazed into the endless sea of fog. "Your material possessions have not traveled with you," he explained. "Objects cannot pass between the Earth and the Aether."

I frowned as I ran my eyes over my red boots, my skull belt buckle, the dog collar on my wrist. He caught my meaning.

"Your clothes are part of your persona. A visible reflection of yourself, not unlike how silvans and jinns wear clothes in your world."

That explained the brand-new tank top. It was officially part of my identity now.

"My spellcraft," I said, scrambling to find a patch of shadow in this world of sun. I hesitantly crawled to the edge of the cliff and fanned some fog away with my hand. I tweaked the darkness along the rock wall. It responded forcefully, slithering toward me and wiggling with a life of its own.

"Your spellcraft is of the shadow," explained the elemental. "Intangible by nature. You should find it potent here. Your necromancy, on the other hand, may be all but useless."

I sighed in relief and dissipated the construct. At least I wasn't completely naked. I could work with that. I returned to my seat and bit into the gourd. It crunched like an apple. Sweet juice filled my mouth. I finished it quickly.

"Eat the other," said Tyson. "I don't need it."

He stood to resume the hike. I ate on the way.

After I was sated, I again considered my host. He was blunt, quiet, and always pushing forward. This was a mission for him, I realized. I didn't say anything and let him lead the way.

We followed the fog's edge. Several times I saw more exotic creatures in the distance, although they were small and unimpressive in scale. A flight of wyverns chased each other and dipped into the sea. A field of balloons drifted along the current, sometimes taking flight above the surface and revealing jellyfish tentacles before succumbing once again to gravity and nestling back into the fog. We also passed over a network of holes in the rocks where worms the size of snakes weaved in and out like rodents.

"Aren't they afraid of digging out through the bottom of the world?" I asked offhandedly.

Tyson glanced at me sideways. "It's foreign to you, but this is my home. The Aether. We cling to the rock but we live in the sky."

I nodded and stared at the ocean of fog. "There must be a whole ecosystem in that mist."

"The drift," he corrected. "Like your oceans on Earth, the drift is beautiful but exceedingly dangerous."

"The drift, or what lives inside it?"

He smiled.

"I've always wanted to see what the belly of a whale looked like," I muttered.

"Bah," Tyson scoffed. "The whales are the gentle ones. Just keep it simple. Don't wander in the drift and you don't need to find out what's inside."

Sounded like good advice.

By the time we approached some huts on the horizon, I was all *National Geographic-ed* out. Civilization was a welcome sight, but I didn't have any illusions that we were safe.

"Where are we heading?"

"A common wayfaring point, frequented by traders and the like. Keep your head down and your eyes to yourself."

I snickered. "You obviously don't know me well."

The road we'd been avoiding skirted closer to the ravine now, squeezing us in. The small row of pinioned huts resembled a hunting outpost, the outskirts of civilization but lacking the structure. Three men huddled around a raised pyre. At first I figured it for a campfire for cooking but it was too large. It didn't take three people to grill a few burgers and it certainly wasn't cold enough to huddle around a fire. Then I noticed it wasn't lit, but the three jinns held up their palms as if they were being warmed.

Tyson frowned. His step stuttered as he considered crossing to the outer road. But he was determined to move on and we were already exposed so he pressed forward.

I followed carefully, not thrilled about getting up close and personal with jinnfolk. "How big a deal is it that I'm a human?" I whispered.

"None at all," he said. "As long as they don't realize."

"And will they?"

He turned to me. "Visitors in your world aren't always easy to spot. And when they are, they should be treated cautiously."

Great. So I was the monster here. *I Am Legend*. Richard Matheson would be proud. Will Smith, too. I frowned sternly as we approached the huddled men. They weren't warming their hands. They were weaving a working. Twitching their fingers and teasing a glow from the center of the smooth stones. A salamander rose from the earth, orange as fire and just as ethereal.

"Mark it," said one of the men.

Another pulled a golden needle from a fold of his shirt. He spoke some words and pierced the lizard with it. Instead of thrashing, the action seemed to give the salamander definition. Form. The needle was absorbed into the thing's body.

They were trapping an elemental. It was like Tyson had said. Aspects were probably caught and traded like *Pokémon* here.

Their precise working accomplished, the men looked up from their fire. I dropped my head and marched forward, following Tyson's lead, hoping we could skirt their whole ceremony and be on our way.

"That's a big one!" a jinn exclaimed, eyes wide. He wasn't fearful, though. He was hungry.

"You do not lie, brother," said another. Calm. Careful.

Tyson picked up his pace and attempted to pass the men. They hurried into our path.

"You here to do business?" asked the calm one. The third still hadn't spoken.

Tyson halted in his tracks. I waited for him to answer but realized the three jinns were addressing me. That made sense. He was a second-class citizen here. A tool more than an equal. I cleared my throat.

"Just moving through," I said.

"You sure we can't talk trade?" asked the first jinn. He was a jittery fellow. Nervous and jumpy. "We could use a battle aspect these days. The damned skags are getting bolder every day."

"No thanks," I said. The calm one eyed me suspiciously. "Keep moving," I told Tyson, putting my hand on his shoulder and directing him. He sidestepped the men and headed past. They fell in step alongside us.

The third jinn finally spoke. His voice was high-pitched and hurried. "You can't protect what you don't claim," he said.

The nervous one chuckled and nodded. "He speaks truth. You can't protect what you don't claim."

Tyson continued walking. I tightened my fist and turned around, walking backward to keep between them.

"Leave them be," rasped an old woman at the doorway of the largest hut. Her leathery skin was wrinkled and worn. Her silver hair was brittle and patchy. For a jinn, that meant she was very, very old. "He is owned by another," she said.

The three jinns immediately backed away, reproached by their mother. I waited a tense moment, knowing for a fact she had power to be worried about. Not because she was big or loud, but because she didn't need to be.

Her eyes were mottled blue and white, like the sky. They studied me curiously, then she said, "You two move along, now. You don't have any business here."

I nodded briskly. Tyson hadn't even paused long enough for that. We stomped away from the huts, meeting the dirt road and staying on it until the hunting outpost shrank in our wake.

I let my shoulders relax. The tug on the shadow eased up. We wouldn't need to fight just yet, but it was only a matter of time.

And then there was Tyson. The woman had said he was owned by another. If elementals served in bondage, who did Tyson swear fealty to? It was clear he had a plan, but I was beginning to second guess the part I was playing.

Chapter 14

The journey was easier going on the road. Despite running alongside the rocky cliff edge, the land was flatter here. My jeans and tank top didn't exactly scream local but the few travelers we passed kept to themselves, possibly more wary of us than the other way around.

Most of the time I kept my gaze on the sea of fog, looking for glimpses of the sky below. I imagined Miami was down there somewhere. I never saw anything. The clouds were vast sheets of matter held together with a kind of surface tension. More familiar cumulus clouds littered the distant sky. It was a sight that defied reason. Beautiful but barren. Constricting but vast. As the sun faded into the growing layer of overcast sky, I saw something even more amazing.

Miles away, a structure extended to the heavens. Floated, even. And it wasn't just a structure but a series of them. Horizontal concentric rings, like roadways, circled a mighty tower. Each ring was made up of hundreds of smaller buildings, jutting into the sky like weathered teeth. The mighty skyline was so far away it was difficult to judge its size.

An entire metropolis nestled in the clouds.

"The capital city of Maqad," said Tyson. "Seat of the shah." He grunted and trekked forward as if his words fully explained everything.

The city was magnificent, perched high above the drift. Pillars led below the structure and down into the fog. I wondered if those were supports, like houses built on stilts. Except what would they be standing on?

I admired the stunning horizon. It looked like a painting except the clouds were moving. (It would've made a killer animated desktop.)

"Why do I get the feeling that's our destination?" I asked.

He smiled at me. "Because that's where the Aether's power base lies."

I frowned. I didn't want to bring up the obvious, but we couldn't exactly fly over there. I didn't consider myself scared of heights in general, but it seemed like ninety-nine percent of anything in this steppe was open sky. It would be hard *not* to fall into permanent oblivion.

"Here it is," said the elemental.

I shifted my eyes to the road. Ahead of us was some kind of bazaar. Red and yellow tents crisscrossed our once direct path like a flea market from hell. Crowds of jinns and elementals wandered the stalls. A blue-painted man haggled with a winemaker. A crone displayed cages of birds that crackled with electricity. Dogs with jagged stripes chased each other, stitching between passersby. It was ten kinds of crazy, and pretty soon we were smack dab in the middle of it.

The crowd was a good thing, I told myself. This was a bustling trading hub. Everyone was too busy trying to make a buck to focus on the human and the rogue elemental. We slalomed through the people with little trouble. I didn't even have to worry about my pockets being picked because my possessions didn't exist in the Aether.

The marketplace was larger than it had seemed from a distance. Rows and rows of tent booths flapped in the wind. I followed Tyson's lead and ignored it all. We escaped through the bazaar and found ourselves in the town proper. Clay buildings constructed in bricklike clumps, mostly low to the ground. The alleys weren't empty but the people here lacked the bustle of the marketplace. The buildings were simple but effective. We headed toward one of the few exceptions—the only one with an arched roof.

Like a church at the center of a colonial town, the tallest building towered over the others, visible from blocks away. It was an impressive mix of clay and stone, but it was also the oldest building around, showing signs of age and even damage. The entire facade was covered in drapery. Steel beams supported a cracked wall. This place was mid restoration.

Tyson threw the thick red curtain aside and we hurried into the public house. Mid restoration was both right and wrong. There was no remodeling going on, but the front wall of the building was half missing. The curtains were a temporary enclosure. Ignoring that, everything else was normal.

The interior wasn't fancy, exactly, but it was decadent compared with everything else I'd seen so far. A deep crimson carpet softened my boot steps. Similar red curtains lined the walls at intervals, framing low booths of cushions. Group hookahs dotted the floor. Men and women sat on pillows and passed their pipes in a circle. Tall, thin cups, flared like hourglasses, clumped around steaming ceramic pots.

I turned to my host, unimpressed. "I can't decide if this is a tea house or an opium den. Either way, no thanks. I'm more of a coffee guy. Cuban, preferably."

"Sorry," said Tyson. "No coffee here."

"Not even a Starbucks?"

A wisp of smoke thickened beside us, growing into a ghostly figure. Most of it was translucent except for the face: vacant eyes and drooping mouth. Tyson mumbled something to the elemental and it nodded and led us to a dark nook. A low table lined the curved red mattress that made up our booth. I watched Tyson sit, half worried his molten essence would set the cushion ablaze. Thinking about it, this whole place was a fire hazard. But nothing happened and I didn't want to stand out, so I sat as well.

"What is this?" I asked.

My voice was jarring, like I was yelling in a library. I kinda preferred the commotion outside. At least that way I knew the attention was elsewhere. But I looked around. Half the crowd chatted in low whispers and the rest seemed content to relax in comfortable silence.

I turned when Tyson didn't answer. He was staring ahead at nothing, moping more than usual. I leaned forward and repeated myself in a forceful whisper. "What is this?"

His red eyes studied me and then flicked to the side table. The smoke elemental appeared with a tea pot. He poured a greenish drink into three hourglass cups and set the pot down with a bow. Then he seemed to waver until I couldn't tell him apart from the ambient smoke.

"Drink," said Tyson, quickly taking his own advice and downing a cup. I picked mine up. The pot was ceramic but I couldn't tell what the cup was made out of. Not bone, not ivory, but something similar maybe. I studied the liquid more carefully. It smelled like tea but more pungent. Little bits of spice swirled in the cup. I scooted further in, rested my back against the stone wall, and tentatively took a sip.

Bitter. Not floral or herbal. Grassy. The flavor was subtle but strangely potent. I had a larger taste and felt invigorated.

Tyson sighed. "Memories. Nostalgia. Is this what it feels like to be human?"

I arched an eyebrow. "It's just tea, bro."

"Tea's important to my people. Look around."

I did again. Groups traded smiles. Others closed their eyes as if relaxing at the beach. Brown-skinned, olive, and black—the crowd was eclectic but harmonious. "I don't—"

"Tea houses are the one place where aspects sit alongside jinns. That woman in purple with the hookah, that bald man in the long coat—they're elementals."

I squinted sideways at them. "I can't tell."

He shrugged. "They even welcome humans in here, as rare as it is." He pursed his lips thoughtfully. "Kita was here twice."

I paused mid sip. The dead paper mage. He was talking about her like he loved her, but he was an elemental. That's why he was going on about human emotion and nostalgic memories.

"She's the reason you're doing this," I said. "Isn't it?"

Tyson didn't answer this time, choosing to remain stoic and mysterious. He remained in his elemental form. Besides the spooky waiter, no other aspect here had. I finished my cup and went to pour another. My eyes fell on the third cup.

"We're meeting someone," I said, not a question but a revelation.

This time Tyson graced me with a nod. He still wasn't talking. I slammed my cup down.

"Listen, I'm all for your plan to bring Connor down. This is your home. You know it better than I do. But I'm not some lost puppy for you to drag around. I need to know things."

His eyes met mine again. "Like what?"

I shifted and leaned on the wall again. "For one, how are we supposed to hurt Connor? He's still a jinn, right? If he walked in here right now, what would stop him from blinking around?"

"The rules you know—jinns can't hurt humans outside of a bargain—that all goes out the window. Those are the laws for the Earthly Steppe. It's different here, even for him. He can't flash around at will. He can't escape to your realm unless he moves to the outskirts in the wild." Tyson killed his cup and smacked his lips. "In the Aether, you'll find the jinn are exceedingly human."

Connor was vulnerable. I could work with that. "So we fight him here."

"We don't need to. It would still be too dangerous. He has too many connections. But those connections are his weakness too."

"You're not making sense, Tyson."

"The Aether is a world built on servitude," he stressed. "Servants for servants. Masters for masters." He narrowed his molten eyes. "And even Connor Hatch answers to another."

Holy shit. The drug kingpin of the Caribbean, the new Pablo Escobar—he had a master? Maybe that's why Connor spent so much time on earth. I couldn't imagine him bowing down to someone in a million years.

I opened my mouth to speak but instead heard an ear-piercing shrill. A man tumbled inside and into a group of pillows and people like a bowling ball. I jumped to my feet and looked to the front curtain. A humanoid twitched a feathery head sideways, staring at me with a single eye like a bird. His sharp beak cracked open and let loose another shrill cry. Then he came at me.

Chapter 15

I wasn't sure what I was looking at. Some cross between a man and a bird and a velociraptor. Besides the avian head, his skinny legs were wrapped tight like a kickboxer's. He wore a heavy cloth jerkin-and-pants combo, but his arms extended into thick plumage that matched his tail. I'm not talking frail, tickly feathers either. These were as thick as cowhide. A fact I became keenly aware of when a quick swipe whipped me across the head and spun me to the floor.

A heavyset man on the other side of the room charged him. The bird creature spun a short spear into his midsection. After impaling him, both feathered arms hurled the weapon overhead, lifting him off the carpet in a smooth arc and slamming him down on the other side. By that point the large man had transformed into a hulking mass of packed dirt. Another elemental.

With the birdman's back to me, I didn't wait. I somersaulted ahead and drew the murky opium-den environs to my fist. The creature turned around as my shadow punch met his stomach. He squawked and flew backward, bowling through the curtain at the entrance. I jumped to my feet and braced myself for a return attack.

The dirt aspect yanked the spear from his torso and

dropped it beside him. Then he shook his head and returned to his seat, casting only a cursory glance outside.

Tyson sighed. "Skag raiders." He said it like he was talking about his tax return. Crappy, annoying, but a necessary and occasional evil.

I turned to all the other tea house patrons. The group that had been leveled were reaffixing their hookah to the bowl and had already rearranged their pillows.

"Is everyone just gonna sit there?" I asked.

One of them glared at me like I was causing a scene.

There was more shouting outside. Quick steps on dirt, weapons clacking together. I turned to Tyson. This was insane.

Another shrill caw interrupted us. Clawed feet scratched the carpet. The skags reentered the tea house. Two of them, this time. One held a short blade.

Tyson huffed. The magma flowing under his rockskin flared. "Oh, all right," he said, standing up. "It looks like this is going to be a distraction." He fell in at my side. A couple others stood as well, including the dirt elemental. I traded glances with everyone in our line. Then I smiled.

These skags didn't stand a chance.

The front facade of the establishment exploded outward. The curtain ripped. The steel framework snapped. Even a new piece of the stone wall broke away. In a flurry of smashing dust, the two skags crashed through the patchwork storefront and landed hard on the sand. The four of us followed outside to assess the damage. The two birdmen didn't get up. I now knew why the front of the tea house had been damaged and shoddily repaired.

Unfortunately, we didn't have a lot of time to bask in our

defense of the establishment. The large alley of businesses was packed with scrambling denizens of the trading port. Some running for their lives, some protecting their shops, and some fighting the raiding party of skags.

"More and more of them," spat the dirt elemental beside me. He charged ahead to join the fray.

I turned to Tyson with a sour expression. "This isn't because of us, is it?"

"Don't be ridiculous. The skags are petty raiders who rebel against jinn rule. They're inconsequential."

I watched the electrified combat. Fists against feathers. Curved swords kept generally lighter weapons at bay. If the skags depended on flight, they wouldn't easily carry heavy weapons or armor. That flight, however, made up for the disadvantage. The birdmen swooped down from above and struck fast before retreating out of reach, only landing and engaging when they had a true advantage. So far they were harassing the townsfolk, but it wasn't a slaughter.

I felt the air beat on my back before I heard him. A huge skag raked at me with clawed feet. I shielded myself with my forearm. Sharp daggers clashed against my Nordic armor. I was knocked on my back as my attacker flew away.

The sun was blazing in the Aether but the sky was overcast enough to soften the light. That softened the shadows too. It didn't give me a lot to work with out here. I backed against a small wooden building that had an overhang.

Two birdmen landed on either side of me. The big one that had attacked me and a woman with a red-tipped tail. They both started squawking and it suddenly felt like I was in the middle of the most awkward mating ritual ever.

Meanwhile, Tyson was chasing another skag down the road.

My two attackers didn't showboat for long. Moving as one, they struck. Redtail swung some kind of multi-pronged short leather whip while the other attacked with a kick again. I called on the shadow and faded into the floor. Both their swipes missed their mark. The skags fumbled to avoid hitting each other. That's when I made my move.

The spot of shadow was too small to change my position much, so I merely sidestepped and caught the woman's whip at the end of her swing. I yanked on it to spin her around and then kneed her in the stomach. As her thin frame doubled over, I clasped my hands together and brought them down hard on the back of her head.

At least, I tried to. The big one kicked me in the chest and shoved me back into the sun. I'd only glanced the woman's head, and she was still on her feet. The big skag jumped over her with a flutter of his wings and tried to stomp me with a heavy landing.

I rolled away, kicked my boots under me, and leapt at him. My fist swung wide as he darted to the side. I stumbled closer to the woman again, who was rearing up with another snap of her whip. I waved my hand at her area under the awning and the shadow went sludgy. Her strike slowed like she was underwater, fighting against the thickening darkness. I easily caught the whip again, pulled her toward me, off balance, and decked her.

She was down this time but I was distracted again. Sharp claws grabbed my shoulders and heaved me upward. The only thing I had a grip on was the pronged whip. I clutched it for dear life but it ripped free from the collapsing skag's hand and I took to the air.

Powerful wings beat over me, each bass drum lifting us higher. I willed a tentacle of shadow up. It snagged my boot and stalled the skag's ascent. He glanced down and snarled, flapping harder. His sharpened toes curled and dug into my skin. I groaned and flailed, just five feet in the air. My alligator boot kicked over the awning. In a heartbeat, the shadow on the floor was snuffed out. My manifestation vanished, letting us take flight. We rose above the crowd. I saw Tyson fending off three skags at once.

I twisted in pain, trying to escape the skag's claws, but it was no use. His legs were strong. He let out a raucous series of chirps like laughter. Then he snapped at me with a pointed beak.

I jerked my head away. The second time his head came down, I shoved the whip into his mouth. He bit down hard but couldn't break the thick leather. His flight veered slightly out of control. My boots came close to the combat below me. But he ripped the whip away and spit it out. In seconds we were ascending again.

Screw this. If I let this wrestling match go any higher, all he had to do was drop me. I tried to pry his claws from my flesh but he only squeezed tighter. The searing pain made me momentarily dizzy. Warm blood washed over my fingers. And I smiled.

Tyson had told me my necromancy was useless in the Aether. That death worked differently here. Well, I wasn't sure how well skags and elementals and jinns bled, but I was still human, damn it.

Both my crimson-covered hands clamped onto the skag's thin ankles. With a force of will, I cursed the blood on my palms. It turned like sour milk. Burning, sizzling. The skag extended his body in shock. Loosened his toes. My chewed-up flesh fell free of his claws, but I held tight.

We were high in the sky now. I scanned the crowd and reoriented myself, finding Tyson below. He was still surrounded. A stream of lava blasted from his mouth but the birdmen dodged the attack. I grunted. We were too high for a freefall, but that status was rapidly changing.

The big skag rasped and kicked his strong legs, trying to shake me off like a bad hangover. I heaved and hopped in the air, doing my best to upset his balance and pull him down. He swerved right and left in the sky, wildly careening toward the ground. I tightened my searing grip and steered him like a parachute toward Tyson. Lower and lower, until I unclasped my hands and dropped like a rock.

I used one of the skags attacking Tyson as a cushion. His bones cracked as I landed on his back. Another lay in a burning, steaming heap of magma. The third birdman swiveled his head from me to Tyson before launching into the sky and retreating. I spun around to find the big skag that had taken me for a ride doing the same.

"Nice friends you got," I told him. "We should really do this more often."

He snorted and fixed his eyes on the crowd. I followed his gaze and saw a man walking through the chaos. He wasn't fighting. He wasn't dodging. He didn't even seem to weave around the brawlers in the road. Instead this man walked in a straight line toward the broken tea house entrance and the chaos seemed to move out of *his* way.

He wore a red hood over his head that ran along his back in a half cape. White fur hugged his shoulders and rested over intricate leather armor, dark with metal rivets. He strolled forward with ease, completely oblivious to his surroundings. Or completely unconcerned. It was like everybody was ignoring him except me and Tyson.

"Don't tell me," I said as the mysterious figure disappeared into the tea house. "That's who the third cup of tea is for."

Chapter 16

The alley was still embroiled in combat, and I could only imagine what the flea market looked like, but the initial tide had turned. The townspeople had rallied and survived the first wave. The skags backed off as they were wounded, and I knew from personal experience that jinns and elementals were hard to kill. When Tyson considered the battle no longer worth attending to and returned to the tea house, I followed him.

Surprisingly, we weren't the only ones. The dirt elemental wasn't back yet, but most of the others were. It seemed like a good portion of the populace thought of the skags as no more than a daily inconvenience. The rush-hour traffic of the Aether. I had so many questions, but the biggest one on my mind wasn't about birdmen or jinn politics.

Tyson returned to the curtained booth in the back. I approached with caution. The man in the red hood rested against the wall with his feet crossed, where I'd been sitting.

A volcanic elemental, a necromancer, and a mysterious stranger walk into a bar... There's a punch line there somewhere—I just don't know what it is yet. Tyson settled down and grabbed his cup of tea. They all had fresh pours. I frowned and waited.

The stranger pulled the red hood behind his head. Curls of black hair. A flash of sky-blue eyes. Bronze skin and a strong jaw, so clean shaven it had that baby quality.

"Be not afraid, friend," he said to me.

Suddenly I felt a little silly standing. A cursory glance around the curtained interior proved no one was concerned with us or the dwindling battle outside. I nodded slightly and took a seat on the edge of the booth.

Tyson spoke low and direct. "I wasn't sure you'd come, Malik."

The man smiled. "I told you I would welcome you home with open arms. It is good you've finally decided to return to your place."

The elemental grunted. "Can't say the same about you, can we?"

Malik's smile was a permanent fixture, as was his confidence. "I'm where I'm always needed." He drank from his cup. Tyson and I did the same.

"And what is it we need?" I asked.

"Entry into Maqad," said Tyson.

"With your mark?" asked the man. "And a human? The officiates would love that."

"That's why we're going in unannounced."

Malik scoffed lightly. "I am no smuggler."

"Aren't you?" asked Tyson pointedly.

Malik smiled.

"Speaking of which," I cut in, "who exactly are you?"

A sip of tea and a pause to savor the flavor. "I'm a visitor to this world," he answered. "Like yourself."

That confirmed he was no jinn, but I'd already guessed

as much. And I'd eat my boots if he was human. "What kind of visitor?" I pressed.

"Is it so easy to forget us?" he asked wistfully.

Tyson grunted and spoke plain. "He's a lost Celestial."

The humor fled Malik's face, disappointment evident. "So direct, my friend. So banal."

The elemental shrugged.

I narrowed my eyes at their implication. "I don't believe in angels and demons," I said firmly.

"Then," noted Malik, "you are half right and half wrong."

I snorted as our guest waved for the servant. The smoke elemental appeared with his hands full, already knowing what Malik required. The wispy servant placed a silver tray of black sand on the table beside a tray with wrapped tobacco. Between them he placed a lit stick of incense on a stand.

After the servant retired, Tyson said, "Malik likes to speak in riddles but, believe me, he is what he says he is."

"Oh yeah?" I asked. "How is the big man?" I pointed up.

The Celestial's smile didn't waver. "Does he always do this?" he asked Tyson. "Make light when he needs someone's help?"

"Seems to be a defense mechanism," agreed Tyson.

I shook my head and sighed. "Well, excuse me if I don't believe you're hiding wings under that cloak."

"We both have wings, Cisco Suarez," said Malik evenly. "You will find yours before you are through, or you will fall at your enemy's feet."

Everyone's face darkened on that grim note. I sipped tea and watched the so-called angel. Malik picked up a cigarette, lit it with the stick of incense, and smoked. Divine.

"Man is a funny creature," mused Malik between puffs. "So eager to believe in nothing but himself."

As he spoke, he traced the stick of incense over the black sand. The lines exposed the silver below in the form of a classic stick figure: a round head, a stick body, arms straight like a cross, and diagonal legs. Malik drew the figure so it faced me, and then drew two more so there were three in a row.

I plucked a smoke from the other tray and extended my hand for the incense. "You mind?"

"Not at all."

Malik handed me the stick and I lit whatever passed for tobacco in the Aether. Unlike the tea, the smoke was harsh and sent me into a fit of coughing.

The Celestial continued as if I hadn't interrupted him. "You have heard of the three beings of creation, haven't you, Cisco?"

I tried to speak but could only manage a nod.

Malik pointed to the tray of stick figures. "Three sapient beings. Humans, Celestials, and jinns. My kind are creatures of guidance." He leaned in to me. "Even when my advice is unsolicited." Malik pointed at the patrons of the tea house. "Jinns are creatures of duty. Service is at the core of their livelihood."

I echoed Tyson's description of Aether hierarchy. "Masters for masters." I took another drag but had already decided I wasn't a smoker. I didn't like it on Earth and I didn't like it in the Aether. "And humans?" I asked. "What are we creatures of?"

"Freedom, of course." Malik flicked ash into the black sand. "Defining traits are central to both empowerment and ruin."

I snickered. My eyes strayed to Tyson. "Riddles," I said with distaste. And then I paused. Had he been talking about me or Connor?

Malik accepted the stick of incense again and took it to the black sand, noting the three figures. "These days, man looks around and only sees himself."

He added two vertical lines to the first stick figure, each leading from the tip of the arm to the tip of the leg. It suddenly looked like a hieroglyphic of a winged man. A Celestial. He skipped the middle figure and added a single horizontal line to the third from one foot to the other, essentially merging both legs into a triangle.

"But if the man in the middle takes a closer look," finished Malik, "he'll find he's not alone."

I brought my cigarette down on the third figure, extinguishing it on what was purportedly the jinn. I dragged the butt through the drawing, obliterating it. "Story time's nice but if you truly wanna help you'll tell me how to crush Connor Hatch."

Malik returned the incense to its stand and leaned back against the wall with a smile. "I thought I just did." He took a final puff and extinguished his own cigarette over the drawing of the angel. It left the human, me, all alone again.

Tyson must've seen my face redden because he broke in. "That's enough talk. We can deal with Connor. What we need is access to the capital. Either you'll help us or you won't. Or you can't."

Malik laughed. "You know better than to challenge me

thus, friend. Believe me, it can be done."

"It's allowed?"

"It is allowed to help you help yourselves. In a roundabout sort of way."

I waved the last of the dying smoke away from my face. This place had a certain charm but I was ready to move on. This was Tyson's show, though, and I decided to let him finish it.

"Tell me," said the elemental.

Malik reached under one of his sleeves and produced a coin of once-shiny bronze. The pressing was uneven and the design rudimentary. All I knew was it was old. He gave the coin to Tyson, who turned it over in his hand. I caught a glimpse of dragon wings on one face.

"You want me to walk in there with this?" asked Tyson sternly.

"The coin doesn't spend anywhere else," said Malik.

"But... you know how they play with his kind."

Malik's blue eyes twinkled as they fell on me. "Experience is a better teacher than I."

I ignored the jab and poured a round of tea. There was only enough for a half cup each. I killed mine quickly. Tyson frowned at his in uneasy silence. Malik sipped and considered his cup. "But then, our tea is done. It's time to say farewell."

I arched an eyebrow. "You know, we could just get another pot."

The would-be Celestial smiled. "Moderation in all things, my friend."

He held up his hand as if to say "You first." I backed out of the booth so he could slide out. Tyson joined us on our feet, and we all considered one another quietly. Muddied conversation and laughter filled the warm room. Malik and Tyson locked wrists. I accepted Malik's arm as well. It wasn't that I didn't like the guy. I just didn't go for this cloak-and-dagger stuff.

"Be careful, unlikely companions," he warned. "Neither of you will be well-received in this duty-ridden world."

"Some duty is noble," said Tyson. "You of all people can understand that."

Malik didn't smile with his rejoinder this time. Instead his lips tightened. "It is often the noblest men who endure the roughest winds. Be sure of your path, my friend."

Malik pulled his hood over his head. The cape wasn't as bright as the lively red curtains and pillows adorning the tea house, nor as deep and luxurious as the maroon carpet. It was a muted shade, faded yet enduring, like dried blood.

His face was darkened by the cowl. Black and nondescript. He was a stranger again. Somehow I could tell he was studying me.

"Perhaps we will meet again, young one." His voice, like his countenance, seemed strangely distant. Deep and familiar, but without the amiable flavor it held a second ago. "Or perhaps not."

He spun his boots stiffly, made his way to the broken storefront, and turned the corner out of sight. Tyson and I took the same path, almost as if drawn to the enigmatic figure, to bask in his grace even if only for a moment longer. Once the sun hit our faces, though, he was gone.

A pathetic screech from above drew our attention. Tyson's reflexes were quicker and he tackled me. A bloody skag crashed into the dirt where we'd been standing. Her wings and legs were sliced up and her neck was bent at an unsavory angle. A few jinns erupted in a cheer as the last of the raiders fell.

Bodies were strewn across the road, but not many. Most of the skags had retreated. It was a low-risk, low-gain attack. One, apparently, built into the culture of the Aether outskirts. It unsettled me how casual everybody was about it. Clearly, this was a wild realm.

"Let's get out of here," I muttered.

Chapter 17

I was happy to be on the north road out of town. The well-traveled trade route took us directly away from the port, moving toward the center of whatever hulking land mass we were on.

"What's wrong with this place?" I asked.

Tyson trudged forward in thought for a moment. "What do you mean?"

"Are you serious? Those attacks back there. How little everyone seems to care about them. What's with the bird people?"

The volcanic elemental hiked his wide shoulders. "The great city of Maqad is the capital of the realm. It's ruled by five great jinn satrapies. Five houses that own the sky islands."

"I thought you said the city was ruled by a shah."

"The king of kings," he said with a nod. "When a shah dies, the satraps appoint one of their own as a successor. They all live within the great city, but they govern the land without all the same."

I watched the trading post shrink behind us. Along the horizon, the floating rings of the capital faded into the hazy sky. "Where do the birdmen fit in?"

"They don't," said Tyson abruptly. "The jinn rulership is concerned with order. Controlling the aspects. Shaping the magic. Aside from that, the fringe races are free to govern themselves, as long as there's order."

"Sounds like a better deal than the elementals get."

"It is what it is. The Aether's a place of great irony. Creatures large and small are born of magic, built of fire and air, yet nevertheless dependent on water. And these last few decades have been the driest on record."

I snorted. "Climate change in the Aether."

"Your world doesn't have a monopoly on greed. Water's a natural resource. The flyers, especially, have always had easy access, but tightening restrictions and drying wells are putting a squeeze on everybody. The conflicts have escalated over the years. Now the ruling shah has banned all skags from the capital, cutting them off even more. They're no match for us, as you've seen. They must continually raid to survive. To steal resources. To protest the satrapies."

"You sound unusually sympathetic to their plight."

"I've long stopped giving a shit about royal interests."

"Apparently." I chewed my lip, trying to take in the politics of the land. Wondering if it mattered. I considered the satrapies and the shah. I thought of Tyson's earlier words. Servants for servants. Masters for masters. "So that's why people live outside the city," I gleaned. "They eschew the safety and convenience so they can be free."

"Jinns and aspects are never completely free. That's a human trait. Aether politics is built on service. Agreements are arranged, service for status. It's the way of things. But it's true that those without such status may choose to serve outside its confines. And of course, there are many fringe races who are all too happy to do so."

All too happy to live outside jinn order. Something told me that's why we were marching in the opposite direction of the capital city even though it was our destination. As we hiked, we split off the well-worn road and made towards rockier ground. Foothills with great mountains in the distance. It would take hours to reach them.

"So by my reasoning," I said, "Connor Hatch is in hock to one of the five satrapies, and we're going to the capital to smear his good name. So who's past the mountains?"

Tyson stopped at the bottom of a foothill. A stone pillar balanced on the ground, perfectly shaped into an even square, like a fencepost. Carved into the unadorned rock were two symbols. An X, and then a character which was newly familiar. A stick figure with an extra horizontal line running along the bottom. Not a man, or an angel, but...

"The enemy of my enemy," grumbled Tyson. Then he pressed forward.

I snorted as I thought about Malik. So his lesson on the three fabled races had actually had a point. This figure represented the jinn. There was no doubt in my mind this sign was a warning, with the preceding X having a crystal clear meaning: No jinn allowed.

I doggedly stuck to Tyson's heels, wondering who would have the audacity to post such a decree, wondering if we really were safer without the civilized structure of jinn law.

The path was long. The going grew more arduous. Rocks skipped under my boots. The slope steepened. At times it seemed like there was no path at all. But I was strangely invigorated, despite not having had a real meal in hours. I suspected the tea was nourishing for travelers in this arid land. It gave us the endurance to endlessly march ahead without thought. I didn't notice the air get drier or crisper at first. It wasn't until I glanced behind us that I realized how high we'd climbed. How desolate the way back was. How committed we were to this ascent.

The sun was harsher at this elevation. The protective haze didn't reach this high and my eyes burned if I looked up. Twin mountain peaks jutted before us on either side like towers. Thankfully, we proceeded on a lower gradient. We crested the midpoint between peaks and a great valley crater spanned the inner mountain, surrounded on all sides by protective cliffs. Our path was one of two that safely entered the dip.

In spite of the rocky terrain, the bottom half of the crater was covered in lush vegetation. At the very center, a great fountain of water rushed into the sky like an inverted waterfall. The mist from the crashing water gave the impression of a mushroom cloud, and although the water didn't rise into infinity, it didn't seem to splash down anywhere either.

"A wellspring," remarked Tyson.

I hadn't realized how thirsty I'd been. I peeled my tongue off the roof of my mouth and tried to moisten it. It felt coated in sand finer than any I'd ever touched. With unspoken urgency, we headed straight for the lush water. The valley was larger than it seemed from above, but we made quick time on the downhill journey.

I jumped into the edge of the pool. Despite the raging swell, the edges of the spring were calm. I submerged my head and drank. The water was heavy with minerals. Delicious. Life-giving. If I could figure out a way to bottle it in plastic and ship it to the States, I'd be a billionaire. After an embarrassing few minutes of debauchery, I noticed Tyson standing outside the well.

Of course. He was an elemental. He didn't need to eat or drink. In my steppe, water killed him. Hardened him until he was just crust. Was that true in the Aether as well?

A passing cloud fell over us. At first, it only darkened the sky. But then I was reminded of our altitude when the fog crept through the bushes and low trees of the valley. It grew so thick I would've lost sight of Tyson had it not been for the illuminated cracks across his skin. Molten orange flowed between the plates of rock on his body.

"At your ready," he said.

I nodded and drank some more. He wasn't the only one getting the spooky vibe but this water was damn good. Even better than the tea.

"This wellspring is generously hosted for you," he stressed. "You don't want to undo your welcome."

I begrudgingly stepped to the edge of the water. "Hosted? What welcome?"

The wall of fog thinned but did not retreat. I could see the elemental now. His red eyes darted to the outskirts of the small clearing. His body was tense.

His eyes weren't the only pair of light in the fog. The others were farther off, but sets of piercing blue, green, and gold surrounded us. It must have been twenty creatures.

"Dragons," said Tyson.

Chapter 18

I hurried out of the wellspring. Stumbling and splashing. It was like someone had walked in on me taking a dump. I wasn't prepared to be accosted by a flight of dragons. Apparently I'd forgotten my life was a third-rate Dungeons & Dragons campaign. But, hey, at least I had my pants on.

"You shouldn't have come here," said a crystalline voice. She spoke with a light but confident air. Thing is, her voice drifted on the mist, somehow snaking through the rush of water at my back but nevertheless hard to place.

I swiveled on my feet and reached for my belt pouch. Damn, when was I gonna get used to the fact that I was unequipped? Even if I hadn't lost it in a clash with Connor, I wouldn't have been able to bring it to the Aether. I zeroed in on a set of purple eyes. They were closest to us. I squared my shoulders to them.

"A volcanic aspect is an impressive guardian," she said, "but you know just as well as I that no jinn passes through High Valley alive."

The figure ambled toward me. She was humanoid. Lithe. The slight sway of her hips practiced and seductive. But I could barely make out something else in the mist. A long reptilian tail snaking from her backside. Large leathery wings extending from either shoulder. The vision in the mist was like a dream: suggestive, frightening, but I couldn't tell if it was real.

I took a step back. The fog passed and the woman came into view right before us. My eyes widened.

Whatever I'd been expecting, it wasn't this.

A tall woman slithered into view. She didn't have wings or a tail, and she was completely naked. Her frame was thin but long, standing a couple inches taller than me. Her arms and legs were ropey but smooth. Small breasts, tight stomach, toned glutes. An active woman, around my age maybe, in great shape and without a single wrinkle marring her pink skin.

Perhaps more striking than her nude body were the tattoos. Her arms and legs were covered with wide inked scales, stockings and sleeves suggesting her heritage. She was barefoot but had metal bands around her feet, legs, and forearms. Small spikes jutted along them in a ridge. Her long black hair was held in place by a tiara with matching horns. A short sword hung on a thin strap around her waist, impressive in its own right. It reflected an azure hue that cut through the fog.

Despite the danger, I couldn't help myself. Something about her exotic markings, casual nudity, and supreme confidence mesmerized me. She converged on us with a seductive gait and it was hard for me to do anything but watch.

"You don't look like a local jinn," she mused, tapping her finger on the hilt of her blade. Then her entire display of control shattered. Her purple eyes widened and she recoiled in shock. "A human!"

Everybody tensed. She drew her weapon. The other dragons converged. Tyson took a protective step forward like a guard dog. The shadow tickled my back as it answered my call.

And then the woman laughed. She turned to her people and laughed for them all to hear. She flipped her blade in her hand and deftly sheathed it. She waved and the fog cleared out of the entire valley.

The rest of the dragons were revealed by the sun, men and woman wearing light clothes that sometimes failed at modesty. The woman with the purple eyes was no longer naked, either. She wore something of a leathery dress like a second skin. It reminded me of my alligator-hide boots. It framed a collar around her shoulders and neck, stretched down over the center of her chest and into a hip belt, and barely covered her waist. The look would've killed on South Beach.

Tyson grunted. "Princess Lilliane, the High Justice." He bowed reverently. "I am named Tyson. The human is Cisco Suarez."

Lilliane snorted. "I'm no princess to your kith. Don't belabor me with titles."

"Breaker of chains," I joked. "Mother of dragons." Everyone glared at me. I pretended I had something under my fingernail.

Tyson cleared his throat. "We thank you for allowing the human to use your wellspring."

"A taste for travelers is not an offense," Lilliane replied sharply. "It's your jinn masters who hoard the resources of the land. I give you leave to rest in our shade, eat of our fruit, and drink of our spring. And then you must press on, before darkness falls and the human freezes."

She signaled to her army who fell in behind her. Despite their scant armor, they were an intimidating troop. Each had black-clawed fingers that could probably do serious damage. Some had shimmering blades at their hips. All ranged from six to seven feet tall.

"You don't understand, Lilliane," said Tyson.

"Oh?" She turned, more curious than annoyed.

"We're here for an audience with the Mother."

The elemental held up the bronze disk, the gift from Malik. Lilliane's eyes narrowed suspiciously. We weren't in immediate danger but the tension returned.

"Wait," I said, dumbfounded. "There really *is* a mother of dragons?"

Chapter 19

The sun beat down in the recently cleared sky, raising the temperature in the mountaintop crater. It didn't help that we were marching uphill, leaving the shade of the oasis below. My boots slipped several times, and I jealously wondered how the barefoot dragons had no trouble on the craggy surface. Tyson was just as surefooted, which made sense considering he was essentially rock himself.

We approached the base of a vertical wall against the side of the valley. The mountain was bare here, revealing its stone underside in the absence of soil and plants. Even though the surface was a natural formation, there was nothing natural about it. The walls were smooth and ornamented with symbols, looking like something out of an Indiana Jones flick. There weren't any columns cut into the rock, but a large cave mouth was shaped into an elegantly pointed arch, complete with frame. Desolate and abandoned, an undiscovered ancient wonder of the world. Notwithstanding us, of course. Or the leathery inhabitants. Sets of eyes blinked in the darkness within, silently standing vigil.

The cave interior was dark and moist, a welcome reprieve from the sun. I smiled as the shadow played around my feet.

"Do not raise your defenses, human," warned Lilliane. "You're safe, until the Mother judges you otherwise."

"It's Cisco," I said with a mock smile. "And that's real comforting."

Still, I had a feeling she was telling the truth and I didn't want to overplay my hand. I relaxed my spellcraft, if only to prove to her I had the courage. Impressed yet?

Deeper in the cave mouth, several tunnels opened up. It was getting darker and darker so I let the shadow seep into my eyes. Lilliane didn't complain. I could see in near pitch black if I needed to. Apparently the dragons and Tyson could do the same. We marched ahead unhindered, following our escort.

We were in what could only be described as a palace. Smooth walls, extravagant but sparse. After the first few normal-looking rooms we passed through, I gave up all hope of finding Smaug sleeping on a sea of gold coins and treasure. These dragons didn't hoard riches, but there was something noble about them. Their heritage, their tradition, their culture. They carried themselves with the self-importance that only monarchs could. I wondered if they ruled over anybody or hid from the rest of the Aether in exile.

Eventually we were led into the throne room. A large space of flat ground opened before us. The rocks on the side walls were carved into rows of seats like bleachers. At the far end was a small dais with a modest chair. No gold-armored guard. The throne wasn't forged from iron swords. The place looked more like the site of a pep rally than a seat of royalty.

In attendance at this quick-and-dirty meeting was a woman on the throne and three standing men. Two held spears and flanked the dais. Just guards. The third man bore a sheathed sword ornamented with gems. His barrel chest was bare and he wore long scale leggings. All were adorned with the tattoos of their kind.

"Brother," said Lilliane, giving the prince a hug and a kiss on the cheek.

"You bring us distinguished guests," he said in reply. An open sneer announced his sentiment toward "distinguished guests." His eyes were black and something flashed in them as he looked me over. I'd never seen or heard of dragons before, but something about these people was eerily familiar.

The two guards watched us too, but in that unobtrusive way that made it easy to forget about them. Eyes forward, taking in the entire auditorium even though there were only the seven of us huddled in a small space.

The prince smiled. "What, pray tell, is a human doing in High Valley?"

"Don't look at me," I said. "I'm just along for the ride."

He watched me like a predator, unsure what to make of me.

"Don't bite, Edric," chided Lilliane. "They come bearing gifts." She flipped the coin into the air and he snatched it with precision.

He studied the token with a measured face at first. Then he curled his upper lip and stared daggers at me, a snarl escaping his throat.

"Where did you get this?" he snapped.

Tyson replied evenly, without aggression. "Does it

matter?"

"It does if you're in league with dragon hunters." His eyes flicked to me again.

The elemental shook his head. "The human is my charge. He doesn't understand the significance of the Roman coin. I merely offer it as a gift."

"This *gift* is an insult to my people."

Despite the threatening air in the room, the smallest of gestures stole everyone's attention. It was the woman sitting on the throne, until now still as a statue. She was old but robust, with short hair and strong features. A robe of loose strips of magenta dragon scales rolled over her shoulders and ran down her body. The layering of strips hid her limbs well, as a child hugging a blanket, but with a slight movement her arm protruded from the cloth and her wrist twisted, hand waiting, palm up.

The gesture stopped the prince in his tracks. He bowed slightly and placed the Roman coin in the Mother's hand. She turned her attention to it, again with only the minimum movement possible. Just a cock of her neck. Then her eyes rested on me.

"It doesn't take a sage to see this human knows nothing of our plight," she stated calmly. Not in admonishment, but as a parent doubling as teacher. "Isn't that right, Cisco Suarez?"

I nodded, wondering when Lilliane had mentioned my name.

"And the elemental is beyond such hunts," she continued. "Even if a jinn master were to command it. But then, this aspect has no master." She rose from the throne, lithe and slow, and stepped toward us. "How is it that a masterless aspect travels to High Valley with a human?"

"It's a long, boring story," said Tyson. "Involving human affairs."

Distaste flashed across the Mother's face. An annoyance, painful but necessary, like waiting for a shot at the doctor's office. Her lips pursed in impatient anticipation, suggesting Tyson continue.

He cleared his throat and addressed her. "We were manipulated by the same jinn in a struggle for power over the human's city. Many friends perished, and our enemy now stands to control the dead."

The Mother soured. "Earthly politics," she said, aghast. She considered me. "I bet you look upon our world with wonder, human, twisting your neck to keep up with our ways. The truth is, nothing is more circuitous and arcane than Earthly politics."

I cocked my head and shrugged, weighing her opinion with mine. "I don't know. Five great satrapies ruling the sky. Animating elementals, hoarding water and other resources, leaving scraps for everybody else. It doesn't sound so unfamiliar."

"Does it not?"

I shrugged again. "Bureaucracies only make sense within the confines of their rules. Anyone looking from the outside in is bound to see something silly."

The Mother nodded. "The ways of the jinn and Maqad veer eerily close to Earth's. The way they subjugate aspects for their utility is horrendous."

Tyson grunted. "It was aspects who built this palace."

Lilliane cut in. "That was an alliance in another time."

"The result is much the same," he maintained. "Just like

now."

"Now?" asked the Mother.

"You detest jinnkind, and we aim to disrupt one in power. Common goals, if you ask me."

She watched the elemental with amusement, not so easily backed into an alliance. "We hate them and their silly ways," she stated flatly. "Even the human has an opinion. But opinions are not strategy."

"I'm not talking about the jinn," I said, trying to steer the conversation back on point. "I'm talking about the bureaucracy right here."

The hall silenced. The Mother crossed her arms. "And what is silly to you about High Valley, Cisco Suarez?"

I spoke carefully, doing my best not to offend but pressing on. "I don't know. On Earth it makes sense at least. Why humans rule the world. But what makes the jinns such hot shit when there are dragons in the mountains?"

Prince Edric stepped forward. "The jinns do not rule High Valley," he spat.

The Mother lifted her hand. "That will be enough, High Sword." I could tell she had to rein in her son's temper often.

"I just don't get it," I continued. "With all the races up here, what makes them fit to rule? Is it just that angels, jinns, and humans were destined for it?"

Now the Mother's cheeks tightened in anger. "That's Celestial talk. It's garbage. All of it."

Lilliane cut in with a cooler head. "Those stories don't account for the plentiful other races in the realms. But even by their measure, you're mistaking the jinn for a single people. We call them so today, but back then many others would've been classified as such, including dragons."

I stared at them curiously, seeing such hatred for a people that they could be counted among. Although I wasn't sure all of them shared Lilliane's viewpoint.

"Let me tell you about the Celestials," snarled the Mother, standing eye-to-eye with me. The queen was shorter than her offspring but every inch as tall as me. "It's the simple story of greed." She drew the Roman coin up between us. "This brought wealth and fame in its day. It's called a dragon, named such for its equal worth in the life of my kind. Your so-called Celestials paid unscrupulous hunters one of these for every head they procured."

Rage boiled on her face. Her purple eyes flashed brightly, and the suggestion of wings blurred in the space behind her. Immaterial, like a blind spot. Stare too long at a light bulb and look away—that afterimage lingers. That's what I saw. Pointed wings. Tendrils snaking from her mouth. I took a step away from her and blinked.

The images were gone, but the uneasy pit in my stomach wasn't.

The Mother smiled and palmed the Roman dragon. "Only this coin isn't alone. It's one of thousands. *Seven. Thousand. Dragons.*"

Angels and dragon hunters. That didn't make much sense. The leathery wings flashed through my mind, and I realized humans didn't think of them as dragons.

"You're talking about demon hunters."

She smiled primly. "We're a small population at our most robust. A thousand by optimistic counts. You can imagine, back then, how that genocide nearly wiped us out." Her eyes flicked to me like a snake's. "Don't worry, little apple. I do not **b**lame your kind for this."

I waited a b**e**at. "The angels."

"That's a **m**isleading word. Celestials merely enforce their dogma o**n** the world. Keep *us* out of *yours*. Give rise to the rule of the jinn. But despite their best efforts, we have persevered. So **y**es, while we detest the servitude demanded by the jinn, ou**r** true hatred is reserved for those who deem themselves ou**r** betters. Those who would have seen us exterminated f**o**r not blindly complying like the jinn."

The threa**t** sliced through the molecules of the air. Efficient. It le**ft** no doubt how the dragons treated friends of angels. I truste**d** my companion wouldn't mention Malik. I wondered ho**w** he meant to explain the coin. If it mattered.

Thousand**s** of years of history raced through my head. Not persona**l** experience but belief. That was about as personal as i**t** got. It shaped everything I was. I'd never believed in a**n**gels and demons, at least not since I was a kid. Malik had to**l**d me I was half right. And it was starting to form a new be**l**ief in my mind.

Angels were supposed creatures of guidance. Compliance, the way the dragons saw it. Enforcers, even. They were real.

All of a sudden the law and order of the jinns made sense. Duty. That was their defining trait the angels favored over the dragons. No doubt that applied to their masterships. Even Connor Hatch had admitted to serving many others in his time. And no doubt those rules extended to their treatment of Earth. Jinns aren't allowed to interfere with humans unless both sides openly parlay with each other. Maybe these safeguards weren't jinn law at all, but angelic in nature. A red line drawn in the sand, staking out territories, creating order. A red line which the dragons had at one time crossed.

And there was the flipside to the metaphorical Roman coin. The dragons. If they had been persecuted for messing with human affairs, killed off by the angels and their hunters en masse, did that not make them the demons of Western folklore? Maybe demons as we understood them didn't exist at all. Various constructs and races of unimaginable horror. Gargoyles. Vampires. Dragons. As long as they bumped in the night, mankind allowed them to fill the role. But it's a two-dimensional role in a derivative B movie. One which relegates evil into something plain and easy to imagine, existing for its own sake. That was what Malik had meant by there being no real demons. Nothing is so black and white.

"We're no friends of Celestials," insisted Tyson. "We merely return one lost fragment of your honor. A token your kind has often accepted. And we ask but a simple favor in return. Smuggle us into the capital city of Maqad where we can properly strike a blow against our enemy, leaving you to yours."

Prince Edric grinned and rapped his fingers on the hilt of his sword playfully. "We will have the truth," he said firmly. "Where did you acquire the coin?"

Tyson shook his head. "No questions asked. It's the word of your people."

The Mother hissed. She knew her people's word. It was the same as hers. It was plain on her face: she didn't like it, but she wouldn't rightly murder anyone who returned a dragon to High Valley. Otherwise no more coins would ever see their way here.

"See them to the dinner chamber," she rasped as she

stomped toward a rear exit. The two passive men followed her.

The prince sucked his teeth into a sneer. Same expression as when he'd first seen us. Word of his people or not, he didn't like it. And if history was any judge, the dragons were oath breakers.

That's when I realized the philosophy of angels and demons—good and evil—was an academic privilege I couldn't afford in High Valley. Like fire and water, danger was danger, no matter which way you sliced it.

Chapter 20

We were whisked to private quarters to rest. Invited to the baths too, but I declined. I wasn't much into the mountaintop spa treatment at the moment. There was something anxiety-inducing about a masseuse with razor-sharp claws.

Even though Tyson and I were alone, I wasn't confident of our privacy. We didn't discuss our predicament. That suited him fine. His usual stoicism played across his rock face, searing magma underneath. Tyson Roderick was all business, staring ahead and minding his own. I had burning questions but they waited.

I spent the time on the ground on my back, eyes closed and thinking. For all their impressive cave-dwelling, the dragons weren't a luxurious people. Their environs were grand without being lavish, and best I could tell they slept on the uncushioned floor. Either that or they weren't overly concerned with our comfort.

After what seemed like hours, they led us to a dinner hall. A relatively small room compared to the rest of this place. Edric and Lilliane were in attendance, as were another man and woman. The Mother was noticeably absent.

We sat at an oval table with benches carved out of stone. Most things in the palace were. The difference was that the table was a smooth dark material, like onyx. Running down the center was a line of food, sitting directly on the surface in overlapping piles. A bed of squashes and bushy purple things. Long, ridged grains. Roasted fowl, bones wrenched apart.

There were no plates or utensils. Everyone just reached into the mass and pulled food toward them, ripping the portions apart with their hands and teeth. My description notwithstanding, it was a surprisingly civilized affair. Not at all like wild animals feeding. It simply lacked the pretense of etiquette I was used to.

"Will the Mother be joining us?" asked Tyson.

"She no longer wishes to be burdened by you," said Edric. "Apparently, *my* wishes do not matter."

Lilliane shook her head. "This is a war room," she explained. "The Mother trusts us to smuggle you into the capital without her oversight. It is a trivial thing."

I put my giant chicken leg down. "You'll help us?"

"It is our word," she said.

"Meet Jax and Tena," continued Edric. "Along with myself and the High Justice, we make up your smuggling team. We leave in an hour."

"So soon?" asked Tyson.

"Like my sister said, sneaking you into the capital is a trivial matter. Unless you'd prefer more long-term lodgings in High Valley?"

"No thanks," I said quickly. "What's the plan?"

"The plan is to let me enjoy my dinner," he said. "I'm unusually hungry tonight. And hungry dragons are...

distracted."

Point taken. I buttoned my lips and looked over the team. Tena was a young girl. She looked fragile but I suspected that to be deceiving. Jax was quite her opposite. Built like a Mack truck, he and Tyson were a good match for an arm wrestling contest. Neither concerned themselves with questions or our personal details. They were soldiers under orders.

Eventually I tried some small talk to lighten the mood. The High Sword and the High Justice deflected anything personal and the soldiers kept to their meals. Even my questions about the food were answered with more snark than information. I settled into silent eating for a while until my questions turned to the mission.

Tyson decided that, even if everyone else knew what they were doing, I at least needed a primer on the area. He spoke between infrequent bites, eating more for company than sustenance. "Maqad is the seat of power to all the Aether." He glanced at the prince but there was no open objection. "The satrapies rule much of the outer lands."

"Wherever they can reach," corrected Lilliane. "High Valley is but one area they stay out of."

"The skags?" I asked.

"That is another," said Tyson. "The skags are nomadic, living in clusters and constantly roving. It makes pinning them down hard, whether they live on jinn land or not. They don't represent a central opposing authority like the dragons."

"They're weak and scattered," interrupted Edric.

"Their weakness is their strength."

The High Sword scoffed. "Weakness is strength now.

Only a jinn aspect would say as much."

I ignored him and followed the line of logic. "So the jinns and, by association, the elementals police the land."

"Where they can," agreed Tyson.

"And how it suits them," added Lilliane.

The elemental nodded. "And the capital, most of all, is guarded well. Officiates police the borders and the streets. Aspects of sand and air. All-seeing dust storms that can be anywhere at any time."

"Anywhere at any time," I repeated. "Sounds like sneaking in will be tough."

"To anyone but the dragons," said Edric, finishing the last of his scraps. The soldiers had been waiting for him, and when the prince stood, they did too. "Let us show you what strength means."

I wiped greasy fingers on my shirt, eager to get moving. Everyone left the table and followed Edric out. Lilliane waited and brought up the rear. The troops wound in and out of increasingly narrow hallways, away from the understated opulence of the palace. We descended into catacombs. The walls became rough, the footing unsteady. Ceremonial crypts dotted the walls, each adorned by a skull with large canine teeth. A few had personal trinkets like swords and boxes.

A chill air rushed through the passage and made me shiver. In minutes, I found out why. The soldiers walked outside onto a makeshift balcony. Really it was nothing more than a stone outcropping and a precipitous edge. A small hidden cave opening in the side of the mountain, with nothing but rocky death hundreds of feet below.

The wind battered us violently. I widened my stance to

steady my balance. None of the others seemed to notice. Maybe that's 'cause most of them had wings.

It was night now. No sun in the sky. No moon, either. Just a perpetual gloom of clouds and gray sky. For the first time in hours, I let the shadow slip from my eyes. Despite being night, it was light enough out here to see.

"This is it," said Edric with a smile. "The moment of truth. Jax, carry Tyson. Tena—"

"Actually," interrupted Lilliane with a glimmer in her violet eyes. "I'll take Cisco with me." She strolled toward me with the same seductive gait as when we'd first met and stopped with her face close to mine. "Put your arms around me," she said and turned around.

I hesitantly hooked my arms over her shoulders.

"You trying to choke me?" she asked with a smirk. Then she unclasped my hands and lowered them under her arms. She yanked my body into hers and hooked my arms over her chest without shame. Her skin was deathly cold. "Now the most important thing," she said with a halfway turn of her head and a grin, "is not to let go."

Then she hurtled off the edge of the cliff with me in tow.

Chapter 21

Air buffeted my face. Butterflies scrambled in my stomach like on a rollercoaster gone bad. I assumed we were rocketing toward the ground but my eyes were shut so it was just a guess. I clung to Lilliane tightly, losing all pretense of modesty. When we swooped I felt the pull of g-forces. I opened my eyes.

Lilliane still looked human, but she didn't. Her body was longer. Large wings stretched from her shoulder blades and caught the air in massive sails of flesh. Her skin was covered in glittering scales now. It still felt the same, somehow, as if it hadn't transformed at all.

We swooped upward and caught the wind. Three more flyers fell in line with us. The scene was even more surreal from a distance. I saw the dragons in their true form. Covered in scales, long black claws, fangs peeking out of faces both human and reptilian. They craned their necks gracefully and stretched with the breeze, looking completely at home in the skies except for the two riders clinging to their backs.

Edric and Tena darted and dove around us, unencumbered and leading the way. Lilliane and Jax settled into a steady beat of flapping wings. Adrenaline rushed through me. The ground sped past at alarming speed. Soon enough it gave way completely. We crossed the edge of the floating island to the endless roll of the drift, making a straight path to the clouds. We lost ourselves in the horizon.

Despite the dizzying speed and incomprehensible heights, what got to me most was the cold wind whipping against my skin. I was in jeans and a tank top, dressed for the Miami heat, and here we were higher than Mount Everest doing a hundred and sixty miles per hour. Sure, it wasn't snowing. There wasn't enough humidity for that, but it felt like it ought to have been.

Edric flanked his sister like a wingman and turned to her. "We'll take the lead," he screamed over the wind. She nodded in full understanding and the prince and Tena swept into a cloud below. After a handful of seconds, we followed.

The fog gave way. For the first time, I could see the capital city. It was blanketed in folding clouds, but still a mile away. We were high above it now, showing me a new perspective of the great metropolis. Instead of the rocky concentric rings of land, I focused on the structures built on top in mud and clay. Interlocking buildings with bridges and roadways. An intricate maze of city planning, the mapping of an irrational mind personified. Sprawl where very little real estate afforded it; the only way to expand was up up up.

Much closer to us (and our obvious destination) was an outpost of sorts. A single floating boulder the size of a house with a small tower growing out of it. Sparse inner quarters were sacrificed for a wide roof platform that dominated the surface. Two figures of sharpened icicles stood guard on top.

"Aspects," she yelled over her shoulder. "They stand watch outside the city."

Edric and Tena swooped down on them from above. The icicles raised their hands to react to the sudden threat but were bathed in sheets of flame spewed from above. The dragons weren't fire-breathing exactly. The heat seemed to come directly from their open palms. It engulfed the elementals and reduced them to water instantly. With precise timing, the six of us touched down on the tower.

"Woo!" exclaimed Tena. "Barely saw what hit 'em."

Edric crouched behind the short parapet and surveyed the capital city with a nod. "Excellent work," he agreed. Everyone else instinctively crouched with him. "And it appears we haven't been noticed by the capital."

I released a sigh of relief I hadn't known I was holding. I unclenched my arms around Lilliane and rubbed freezing palms together. I noticed the traces of water on the stone. "Are they...?"

"Dead?" asked Lilliane. "Aspects don't die. Not like you or me."

I turned to Tyson, wondering how he felt about it.

"We merely return to our inherent forms," he said without emotion. "Free but inanimate."

"Isn't that bad?" I asked.

"It's not good or bad. It just is."

I frowned, wondering about our mission, not fully taking in the ramifications until now. Would we be killing jinns? Strangers? Friends? What exactly did Tyson have planned?

"We need to wait for the next patrol to pass," said the

prince.

I nodded with a shiver and rubbed my arms to get my blood moving. "How long will that be?"

"You should get inside," said Lilliane. She took my arm and led me down a hatch. A short stairway circled into a sheltered area devoid of personal effects. There was a small fire pit along one wall with a chimneyed exhaust. The High Justice waved her hand and flame roared to life within.

"Cool trick."

"Sit here," she said, plopping me right in front of the fire. Then she straddled behind me and hugged me from behind. I flinched as her cold skin pressed into my back. She ran her hands over my chest. "Are you freezing, Cisco?"

The magical heat I'd seen the dragons use seemed to emanate from her palms. They rubbed over me, massaging the feeling back into my flesh. Stirring other feelings as well.

"What do you think, when you look at us?" she asked, rubbing the length of my arm.

"What do you mean?"

"You know what I mean," she said. "You know what we are to your kind."

I gnawed my lip. "Demons, right? You want me to call you demons."

She shrugged coyly. "It's a word many of us are known by." She traced her fingers up my arm and across my shoulders. Heat ran through my body.

"Well, you've got the whole temptation thing down. I'll give you that much."

"I'd be offended if you thought otherwise."

I grunted. "If you really wanna know, I don't buy into

Chapter 22

The floating city reached starkly against the gloom. The buildings' edges cut away the dense fog, leaving no doubt that the elements were mastered by this great civilization. Several rings circled a large central tower that dwarfed every other structure tenfold. It was an impressive sight, even in the low light and at a great distance.

Rolling blankets of fog reduced visibility but the dragons had a keen sense for danger. We avoided increasing obstacles, almost by instinct, with only a glimpse of warning. Massive sails guiding boats on the thick drift below. Other outposts dotting the sky, piercing blue emanating from the elementals. Each time we would veer away from notice as the dragons flew effortlessly toward our destination.

At one point I was surprised by a party of skags who drifted close. They bayed and squawked. Lilliane just laughed.

"They see us for what we are," she said. "They dare not attack."

For a while it seemed as if we would just fly straight into the city. Then I noticed the structures along the largest outer ring. There were no walls, really. Normal walls were pointless around a floating city. But a tight network of lookout buildings and tariff gates served as wall enough.

"The tower," I said, picking out the highest point of Maqad. "Can you fly us to the top?"

Lilliane shook her head as the wind buffeted past. "Impossible. That's the seat of the shah. It is too well guarded."

"So how do we get over the checkpoints?"

"Not over," she said with a smile. "We go under. Into the drift."

With those words her only warning, she dropped sharply into a dive. Straight down. Through the small clouds that whipped in the wind, sure, but toward the deeper fog. The solid mass that hugged the bottom of the Aether like an ocean.

"The drift? Isn't that dangerous?"

There was no time for an answer. The four dragons, with Tyson and me in tow, plummeted into the surface of smoke. It parted and swirled away from their wings, but folded back over itself and filled the gaps immediately, blinding us. I charmed my eyes with a bit of shadow but it barely helped. This wasn't darkness I was fighting against but something solid, and my ride didn't come equipped with fog lights.

Still, the dragons knew where to go. Or they faked it anyway. I caught sight of the others for seconds at a time before the fog buried them again. They kept in tight formation as if in wordless communication. Tyson was the easiest to spot because of the faint glow drifting beneath his skin.

"It's hard to breathe," I told Lilliane, who seemed not to

notice. The air was thick down here, like it was more than air. Visions of being pulled underwater by a mermaid unsettled me. I wasn't so sure Lilliane was any better. "How long do we need to stay down here?"

"Keep quiet," she said. "We don't want to attract the notice of drift serpents. Our fire would spark too much interest from the capital."

I shut my mouth, message received. If there was something the dragons were afraid of, I didn't want to see it. And I certainly didn't want to blow our smuggling operation before we were even in the city.

But there must have been a reason people didn't sneak into the drift all the time. Slowly but surely, I began to sense we were surrounded.

The dragons spread their wings and glided silently, pointing to our flanks. They sensed it too and tried to fly quietly. It was an amazing display of coordination, but we were sinking.

Worse, the air was getting too thick to stomach. It was there, all right, but there was just too much other junk mixed into it. My lungs rejected the substance. I gasped heavily and wished I'd had my breathing mask, but I couldn't take normal objects into the Aether, much less magical ones. I was screwed.

"I can't..." I started, then broke into a fit of coughing. The hacking sound was fifty times louder than it should've been. I mean, there was no echo down here, but the fog carried the piercing sound like it was a physical thing.

"Shit," said Edric.

Suddenly a wall of air blasted us. It was hot and moist and putrid. The wind cleared a pocket of fog in an instant. A giant face loomed before us, a single gargantuan nostril twitching at the end of a heavy exhale.

Oh. Crap. Noodles.

Lilliane and I were framed within the small clearing of air. Some sort of elongated squid head was in there with us. A black beak, a blowhole, marbled inky eyes. Its body extended behind like a snake, not scaled but smooth. A Victorian sea creature and Lovecraftian horror wrapped into one. Rows of tentacles marred the otherwise mirrorlike surface, lazily dragged jellyfish legs.

In a shimmering blur, Lilliane drew her short sword and whisked it at the goliath. The face recoiled, untouched. Then it screeched at jet-engine decibels and dashed past us. The massive body snaked behind it like a long whip. Going and going and going.

"This thing really is a serpent," I said in shock.

"And its beak will snap you in half," she added, kicking her wings and pushing up. As the pocket of air collapsed, I caught sight of the other dragons doing the same.

Even immersed in fog I knew exactly which way was up, and we headed straight at it. I wasn't sure where we were in relation to the city, but it didn't matter. Anywhere was better than this stifling hell pit. The dragons pounded furiously upward in retreat.

Another blast of air cleared a swath below us. Another screech, this one distant. Whales communicating across miles of ocean. Just below, the end of a tentacle whipped into the drift. Then there was a loud scream at point-blank range. It shook us.

Despite Lilliane's wings beating heavily, the serpent's head rolled nearer with an effortless push. The beast spun in a horrifyingly graceful loop before turning and heading straight up for us, beak open.

"I have to blow our cover," said Lilliane. "We can't outrun it." She slowed and spread her hands, calling a warm glow to them.

"No!" I screamed.

I was doing the same thing as her, but forcing shadow into my hands instead of fire. I could take care of this thing. Well... I *couldn't really*. But I could keep it off our backs long enough to get into the capital.

I thrust a shaft of darkness at the thing's face. The spear glanced off the smooth flesh. I sent out another missile with similar results. I concentrated, improved my aim, and sent another. The beast covered its eyes with some sort of opaque lens, blinding itself but protecting them while on the attack. Although my aim was true, I couldn't pierce the protective barrier.

"You can't stop it," said Lilliane. She spawned a stream of fire from her palms. A bright, lashing explosion of powerful magic. But it sputtered and crackled away in the fog. A match lit underwater. "It's no good," she said, panic overtaking her voice. "The drift. We're too deep."

With a wild surge, she flapped for the city again, but our pause had cost us too much. The drift serpent was incoming. ETA in ten. Nine. Eight.

Like a bullet, the High Sword shot past us from above. The unmistakable flash of light from his royal blade left a contrail behind him.

"Brother! No!"

The metal clanged against the serpent's carapace. It was a slashing strike, designed for a quick getaway in hopes of deterring the charging monster. Easy in, easy out, with no intention of making a real stand. Edric seemed an adept tactician and fighter. One that knew the name of the game was buying time, not total victory.

Unfortunately, Edric had misjudged the great speed of the behemoth.

The dragon's body pounded against the serpent's face, bumping and rolling to the side in a wild spin. His short sword snapped from his grip. The unstoppable locomotive barreled forward, unimpeded by the insects on its windshield. Five seconds till impact.

"I won't have you die for me," I said. "Keep flying." Lilliane was too focused on beating her wings to give me much notice. Which helped me out.

I stared at the juggernaut below and unhooked my arms from the dragon. By the time Lilliane spun around in shock, my arms and legs were loose, flailing in the open drift, still shooting upwards from momentum but rapidly giving in to gravity. Lilliane flew higher. The other dragons were gone. And a force of nature like I'd never seen was rapidly coming up from below.

Chapter 23

As the fog collapsed around us, the serpent's blowhole opened another pocket of air. The rush of wind buffered me against the unrelenting fog. It was warm but vile. The breath carried particulate from hundreds of feet of drift-serpent innards. Hundreds of feet of phlegm, parasites, bacteria, and whatever else clogged up the giant snake-squid's airways. It was the mother of all burps and I nearly passed out from the impact.

But there was a much greater collision on its way. I was in the air. Wingless. A freight train was a second away from smashing into me. The behemoth adjusted its course a hair. Not a direction change, just a fractional adjustment, one drivers constantly make along straightaways. The slight movement aligned its gaping beak with my center mass, and I suddenly wondered why I thought I could do better than Prince Edric.

Then I suddenly remembered I was Cisco fucking Suarez.

I willed a wall of shadow into being. It wasn't meant to stop the thing—nothing could do that. The shadow was for me. I placed it just above me at a gentle angle. Only a few seconds into my physics experiment, I was still traveling upward. I hit my own wall and rolled away from it, still ascending, but nudged to the side, out of the path of the sharpened beak.

The squid face hit my wall a split second later, passing through as easily as the drift. Another insect on the windshield. And then it was my turn to splat.

Things were different for me. My wall had been motionless. Edric had been even worse. He was actively charging downward. Two bodies moving into each other can easily double the force of impact. It's what makes head-on collisions so deadly. But I was the bicyclist on the side of the road. The one moving *with* the flow of traffic. The one *lessening* the impact.

The wind left me as I slammed into the serpent's face. A yard to my right, the gargantuan beak snapped shut. The sound alone dazed me. Worse than a gun firing by my ear. The sudden crack filled me with great confidence that this thing could snap a steel beam in half if it were so inclined.

Just as Edric had, I tumbled to the side of the serpent's face. But I got my hooks in. My right hand caught hold of something wet and slimy. A precarious hold, mind you, but it stopped my fall.

And just like that I wasn't the fly on the windshield anymore. No. I was that spider. The one that crawls out in a panic as the car reaches speed. The one that hugs the windshield tight until Mr. Toad's Wild Ride comes to an end. The one who hangs onto that porous glass surface with an unbelievable size-to-strength ratio in every one of its eight legs.

Eew. I hate spiders.

I clawed my way to the center of the squid's face, pulling

up on my handhold: the circular muscled blowhole. It tensed as I put pressure on it, then quickly clenched shut, dragging me another foot to safety. I widened my stance and pulled my alligator boots under me.

At least, that's what I tried to do. One of my legs was caught. A tentacle had me, just below the knee. The floppy thing had reached up from somewhere along the neck and clung to me. An elaborate defense mechanism. I was a booger stuck in the serpent's nostril hair, waiting to be picked.

Lilliane swooped down, folded her wings over her body, and landed hard with a backflip into a crouch. Her blue sword flashed through the tentacle cleanly. I was loose.

"Now what?" she asked.

I unwrapped the ribbon of tentacle and let it go in the wind. We both rocked to the side as the serpent slowed. Beside us, the dark lens over the eyeball rolled open, and a giant orb focused on us.

Lilliane's sword was quick. It came down hard and true, but the lens snapped shut in a literal blink. The sword rang out uselessly. Metal on metal. Lilliane grabbed the hilt with both hands and tried again. Nothing doing.

Two more tentacles came from the deep.

"Watch out!" I said. The dragon turned her attention to a problem she knew how to solve. Her strikes kept the defense mechanism at bay. The rest was up to me.

I considered the blowhole. Sealed tight by a giant internal muscle. Then I checked the eye. I rested my hand on the lens. It was crystalline and black. A beautifully smooth substance, perfectly thin and perfectly curved, but hard as titanium. I traced my fingers around the curvature to where it met the face. Looking for an opening. If I could just get a grip on the leading edge of the lens, maybe I could pry it away.

The wall was shoved in there tight, though. And deep. I squished my fingers into the moist flesh at the edge of the eye but couldn't reach down far enough to find the end of the lens. The damn thing was simply too massive.

"A little rush, please," said Lilliane, dashing to the side with a spinning strike. She was under assault by several tentacles now. One had hold of the bracer on her left arm. The others weren't just grabbing anymore but whipping at her face. It was all she could do to keep the jabs at bay.

The shadow enveloped my hand. It came quickly and forcefully. It surprised me, almost. I wrapped my fist with layer after layer. A boxing glove of sorts, except the thickness added to the punch. And when I was ready I stood over the eyeball, lifted my hand to my chest, and let it fly with an ear-piercing grunt.

The blow rocked me. Solid and firm against what should have been glass. The black lens dispersed the force across its entire frame. My hand jarred away from the punch without leaving so much as a mark. The lens was perfectly suited to deflecting this kind of damage. I had to change my tack.

Shadow, by its nature, is nebulous. Making it wax and wane, making it sway and drift, these are the fundamental stages of shadow spellcraft. Manipulating it into solid form is where the real power starts. Walls. Wrecking balls. That can take a lifetime to master.

But recently, while fighting a nigh-immortal wolfman, I'd done something different. I'd taken things to the next level. It had just about exhausted my body beyond all measure, but I'd pressed the shadow into a sharp edge.

Imagine that. Something as evanescent as shadow, cutting like a knife.

That had taken a kind of power I was only recently coming to terms with, but I knew I had to try it again. Lilliane's blade hadn't worked, but it was metal. The physics made sense. Against an orb like this, I needed to reduce the impact to the smallest point possible if I had any hope of piercing it. Like cracking an egg.

I folded the shadow in my palm. Let a bit of it drip from my hand and folded that over itself. I was a knife maker, forging from shadow, strengthening my creation by pressing layer after layer together. But something curious happened.

The Aether is made of fire and air. The Aether is immaterial, like my magic. Tyson had said my spellcraft would be powerful here, and I hadn't even pushed it yet.

I willed a knife, but the Intrinsics answered with a sword. The energy coursed through me like I was made of copper. A stronger conduit than ever before, the spirits somehow reached me even in the Aether. And before I knew it, a strong blade shone the color of amethyst in my grip.

A straight Italian longsword, thicker at the base than the point, with a modest straight guard. It wasn't a clunky Final Fantasy sword with gems and a blade as thick as a tree but it wasn't shabby. Its double edge should cut just fine, but I was especially interested in its point.

I didn't hesitate. Somehow I knew the power I wielded. I knew this would work. And I smiled as I brought the magical weapon down into the center of the serpent's black lens.

I'd expected a crack. Shattering debris. I didn't get that. Neither did I get the smooth entrance of a light saber. But I did puncture the protective shield.

With a pop of resistance, I buried the blade into the eye, right through a pinhole in the lens. The serpent jerked and wrenched its eyelid open. The sudden movement tore the sword from my hand, which I would've thought impossible. The lens retracted and dragged the amethyst energy across its soft eye tissue, causing a massive amount of self-inflicted damage. The sword fizzled out, the serpent screeched, and his entire mass twisted violently, throwing me off.

I plummeted into the drift. Loose. Alone. The High Justice was swift. Lilliane scooped me from the air and veered up, dodging the flailing tentacles of the beast. The serpent lurched and tumbled, a skyscraper being demolished. We sped a tight circle around it to the safe side and shot to the surface.

"That was a hell of a plan," she said, thin lips in a tight smile.

"Who said anything about a plan?" I shot back. "If I had taken the time to think about it, I wouldn't have jumped."

She laughed as the drift thinned. Her compatriots rejoined her. The prince was there too. Less his jeweled sword, but alive.

"Keep it down from here on out," he ordered.

There was another deep roar from below. The serpent had made enough noise to wake the city, but I figured it was part of the soundscape in these parts. By comparison, a few dragons darting through the drift would be overlooked.

It was still too thick in the shallows to see the underside of the city, but I did catch a part of it. The vertical pipes that dropped into the sea from above like giant tentacles. I'd seen them before. At a distance, they'd looked like stilts supporting the structure. Up close I saw they weren't metal but a textile of some sort. Strong cloth, like a sail, folded around a ribbed skeleton. The pipes were patchwork in places where they'd been repaired, and extendable, probably built from the top down and slowly dropped into the deep. I wondered what they were for as we quietly slalomed between them.

Edric pointed at his eyes and then to another pipe. This one was wider than the others. Several arms lengths, maybe. The dragons nodded and descended sharply. Then we swooped up, toward the pipe opening at the bottom. Closer and closer we raced. We were going to go straight up the pipe. But we weren't going to fit.

Ahead of us, Edric's wing's flashed into mist as he entered the opening. Without his wingspan he was an easy fit. I went next on Lilliane's back. She simply folded her arms into her body as her wings disappeared. Our ascent continued unabated. Ribbed walls flashed past us, feet away. Lilliane leaned this way and that to stay centered and on course. I was terrified of dragging her off balance. I held my breath.

I gave it about twenty seconds of an upwards freefall. Then we emerged into a subterranean chamber at the head of the pipe. Individual masses of water, bulging bubbles the size of men, stood in rings around the pipe openings. The four dragons shot several yards into the sky above, spread their limbs and canted to the side, and landed lightly on the floor between the elementals.

Lilliane unclasped my arms with a showy wink. We were

surrounded, near as I could tell.

"Don't worry about them," she said. "They're worker aspects. They won't even react to our presence."

I took in the whole chamber. Well after well of openings in the floor. Pipes leading down into the drift. She was right. Every single bulbous water elemental toiled without noticing us. They didn't have eyes or mouths or even limbs for that matter. Not that I could tell. But it was obvious they were focused on the task at hand.

"They're drawing water from the drift," I said.

"It's an ingenious operation," she agreed. "The source of the capital's water. And the reason they harvest so many water aspects."

Tyson grumbled beside me, relieved to again be on solid ground.

"I knew there was a reason the Mother agreed to help you," said Edric. He surprised me by flashing an approving smile. "High Valley doesn't help those who can't help themselves." He surprised me again by clapping my shoulder. "We must leave you now. You've been successfully smuggled into Maqad. What you do from here is your business. If you give even one jinn bastard hell, it'll be worth it."

Jax and Tena laughed bitterly. The rush of traveling through the drift and facing down a behemoth was clear on everyone's face.

"You know where to go from here?" asked Lilliane.

"I have an idea," answered Tyson.

She watched him for a moment, unsure how to respond. Or maybe unsure of something else.

The prince turned to Tyson. "On behalf of the Mother,

I deeply thank you for returning the Roman dragon to us. Whatever your purposes."

"And whoever you serve," Lilliane added under her breath.

Edric smiled. "Someday, Tyson, you must tell me where you acquired it."

The volcanic elemental ground his teeth shut in reply. The prince chuckled, then lightly hopped into the drift pipe, disappearing from sight. Jax and Tena followed.

"Maybe we'll meet again, Cisco," said the High Justice. "If you don't get yourself killed first."

"If I don't get killed, I'm not staying in the Aether. That's for sure."

She nodded. "Then perhaps in your world. If the law allows it."

She coated the last statement with sarcasm, showing she put little stock in "the law."

Celestial law. Demons interfering with mankind. I wondered what I'd gotten myself into. Before I could reply, Lilliane stepped into the well and fell from view.

Chapter 24

Tyson waved his arm with a wordless "This way." We ducked into a doorway that led to a similar chamber of the same size. Wells, water elementals—the same operation. It must have been a maze of interconnecting passages and drift wells, but Tyson wasn't bothered by the scale of it. He just plodded ahead as if he'd been here before, knew the way, and set himself on autopilot to ignore the drudgery.

For my part, I couldn't help but be amazed. A single elemental would be a marvel back in my world. I wanted to spend hours studying one. What would happen if I touched them? Could I jump inside the bubble of water? Could they talk? And if so, what did they have to say?

As we navigated the subterranean basements of Maqad, it was still impossible to truly understand the scale of the city. This was infrastructure. A sure sign of something larger. Something planned. But it was just the underbelly.

We headed up a flight of rock steps. Then another. The water elementals gave way to more humanlike workers manning steam chambers. Tyson swiped a white cloak from a wall hanger and dropped it in my arms.

"Put this on. Keep your head down."

I threw the long cloak over my shoulders and hooded my

face. It did a good enough job of making me blend in, but the fabric ran a little short. My red alligator boots clashed below the high hem. But who said jinns couldn't make fashion statements?

Tyson went incognito himself. For the first time in the Aether, he shifted into his human form. Wide-shouldered in an elegant white suit.

The stairway took us another level up before ending, forcing us to navigate the next floor. The walls and ground were natural. Rock formations, not dissimilar to the palace in High Valley but lacking the layer of polish. It gave the impression that we were still outside, in the sense that a sewer or subway tunnel is outside. Some level of shelter without the niceties of modern living.

The halls on this level were wide but barren. Access tunnels, used when needed. Probably built with the berth to shuffle machinery and cargo back and forth. Regular doors dotted both walls. Indeed, a train of several floating cargo beds approached us, a wispy elemental at the head and tail, no doubt carrying the load. That's also when we got our first glimpse of security. A featureless golem made of sand wore a pointed bronze breastplate. A curved sword of the same metal was hooked horizontally into the breastplate as if sheathed on a magnet. The only other piece of metal on the thing was an upside-down triangular mask with eyeholes. No eyes, strangely enough. The elemental itself was nothing but sand. With and without form at the same time.

So these were the so-called officiates.

Tyson's gait stuttered for only a second as he made his decision. He stepped to the side and continued advancing.

As before. Another boring day. Nothing to see here. Despite wanting to get a closer look at the officiate, there was something sharp and intrepid about it. I didn't want to risk it. I stared at my boots as we slid past the convoy. Each of its steps grinded like dirt against metal. I could feel its eyes on me.

Time slowed. Adrenaline beat through my system. Something was wrong. We walked unmolested for another ten seconds.

I picked up the pace slightly, pushing against Tyson's back and hoping he got the message. Then metal scraped against metal behind us. I turned to see that the convoy had paused. The officiate had drawn its sword. It made a quick chirp, like a question. Not a language as far as I could tell but clearly addressing us. I turned to Tyson to catch him slipping sideways into an access door.

Genius plan.

I wasn't feeling especially creative so I rushed in after him. As we slammed the door shut, the chirp repeated, but it was long and drawn out this time. An alarm whistle.

"This is gonna be the shortest undercover operation ever," I said.

Tyson burst into a sprint.

I waved my hand, thickening the shadow on the floor, gumming it up for anybody who tried to pass. It wouldn't stop anyone for good, but it would give us time. I barreled after the volcanic elemental (who was faster than he looked). We darted through a perpendicular tunnel and into another room. Our scramble almost came to a halt in a utility closet, but we quickly found another door that led into a warehouse of sorts. The floor was busy with worker elementals. We were ignored as we raced past. We climbed a metal staircase that led to an inner chamber, and suddenly we were in a drab office suite.

I mean, it wasn't like a cheesy strip-mall dentist's office or anything—1980s carpet, bland art decorating the walls, waiting room music—but it was the Aether's version of that. A dull workplace with absolutely no soul. A place where coworkers probably complained about Mondays and lunch meetings and printer toner. Our appearance seemed to be the highlight of the day because all the employees stopped what they were doing and watched us with rapt attention.

Luckily, they were either too busy or too bored to do anything *but* watch. We hustled through the corridors without objection, and even the officiate's chirps were out of range. Tyson found an outer doorway. Daylight. The next thing you know, we were on the streets of Maqad, an early morning sun blazing down from above.

Color me impressed.

The capital city was a cross between a French castled village and a Brazilian slum. Stepped buildings towered over each other in rows, all artistic masterpieces made of stone with tiled and tented roofs and elaborate entryways. As the structures piled higher they became more makeshift and tattered. Open patios walled with battered cloth. Patchwork modifications. There was a lot more metal than I'd seen in other Aether structures, too. The larger buildings had skeletons strong enough to support the rampant outgrowth.

The roadways were narrow and packed. Jinns and elementals passed in carts and frequented various roadside establishments. Everything was so huddled and claustrophobic it took me completely off guard when we

walked right up to the edge of the world. A short stone wall
was all that was between us and a drop into the drift
hundreds of yards below. Nothing but open sky. Okay, new
rule: Eyes on the ground in the floating city.

From this vantage, the sprawl was more vividly realized.
What I had assumed were concentric rings of land were
really a series of smaller islands, not unlike the Florida Keys.
Small but firm bridges crisscrossed between the stray rocks,
connecting them in a spiderwebbed network. These bridges
were mostly wide enough for a person at a time. Any
hauling of goods or work traffic needed to route through
the main roads around the ring where larger bridges were
available.

The chaotic scribble of streets was the perfect place for
two shifty pedestrians to get lost in. A few alleyways, a
hopped wall, a bridge or two, and even I couldn't tell you
where we'd come from. Just like that, one moment to the
next, we relaxed our pace.

"We did it," I said with relief. "We're here."

Tyson nodded, pressing ahead with long strides.

"So what's next?" I asked. "What's the master plan?
Which, by the way, you've kept quiet about for too long
now. I've been way forgiving about that."

"You want to hurt Connor, don't you?" he returned.

"Of course. But I need to know where we're going."

Tyson pointed. "The center of the city."

Okay, if I made it sound like the place was a maze, that
was true. But there was a small measure of order to it.
There was a central island. The concentric rings of land
circled it, leaving no doubt as to the location of the center.
And if that wasn't enough, a tower loomed over the entire

city so vast in stature that you could see it from anywhere. The grand centerpiece. The seat of power and guidance and governance for all residents.

The tower rose up as a straight spire, but up close its patchwork structure was apparent, just as with all the other buildings. Sails and fans hung from windows, balconies jutted out into the sky, boxy sub-buildings protruded from smooth walls—it was a masterpiece of the absurd. A hundred disparate buildings were glued together into a massive column. A city taken to its very extreme at the nucleus.

"The tower?" I asked. "What are we gonna do, file a police report?"

He stopped at the ridge of a highway. A double-wide bridge of rock crossed over from our strip of land to the innermost ring. "It all leads to the tower," he said obliquely. Then he hopped down onto the road and headed across.

I sucked my teeth. Tyson obviously wasn't a team player. He didn't like sharing details. It was a wonder he ever worked with the Covey at all. But he was being ordered then. I wondered if he was similarly enthralled now.

Lilliane had suggested as much. Tyson had a master. Tyson had his own motivations. Why was I so blindly accepting his were aligned with mine?

I'd killed his allies, after all. Kita Mariko, the paper mage. The elemental had a close bond with her. It still seemed to affect him. Everything that had driven me thus far had been for revenge. What if the same thing was driving Tyson?

Part of me wanted to ditch the plan. Leave the big lug to his own grumbling devices and say screw it. But where did that leave me? Stranded in the Aether, that's where. Literally between angels and demons.

Besides, that revenge thing I mentioned? It was a strong force. A part of my being now. Something I couldn't turn away from. I'd walked out of traps unscathed before. If Tyson was leading me into another, it might get me closer to Connor than I was now. Was that so bad?

It didn't look like I had much choice. And this was coming from a guy who hated having his arm twisted.

I blew out a sigh, frustrated but futile, and crossed the bridge ahead.

It turned out the inner ring wasn't directly connected to the tower. We got a firsthand view of that as we rounded the expensive residences lining the lush block. Green grasses and plants, out of place against the sudden drop of sky beside them. Various drawbridges and gates led across to the tower. My inclination was that we were looking for an easy way in. My inclination was wrong.

"This is it," announced Tyson, stopping at a metal gate across the street. A large villa and yard were protected behind a high stone wall. The only view inside from the street was through the bars of the gate.

Something like this, you expect a security console or something. A speaker. A camera. A giant lock at the very least. Not here. Instead, standing at the meeting of both swinging gates was a single mound of earth shaped into humanoid form. Its rocky skin was littered with compacted soil. Its face, clay. But the security guard wasn't the only precaution.

I squinted. In the sunlight I couldn't fill my eyes with shadow, but I could barely see the air shimmering between the metal bars. I followed the distortion to the planes above the stone walls. Some kind of force field protected this place.

"Okay." I crossed my arms. "How do we get in?"

Tyson smiled for the first time in forever. "Easy."

He walked right up to the earth elemental and grunted. The clay man bowed and stepped aside. The magical field flickered brightly and vanished. Then the metal gate opened on its own, no pistons or anything.

Tyson turned around. "You coming?"

I crossed the street and frowned as I stepped into the yard, wary of active wards. "What... did you just do?"

"I merely asked for entry," he replied. "Cisco Suarez, welcome to the Aether home of Connor Hatch."

I stood stunned as the earth elemental moved to close the gate. We were here.

Chapter 25

The ease with which Tyson Roderick strolled into Connor's estate was troubling. It was the first real confirmation of the itch I'd been feeling. Lilliane's warning. The jinn hunters leaving him alone. This entire time, I'd thought Tyson was a rogue elemental. Outcast and alone.

But what if he wasn't?

Smoke rose from his eyes as his skin smoldered. His face hardened. His clothes burned away.

"You still work for Connor," I muttered, taking a step away.

The metal gate clinked into place. The earth elemental paused, now on our side of the gate. He watched us with a puzzled expression.

Tyson spun with a closed fist. I jumped backward but he wasn't going for me. He smashed the security guard square in the chest, sending him into the gate. The metal screeched off its hinges; the earth elemental splayed out in the street. He hadn't had time to get the force field back up.

"Watch for more," screamed Tyson.

The figure of dirt and rock in the street didn't crawl to its feet. It simply grew upward, a mound of dirt rising into shape. He lowered his head and stepped toward Tyson, but the volcanic elemental let loose a spray of lava from his mouth. The clay man sizzled, melted into a mound, and hardened into a glassy crust.

I checked the yard but it was clear. The tall double doors of the house, however, cracked open. Two glowing beings of fire casually stepped outside.

"What is this?" I yelled. "What are you doing?"

The big man turned to me, that stupid grin plastered across his face, like once the joy was here, it was never leaving. "Having a little fun," said Tyson. Then he charged the doorway.

The fire elementals transformed into spears of flame, darting off the porch at opposite angles to surround Tyson. I sprinted forward and one turned to me. A flaming hand jutted my way and sent a crackle of fire.

I lifted my palm and willed the snowflake tattoo to life. Turquoise energy answered in an instant, forming a two-foot semi-spherical shield. My magic easily deflected the fire.

Tyson swung a fist at his opponent but the fire was immaterial. His arm passed right through without effect. The fire elemental, in turn, seared Tyson's rockskin. It was accustomed to standing up to magma, so that did little damage as well.

I was in a similar stalemate. In the bright sun of the Aether, there wasn't a whole lot I could fight with. My shield, however, deflected whatever fire came my way. The difference was I would eventually be a step too slow and get burned. And that was an experience I wasn't looking forward to repeating.

I charged the fire elemental, feinting with a haymaker.

He flinched away but only partially, coming at me with a spray of fire. I gritted my teeth, ducked my head, and barreled right through the being. So fast the intense heat did little more than singe my clothes. On the other side, I threw off my burning cloak and rolled onto the covered patio.

Tyson had meanwhile retreated the opposite way, to the street. His opponent barraged him with searing missiles that had little effect. Tyson grunted and lifted the dead mass of the security guard and heaved it at the pursuing elemental. A shockwave of magic—superheated earth—roiled through Tyson's arms as he threw. The dead clay of the earth elemental broke apart into dust and showered the burning attacker, smothering him with dirt. Tyson belched a layer of lava and buried the fire man, extinguishing him in an instant.

That gave me an idea. Shadow spellcraft works in the absence of light. Fire is usually the antithesis of my power. But I'd recently learned I could spend an inordinate amount of energy channeling Opiyel's power. I recently learned that I could counter fire, cut it off, if only for painstaking moments.

But this super-powered shadow magic in the Aether was a different story. And the shade of the patio roof was all I needed. As soon as the fire elemental stepped up to me I surrounded it with shadow. Forced it in with both hands. It struggled and spun in a panic, caught in a death grip. I clenched my teeth and channeled the shadow through my spirit form, packing it tight. Negating the fire like a black hole.

The fire elemental winked out in a silent implosion. I

made it look even easier than Tyson had. As he stomped past me into the house, I cracked my knuckles and matched his smile. "I could get used to this," I said.

I admired our handiwork outside. Then I raised my shield, anticipating an attack. Shadow gloved my fist in case anyone got it in their head to wrestle. Basically, I was ready for a blitzkrieg.

What I didn't expect was an empty house.

It seemed the gate guard, the force field, and the roving fire elementals were the sum of Connor's security. Not too shabby, when it came down to it, but I was almost disappointed. By the time I inched inside, the welcoming living room was destroyed. Low chair frames flattened. Countless pillows ripped and feathers drifting through the air like in a John Woo movie.

I followed the sound of crunching and crashing, wary. They weren't the sounds of battle. Combat was frantic and hyper, with grunts of pain and cries of surprise. This sounded more like one of those YouTube videos where someone smashes an X-Box with a sledgehammer. Heaves of steady, patient effort. I followed the trail of destruction until I reached the kitchen. Fine china was scattered across the floor in shards.

"What the hell are you doing?" I asked. "Your big plan is to trash his place like an angry teenager?"

The creature of rock and magma didn't answer. He lifted the icebox above his head and slammed it into a cute little breakfast nook.

"I have a good one. We should wait until Connor falls asleep. Then steal his car keys and drive to the store and buy cigarettes."

Tyson ignored me. After he was bored with the kitchen, he cleared out and hit the steps upstairs. I checked outside. The quiet street was finally stirring. I guess you couldn't really have free run of the neighborhood without some consequences. I ran upstairs and found Tyson in the bedroom. Everything was ripped apart.

"Okay, you made your point. Now let's get out of here. Connor's not here."

The elemental smashed fancy-looking glass orbs on the shelf. "Of course Connor's not here. He's in the Earthly Steppe. We're trying to get his attention."

A shrill alarm rang out in the distance. The same sound the officiate in the underground had made.

"I get it," I said, "but I think we've just found the wrong kind of attention."

Tyson lowered his shoulder and charged right through the wall into a neighboring bedroom. "Good. That will hasten the process."

I scowled and ran to the hall window. I could see them already and they weren't playing around. A score of sandmen. Officiates wearing bronze with their swords drawn. Their legs didn't march down the street so much as shift, one ahead of the other as a solid mass.

I stomped toward Tyson. "There're too many of them out there. If you wanted Connor's attention, you got it. There's no point sticking around any longer."

"I can always do more damage," he countered.

I couldn't believe him. I mean, I thought I was the reckless one. The one who ran on spit and strength. Who never put two minutes of thought into a single plan. I had a reputation for wanton destruction and carelessness, but even this was too much for me. It was like Billy Idol and Marilyn Manson sharing an expensive hotel room. Way unnecessary.

"This is bullshit," I told him. "And I'm done until you tell me what's going on."

He ignored me until he noticed I was climbing out the second-story window onto the roof. "Getting Connor's attention is the plan," he said.

"Then mission accomplished. I'm outta here."

"Stay."

I crouched at the edge of the roof and slid down the wall to the ground. The officiates announced their entry into the front yard with warning chirps. The overturned metal gate groaned under their weight. At the side of the house, I made a bee line for the stone wall and vaulted over it to the outside. I caught a peek of Tyson jumping off the roof in tow. Good, he wasn't a complete idiot.

I ran along the wall, sticking close to the low shadow. With any luck the officiates would make clearing the villa a priority. We'd simply slip down the street and disappear.

Right before I was clear a single officiate turned the corner of the property. Damn, they were organized enough to lock down the perimeter. The sandman opened his mouth to alert the others.

My fist rammed into the plate on his face. Shadow packed into the punch, shoving the triangle right through his head, cutting off any alarm before it began. The piece of bronze bounced on the street behind him.

Unfortunately, displacing the thing's head didn't seem to have any effect on the rest of its actions. The officiate jabbed at me with a sword. My tattooed forearm caught the curve of the blade and forced it outside.

The parry gave me enough time to pull my hand back and try another punch. This one connected in the center of the chest, on the breastplate. Again the force knocked the metal into the sand of its body. There was too much surface area this time to force it all the way through, though. I pounded again, tapping the darkness.

The breastplate sank through the back of the elemental, but the sand of its torso folded around my arm. The grains compacted around the small bones of my hand and squeezed.

I grunted and parried another swipe of the sword. I channeled the Intrinsics through my fist and coated my arm with a protective layer of shadow. I drew more and more power into my arm. Then I balled it into as tiny a space as I could. The mass of spellcraft grew as unstable as a hunk of uranium.

The officiate's sword arm lengthened and wound around my guard. The sharp blade sliced against my ribs. Warm blood rushed down my side. My shadow bomb wasn't ready but I had no choice. I let the energy go and shied away from the sandman.

The ensuing explosion was a painful mixture of pure energy and grains of abrasive sand. The bronze sword launched two blocks into the air and the armor hit the dirt. I took some of the blast but flattened into the shadow as soon as I was free of the sandy grasp. By the time I rematerialized, Tyson had caught up.

"So much for slipping away," he said wryly.

I moved around the corner of the wall. The other officiates were no longer on the perimeter. They'd probably be in the house by now. But that was only a few seconds' head start.

On the street, a whirlwind picked up dust. All the scattered grains of sand slid toward the center on a breeze.

"Don't tell me..."

Tyson waited with his arms crossed.

"Screw this." I sprinted down the street. Tyson sighed and came after me.

More alarm chirps. The officiates flooded the street now. The one I'd exploded reformed. Maybe half of them stayed on Connor's grounds to search it, so there was that small bit of fortune, but that meant ten were still after us.

We hustled along the curvature of the inner ring. Unfortunately, there wasn't a lot of space. Large houses on the left and right. Ample yards, sure, but that was all. Not much in the places-to-hide department.

All that changed when we crossed a small walkway to the next island in the chain. This one had heavier buildings of stone. Several stories high at the outset, with stacks behind them leaning closer to the tower. This was a more urban habitat. A marketplace of sorts.

I split down the first alley I saw. Turned at the back of the building. Ran under a second-story bridge and climbed up the sloped ground to the next level.

The chirps stayed on us. I peeked over the bridge and saw the officiates coming down the alley. A few of them spun like dervishes until they were whirlwinds. Literal Tasmanian Devil tornados. Those took to the air and ascended to the roof of the building we'd passed.

No time to gawk. We raced further down the street, avoiding dead ends and open areas. We turned down a tunnel that led toward the tower. An indoor bazaar swarming with people. I brushed through them, losing track of Tyson. Behind us, the chirps of the officiates split the crowd.

I rushed to a wall and climbed a rickety metal stairway. The unassuming door at the top was unlocked. Tyson scrambled up after me. I held the door open. As he jumped in, one of the officiates turned our way. I shut the door quickly, unsure if we'd been spotted.

We ran along an outer balcony with a series of closed doors, like apartments. I was more interested in what was below us. I lined up with a pile of dirty laundry and hopped down, bouncing safely from my back to my feet. Tyson landed beside me on his knees, skipping the laundry pile altogether. We darted down the small alley, searching for escape.

It wasn't my eyes that found it. It was my ears. A discordant caterwaul drew my attention to a garbage pile down a dead end. An alley I'd normally avoid. A black cat sat against the back wall. *The* black cat.

I grabbed Tyson as he ran past me. "This way."

He skidded to a stop and glared at the alley with a half-hearted shrug. "Your funeral."

"This is the way," I urged. "Trust me."

"How do you know?"

"I just do."

He glanced at where we'd come from. The officiate chirps in the distance were still close, but they weren't bearing down on us anymore. A couple lucky turns and we could get away from them. Maybe my lucky black cat was exactly what we needed.

I moved into the alley. The cat, ever aloof, darted into

the pile of trash.

"Oh, come on," I complained. I dashed ahead into the shadow, covering several yards like they were one. I solidified against the back wall but the damned cat was gone. I swear, it had to be a ghost.

I paused. Was this like one of those movies where no one else could see the cat but me? Was I Haley Joel Osment, except with cats instead of people? It wasn't exactly a strong premise for a feature film.

"Well," concluded Tyson, standing at the wall, "I guess the only thing left to do is wait for them." He didn't seem too broken up about it. The same as back at the house. It was like he wanted to get caught.

"That's suicide." I bit down and searched through the garbage. "There's something here."

Tyson crossed his arms and watched.

An annoyed meow interrupted my digging. The sound was muted. It had come from behind the wall. Through it.

"You heard that, right?"

Tyson watched the alley entrance without answering.

I tried to shift a wooden palette that leaned against the stone wall, but it didn't budge. When I crawled around it to check underneath, I smiled.

"Come on, big guy," I told the elemental. "Looks like we live to fight another day."

The palette hid an open doorway in the wall. One that was missing an actual door. I slipped through with ease. Tyson had more trouble but we squeezed through before anyone made it into the alley.

I looked around. We stood in a private garden surrounded by high walls. It was an exquisite estate but untended. Ivy ran along the floor and walls and hung from trees as loose vines. We hurried through the lush vegetation. Around the corner of a building.

A few bushes ran parallel like a hedge maze without being purposely convoluted. I spotted the cat past a dry fountain. As we followed it kept ahead. Moving down steps that curled against a rock face, leading down the side of the island rather than up through the buildings. The chirps of the officiates faded into the distance.

"What did I tell you?" I gloated. We were on the edge of the drift, hugging the rock wall on a narrow ledge. The fog swirled below. Our path disappeared into a tunnel cutting inward, through the island. The cat disappeared inside so we did too. It strolled out the other side into the sun and rounded the corner.

As Tyson and I made it into the lower courtyard, all the adrenaline that was starting to melt away came crashing back like a waterfall.

Three jinns surrounded the black cat. Two held spears to it. The third man watched with a sly smile. Connor Hatch.

It was safe to say our cry for attention was a success.

Chapter 26

My boots scraped to a stop in the small courtyard. Large buildings and walls towered over us on all sides, hiding us deep in the recesses of the city. Ants crawling through cracked stone. Despite the sun, our depth ensured there were enough shadows on the walls and ground to work with.

The cat growled at the jinns. He didn't hiss or spit. He flat-out growled. A spear poked his way and his paw batted it lightly to the side. Another came up behind him. The cat sidestepped and flipped around.

"Just when I think you're getting predictable, Cisco," said Connor, "you show up here, of all places. With an old friend. And..." He arched an eyebrow at the cat. "That thing."

One of the jinns stabbed her weapon forward. The cat darted under the thrust and jumped at her face, slashing claws like razors. She yelped and recoiled but caught the cat with a backhand that sent it to the floor. The two jinns hurried to keep it contained between them.

"Home at last, Tyson," said Connor. "That's not entirely surprising, I suppose. But that business at the villa was reckless."

"Preaching to the choir," I said.

"And this," said the jinn, turning to the stray animal. "We don't have cats in the Aether. And we certainly don't have zombies. You've brought some kind of spirit construct with you, haven't you?"

I narrowed my eyes in defiance. I had no fucking idea what I'd brought with me, to be honest.

Connor Hatch's lips tightened. "Well, we can't have that." He lifted a palm and doused the cat with a lance of fire. It attempted to hop away but the flames were too hot and too fast, just like at the hotel room. A strangled cry cut out before I'd moved a step. The flame subsided. Black, oily smoke danced on the floor where the cat had been.

I halted mid step. I expected the cat to bound away but it was gone. Just a swirl of remains. "It can't be," I said, stunned.

Connor chuckled. "Don't tell me you'd adopted the mangy thing."

"You bastard!"

I charged straight at him. A jinn swung his spear in defense. I dove into the shadow and slid past him. I appeared right in front of Connor, teeth clenched, death in my eyes, and one single thought on my mind. Something Tyson had told me.

In the Aether, jinns were all too human.

My fist connected with Connor's face. He couldn't disappear or blink away. He took the punch and stumbled.

Before I could get another swing at him, I felt the presence at my back. I rolled away as a spear point rushed past me. I grabbed the woman's weapon and yanked it around, knocking her to the ground. The other jinn charged me. I spun the blunt end of the spear to knock his weapon away and slammed a fist of shadow into his chest. Unlike the hardy officiates, he flew backward into the wall.

"Enough of this!" screamed Connor. He fired a stream of flame at me. My magical shield kept the fire at bay. The two jinns backing him up recovered and regrouped. Their arms burst into flames as they prepared to attack.

Great. Two more ifrits. These jinns wouldn't be brushed off as easily as the fire elementals. Still, they were younger than Connor. Something told me they were lackeys. Distant cousins at best. They couldn't have been as good as him.

I pulled the shadow into me and tightened my grip on the spear. "You know what the most surprising thing is?" I asked Connor.

He leveled his eyes at me.

"That you came here with only two other jinns."

Amusement played across Connor's face.

"We're gonna rip you apart," I said.

He scoffed. "There's no 'we,' Cisco."

I turned to Tyson. He watched with his head lowered.

"You gonna just stand there?" I asked.

"That's all he *can* do," laughed Connor. "Elementals can't attack jinns. He can't help you. He's subservient."

"Screw that, Tyson! This is what you've been waiting for. We can take him together."

The elemental raised his head with a grimace. Connor's eyebrows twitched with excitement. Then Tyson retreated back into the tunnel.

"What the?!? Where are you going?"

The jinns chuckled. "Don't wander too far," called out Connor. "We'll be having serious words in just a bit."

I growled, like the cat did. I was fed up. And even though it was now only a wisp of dark smoke coiling on the ground, I wasn't gonna go out like that. Not in the Aether, where my shadow magic was amped up. Not when I had Connor in my clutches.

I stepped into the shadow and drew it to me. I tapped into the Intrinsics and cloaked my arms in darkness just as the two jinns wore fire. The shadow lapped over me in waves. As I approached, I stepped into the oily remains of the black cat. The soot joined with the billowing shadow and crawled along my skin. A rush of energy pulsed over me. I dropped the spear with a smile.

The two ifrits struck as one. One with a fiery spear, the other with a blast of heat. I held a hand out at each of them and froze their attacks midair. Connor's eyes widened. His troops shoved against my power. I clenched my fists and the fire on the spear and in the air extinguished. The flames on their skin snuffed out and their jaws dropped.

I brought both hands together in a clap. The two jinns flew through the air and collided right between me and Connor. They fell to the floor, dazed but scrambling to fight back.

The spear came at me again, attempting to keep me at bay. I grabbed it and sent shadow along its length to its owner's hands. He released it and doubled over, clutching his wounded hand. The other launched toward me. I flung the spear and plunged it into her chest. She gasped, staggered on her feet for ten seconds, and collapsed.

The sword I'd created in the drift extended from my hand now. Connor took a step backward and summoned fire to his hands. The impaled jinn lay still on the ground. The other guard was on his hands and knees, panting. I stepped forward with a look of judgment on my face. Connor watched in shock as my sword came down and beheaded the jinn at my feet.

He hissed in frustration. "You never cease to be a major pain in the ass."

"I'm more powerful here," I said.

His face reddened. "You fool. You idiot. I'm more powerful here too."

His hands came together in a wall of flame. It bore toward me like a bus. I had to dissipate my sword to erect a barrier of shadow. The light slammed into the darkness and the ground shook. My boots dragged a few feet across the ground.

The light of his fire was killing my shadow. I'd been here before. I'd reconstructed it as easily as he killed it. What was once taxing in the Earthly Steppe was trivial in the Aether.

But Connor's fire was stronger, too. More forceful than the elemental blasts. More searing than anything his guards had conjured. My shadow was stout, but cracks of light burst through. Once that happened, it was game over. My shadow fell like a crumbling dam.

I dove to the ground under the burning oblivion. I sent spears of shadow up from the grass. One, two, three. Connor fended them off with fiery hands. This was gonna be harder than I thought.

"Cisco!" yelled a voice from above.

It was Tyson, a few stories above us now. He leaped over a short balustrade into the open air. As he fell, a bronze sword streamed through the sky on a trail of sand. It grazed the elemental's shoulder and nudged him off his trajectory, sending him flailing into a wall. After a hard bounce he tumbled unceremoniously. He dropped two more stories and hit the ground. I had to jump out of the way to avoid being flattened.

Chirps flooded the airspace above. Spinning tornadoes of sand and bronze spilled over the raised walkway and converged on us with earsplitting whistles.

I tightened the shadow around my fist and snarled at Connor. He seethed right back at me.

"Don't do it," warned Tyson, sitting up and raising his arms in surrender.

More tornadoes came into view and touched down. The entire chase party of officiates, twelve of them, landed between us. Three held swords on the volcanic elemental. Three on me.

And then, surprisingly, three held swords on Connor Hatch.

The ifrit rolled his eyes and crossed his arms in annoyance. The fire on his hands died out. The officiates chirped at him but he didn't respond. A soldier checked the headless jinn and then the one impaled by the spear. She was still hanging on.

One of the officiates was jabbing me with his sword, as gently as possible given the circumstances.

"He wants you to release your spellcraft," translated Tyson.

I sighed, nodded, and did so. It was clear the officiates were arresting everybody indiscriminately. And as even more piled into the air above us, I knew this was a losing battle.

As they rounded us up, I grumbled to Tyson. "Where

are they taking us?"

He lifted his head, grim and determined. "To be judged by Connor's master. The shah himself."

Chapter 27

The three of us paraded down the street with officiates at our sides. One held my right arm in packed sand, another my left. Tyson and Connor marched ahead, similarly subdued. The six officiates were led by another unit of six who cleared the street and directed the crowds away. We were tailed by yet another six who brandished their weapons plainly in case we got any ideas about running.

Combined with the giant city spire stretching above us, the seat of the shah and the destination of our march, the justice of Maqad was an impressive display of power.

I'd been captured before. Bound, beaten. This was the first time I admitted escape wasn't an option.

I'm a fighter. Handcuff me. Chain me down. I'll do anything I can to break those links. One captor. Two. Hell, three's not a crowd, it's an every-man-for-himself cage match. I thrive under daunting odds. Even when the Covey had me on the cold tile floor of the Star Island house: gutted, spent, contained in a circle of power, drained by a brick dust pentagram, grievously outnumbered—even when the situation was so bad that death had been the only option—I had fought back.

But here, escorted by the capital officiates in their grand

kingdom, I knew bruising wasn't in the cards. I'd only seen a glimpse of their power, simple but effective. And their numbers were even simpler. Eighteen now. More inside the tower.

Connor and Tyson seemed to come to the same conclusion, but their reactions were curious. The jinn was calm. I only caught his face once or twice when he looked back. Unafraid. Not angry, exactly, but pestered. A rich man holding a parking ticket. The volcanic elemental was even more stone-faced than usual. He silently accepted this fate, keeping his head down and marching forward with implacable rhythm.

That made me the obvious man out. A human surrounded by primal beings. Your friendly neighborhood audience surrogate. Captured by a foreign army and subject to foreign law. I had no idea where this was leading.

The wide thoroughfare cleared free of spectators as we crossed to the edge of the inner island. A metal gate swung open and the road dead-ended, a sheer drop into the sky without so much as a warning sign.

Across the sky-moat was the tower. From this close the ground floor looked like a haphazard cluster of dwellings stuffed together. Wood, metal, and textile patched over every conceivable surface in so many layers I couldn't even see the island the tower sat on except for the rock outcropping below. A drawbridge hung on the other side. It wasn't extended to walk on, but it wasn't in the "up" position either. Rather, it was in a "down" position, hanging limply into the barren emptiness of sky. At the officiate's order, the drawbridge lifted and locked into place. We crossed.

After passing through a slew of checkpoints and gates, the inside of the tower wasn't nearly as mazelike as I would've guessed from its outward appearance. The core of the structure was open and streamlined, with various halls clearly delineated.

Our party stepped onto a large central dais circled by a stepped stucco wall. The six sandmen lined us up. Only four of the remaining twelve stepped up with us because of space limitations. Then the entire slab of stone rose from the floor, straight into the air.

"Huh," I said. "A magic elevator."

We passed through a round opening in the ceiling and picked up speed. Level past level, we headed upward incredibly fast, without any of the stomach butterflies you get from good old-fashioned physics elevators. The platform slowed and came to a gentle stop in half a minute, with quite a few stories still stretching above us.

An officiate chirped and we stepped off the dais into an extravagant bathhouse. Arched walls with geometric columns, brushed designs, and repeating tile patterns. The floor was marble (or the Aether equivalent) and hot baths were carved into the floors of alternating bays. Each was empty but meticulously cared for. We shuffled through to a private hall and found a grand bath with deep blue water. It was so blue it was opaque.

A single figure stood outside the pool. A lanky man with a hooked nose. He had bad skin, rough and sun damaged. He wore a fine robe of red and green, ornamented with some kind of metallic seam. He held a purple cloak in his hands.

One of the sandmen saluted him and communicated in a

series of chirps.

"This is unacceptable," said the man in a whiny voice.

More chirps.

The man raised his hooked nose to study us. He was jumpy and flittery, without the air of royalty. "The bathhouse is a sacred chamber."

"Let it be," called out a voice. This one was stronger. More aggressive and coarse. It dripped with authority and I knew it was the shah before I even turned around.

The top half of a bald head sat on the surface of the blue pool. A crocodile in wait. The man had a ring of fat around his head with shriveled, pointed ears. His eyes were so beady I couldn't tell their color. The complete lack of eyebrows drew more attention than the eyes themselves. His mouth peeked above the surface again to speak.

"We asked for them directly," said the shah. "Although, we admit, we didn't figure they would be captured so promptly."

The shah lifted fat, stubby arms out of the water. Large bracelets clinked together. Thick, carrot fingers covered with rings. Then slowly, like the elevator, the man rose out of the water and floated in mid air.

I didn't know what had me more off guard. The levitation or his size. He was huge. Eight hundred pounds if he was an ounce. Completely naked except for shiny metal links around his shoulders and neck. A far cry from Lilliane, trust me. Thankfully his bulging lumps of mass drooped down modestly. That didn't change the fact this was a dumpster-fire I couldn't look away from. Each thigh was wider than Tyson Roderick, but the jinn was short. His round mass made his limbs look stumpy and insufficient.

As the blue water slicked down his unevenly colored flesh, the shah drifted beside his aide and waited with outstretched arms. The purple cloak was laid over him. It wasn't a full cloak so much as a cowl in two pieces. One for his head and one for his shoulders. The metal necklace was adjusted to rest atop the cloth. A matching loincloth was wrapped around his waist. The belt portion disappeared into the shah's girth, leaving only a length of runner cloth hanging below his belly to his feet.

Not once did the shah bother touching the floor. He floated a foot and a half above it. Even so, his aide was taller than he was.

"Let us address business immediately," he proclaimed.

"Of course." The aide bowed deeply and jerked his head at the officiate.

The sandman escorted us through a doorway and then another, leading us into a sort of viewing room. It reminded me of the Mother's chamber in High Valley. Not nearly as rudimentary or spacious, but an empty seat of power.

We were shoved before a throne with spikes rising from the back. Stacks of books and scrolls were filed away on shelves behind it. The aide took his place beside the chair and waited for the shah to float to his seat. Rather than lower himself into it, the throne rose into the air on the same magic current and fit around the shah's body. Then various items drifted from the shelves and took their places surrounding the king. Hardbound books opened to various pages. Partially unwound sheepskin scrolls. A bejeweled scepter of gold. All the objects hovered around him like *Gradius* options.

"Please tell me you've watched *Dune*," I whispered to

Tyson.

The aide glared at me and one of the officiate's holding my arm tugged in warning. Either I wasn't supposed to talk or jinns weren't into sci-fi epics.

I licked my lips and loosened my shoulders, waiting for things to play out. The aide dismissed the extra officiates, leaving only the six holding us. According to back-of-napkin math, my odds were improving. But something told me the shah himself wielded far more terrible power than anyone else in this room. I still didn't harbor hopes of fighting my way out of here.

"Combating royal officiates," started the shah. His eyes scanned a scroll to his right as he spoke. His voice was wandering, only half paying attention. "A jinn killing. Multiple aspects abolished. Vast property damage in Tree Song."

"I can explain," I said.

"Quiet!" he shouted.

The command hit me like a sonic boom. I stumbled. Probably would've fallen to the floor if it weren't for the sandmen propping me up. I strained to focus and noticed the shah was staring straight at me now.

"We have not given you leave to speak, human." He took in a long, raspy breath. "There is always an explanation, but we are not thrilled to have it from a lot of criminals. There is only one trustworthy person standing before us and we will hear it from him." The shah turned to his loyal subject. "Subjugate Connor Hatch, it has been a long while since we have seen each other."

The jinn flashed a cool smile. "I only regret our reunion is under such circumstances, Master." Connor bowed as he finished the statement.

I was in a stupor. I'd never imagined Connor Hatch could come off so subservient and agreeable. This wasn't just duty, it was ass kissing.

The shah snorted. "The circumstances are not surprising given your love for everything Earthly. We have warned you about the human realm, have we not?"

Connor kept his gaze averted. "Wise words, as I remember. But my profit there has been your profit here."

The giant man on the throne pursed his lips, neither agreeing nor disagreeing.

"I see you are not holding a full court," noted Connor.

"No," said the shah. "We feel it tidier to keep this ugly business in house. No reason to involve the satraps."

No reason besides a fair trial, maybe.

Connor nodded agreeably. "You are ever wise, and I am ever your servant." He flicked his head to the officiates. "That being so, are these really necessary?"

The shah sighed. "No, we suppose not."

He glanced at his aide who in turn jerked his head at the officiates. The two sandmen released Connor and exited the chamber. Tyson and I were still bound. I was starting to get the feeling this trial wouldn't be the pinnacle of justice.

Connor Hatch smiled at me and brushed sand off his arms. Then he strolled closer to his shah.

"Really, Master, I appreciate your zeal for order, as well as the assistance in the apprehension of these two interlopers, but this is my mess entirely. I own up to that. If you release them to me I'll see to it they never disrupt any Aether business again."

The shah frowned. His chair swayed up and down on a

current. "That is not possible, Subjugate. If this were only about a single rogue aspect we would not have demanded your presence, but we cannot submit a human to you as such. He is not your property."

A sigh of relief escaped my lips. Being released into Connor's control on his home turf was just about the worst thing I could think of.

"Besides," said the ruler, "it is not every day that a human sneaks into Maqad. We will hear of this business."

Connor shrugged. Not in objection or ill humor. The shah's decision didn't seem to matter to him one way or another.

"Fine then," he said. "I'll go through the whole boring ordeal as I know it. As long as you have patience for it. But you should know that I know nothing of their plot. I am not part of their crimes."

The shah cleared his throat. "What is criminal and what is not will be decided by us alone. We warn you, we will have somebody's head for this. It is high time we get started. Before the rule of the capital, each of you are to answer for this madness. Let the trial commence."

Chapter 28

The floating throne listed as the shah leaned into a heavy book. "Go on, then."

Connor nodded and bowed. An edge of confidence was shaved from his demeanor, but it hadn't fled him completely. The jinn knew well enough to take this seriously, whether or not this was his playing field.

"The battle aspect was one of mine," he started. "A long, long time ago. Eleven years, to be precise."

The shah's hairless brow hardened. "Years?" asked the shah in disbelief. "In the Earthly Steppe, an aspect cannot be held for more than seven days and seven nights. You know the law."

"Of course," Connor hastened. "I obeyed the law. I summoned the volcanic aspect for one small thing or another. Then I banished him. His actions since then have been someone else's."

"That's a lie," I said.

The aide stomped toward me and grabbed me by the mouth. I jerked toward him but the officiates tightened their grip. The aide spoke in a commanding whisper. "You will remain quiet or the officiates will fill your throat with sand. Is that clear?"

I scowled but held my tongue and nodded.

The aide leaned his hooked nose close to my face as if he could see through me. Then, satisfied, he released me and returned to his ruler's side.

The shah sighed impatiently and turned back to Connor. "So you assert freedom from all the aspect's crimes."

"I do, Master."

I nearly growled. I wondered why Tyson didn't speak up in his defense. But he was familiar with the rules here. With his second-class status, he didn't want to make things worse. Like I was doing.

"How was the human introduced to the aspect?" asked the shah.

Connor tilted his head to concede a fair score. "That, I freely admit, was my work. This human is a formidable animist and there came a time when he faced off against several of my supporters. The volcanic aspect was necessary for this task, which was over a decade ago."

The ruler's beady eyes looked me over with suspicion. It was clear my presence was a bigger deal than Tyson's. Maybe that meant I was special. Like a zoo animal.

"And this human has grievances with you?"

"Unfortunately," said Connor. "The empire that brings wealth to this state is a ruthless one. The human came to odds with a vampire in my employ."

"Nether creatures," he spat.

"Only for Earthly business," tempered Connor.

"The whole business offends us." The shah frowned as documents circled his throne. "Still," he added, "your pursuits have not proven illegal." For the first time, the shah turned to Tyson. "Who is your master?" he demanded.

Tyson lifted his head and squared his shoulders. "I am in service to Connor Hatch," he answered plainly.

"An obvious lie," remarked Connor.

The shah shook his head and squinted at Tyson. "You do know, aspect, that speaking against your master is a crime punishable by death? And lying to us, worse."

The elemental grunted. "I speak only the truth."

"Then you are damning yourself," muttered Connor. I wondered why the shah's aide wasn't snapping at him to shut his mouth.

After a moment of reflection, the shah spoke. "We tend to agree. But we have decided to hold a trial, and hear one we will." The throne drifted to the side so it hung before the elemental. "Levy your charges, Tyson Roderick."

The magma under his rockskin pulsed brightly. "For a decade, and just until five months ago, I was part of a group called the Covey."

The shah arched an eyebrow. "A decade, again." The entire throne pivoted forward so he could inspect the elemental closely. It should've tilted his enormous girth off balance but hey, magic's magic. "Tell us," started the shah, "how it is that a battle aspect, albeit a powerful one, is able to remain in the Earthly Steppe as you did?"

"I was summoned by Connor Hatch. Once in place, he utilized an artifact. A heartstone. Once its strings were in me, his mark no longer mattered."

"Ridiculous!" chimed Connor. "Heartstones influence the raw emotions inherent in humans. Elementals don't have hearts."

Tyson sneered at the comment but held his tongue. I watched him, molten rock and all, and knew I'd seen feeling in there once or twice.

"That's not true," said Tyson finally. "Because of Connor's interference, Kita Mariko is dead. I loved her."

"Loved?" mused the shah.

A hearty chuckle came from Connor's lips. He didn't stifle it in any way. In fact, he grew bolder until his laugh filled the room. It seemed contagious because the aide snorted in mirth a few times. Even the shah couldn't disguise the smile on his lips.

"Tyson Roderick," said the king, "after your time on Earth, we do not doubt that you have experienced much for your kind. We would even grant you an indulgence or two. But to spew nonsense about the ways of love is tantamount to treason."

Connor hungrily took in the admonishment. He held all the cards here. He knew when to speak and when to let the silence do so. This was a task he had well in hand. I could only hope Tyson had some sense of the task as well.

"What of the humans, then?" asked the elemental. "Kita Mariko. Emily Cross. Their hearts and minds were stolen too."

The shah leaned back on his throne and flicked his beady eyes to Connor. "We have to say, Subjugate, this talk of a heartstone concerns us. Service is sacred. Noble because it is voluntary. Coerced, perhaps, but willing. Using spellcraft to short-circuit free will runs rough with the law."

"The animists dealt with me plainly. I outplayed each of them. Jinn law was not broken."

There it was. Jinn law rearing its head. I'd often wondered why, exactly, jinns were forced to jump through the hoops they did. Connor had never been able to attack me directly until I entered a bargain with him.

But then I thought of the dragons. Demons in our world, like the jinn, but demons that crossed the line and interfered where they shouldn't have. Hunted by angels in return. Meanwhile, the jinns thrive as they obey the law.

Because it wasn't jinn law. It was Celestial law.

Tyson continued to state his case, undaunted. "There's also the Horn of Subjugation. Much of the Covey's early directives revolved around acquiring this artifact. A wraith bound to the Horn can turn other necromancers to his will. A slave enslaving others. It's the very opposite of the law."

The shah's face hardened. "Do not presume to educate us on what is and isn't the law, little aspect." But the wrinkle of concern on his face was evident. "What does this one speak of, Connor?"

The jinn smiled nervously at the mention of his name. "The power over the necromancers is the wraith's work, not mine."

"A loophole," leveled the elemental. The aide flicked his glare to Tyson but didn't silence him. "The humans the Horn enslaved never bargained with Connor. In his time on Earth, he built up a Caribbean drug cartel that kills indiscriminately. He used the Covey as enforcers to sway Miami business and politics. And worst of all..."

Tyson Roderick took a bold step toward the shah. The two officiates chirped in warning but the shah lifted a grubby hand. The soldiers gave Tyson enough slack so he could kneel.

"Worst of all," Tyson repeated, "Connor Hatch created me."

The beady eyes of the shah sparkled.

"I've ravaged the Earth," said Tyson. "I've ravaged the Aether. And I'll continue to do so as long as I serve Connor Hatch."

"Lies!" charged Connor, losing his cool for the first time. "He has no proof. He's a rogue aspect, acting on his own. A law breaker. He brought the human here. That's crime enough!"

"He is not the only one on trial," returned the shah. "Am I to suppose you weren't involved when you were present at their apprehension?"

I didn't expect the accusation. Maybe there was animosity between Connor and his master. Or maybe the shah just wanted to make sure his reputation would remain spotless. It seemed to be an opening.

"I was defending my home. The elemental set this up."

The shah chuckled. "Perhaps."

The ifrit's face darkened. "You are a great man, my master. My shah. But even you have no grounds to judge me based on an aspect's mad ramblings."

"Then," said Tyson, still on his knees and bowing deeply, "rely on the word of the human."

The room went quiet. I didn't know Aether justice but I had a sense the burden of proof had shifted. I had a sense that I, as a human, was an intruder, but a somewhat distinguished one.

"You asshole," I whispered to Tyson. "This was your plan all along. You wanted to be captured by the officiates."

So the scarecrow had a brain after all. His damn temper tantrum at Connor's house fell into place now. He'd been waiting for the officiates to arrive. He only ran to chase after me. His plan was to get attention and get caught, but to make sure he got caught *with* me. Tyson, as an elemental, could never get an audience with Connor's master. The shah was much too important. Tyson needed a jinn or a human to stand for him to even have a chance at justice. Otherwise he would've been tossed back to his old master like a dirty towel.

Connor Hatch stood with his jaw open. He sensed the moment too. The shah traded hard stares between him and me. I couldn't tell who he was more angry with, but it was priceless to see Connor at a loss for words. That, at least, proved Tyson was on the right track.

Slowly, the intricate throne drifted my way. The books and scrolls receded to the background, leaving only the jeweled scepter within his reach. The shah plucked the golden implement from the air and lifted it to my chin. He turned my face to study it. After a moment and a frown, he released the scepter to the air again.

"And you, human. You can attest to these charges?"

I spoke without hesitation. "I can. Connor's politics have resulted in the deaths and manipulation of my friends and family."

"I conceded that much," said Connor. "That was the work of Tunji Malu."

"A Nether vampire," said the shah. "Harboring Nether creatures is unclean. The jinn are barred from the Nether and its business, just as it is impossible for Netherlings to come to the sky."

"But the Earth is a middle ground, Master. The convergence of the steppes."

"My mother and father," I protested. "My girlfriend. My partner. All the people I killed as his undead hit man. They can't all be loopholes."

Connor shrugged solemnly. "I don't deny partaking in Earthly affairs, but Earthly affairs are what Cisco fell victim to. Not me."

"This has already been discussed," muttered the shah. "We wish you to address the aspect summoned to your world. Can you confirm his account?"

I wasn't sure what he was getting at. Was the entire crime simply that Connor had brought Tyson to the Earthly Steppe for more than seven days and nights? I didn't get it but I didn't want to falter and show weakness.

"Ten years ago I was ambushed by the Covey. Tyson was there. He was there six months ago, too, protecting Connor's interests. I saw him die twice, only to return as a member of the Covey."

"But was he resummoned?" questioned the shah. "Multiple aspect summonings are commonplace."

"He was there the whole time."

"But you said yourself he was killed twice. Sent back to the Aether. The only way for an aspect to return to your world would be a resummoning."

Connor Hatch chewed his lip during this interrogation. I berated myself for not being able to read his thoughts.

"I saw the heartstone," I offered.

Drool dripped from the blubbery shah's lips. "The aspect binding," he said. "Did you witness the aspect binding?"

"I destroyed the stone. I saw Tyson rip off his heart locket, the artifact's anchor. The others wore them too. It's why I killed Kita."

He arched a brow. "*You* killed?"

"Connor forced me to kill," I amended.

The king relaxed back into his throne. He grabbed a length of purple cloth hanging from his shoulder and wiped the dribble from his chin. "We are not hearing evidence," he ruled. Connor breathed a sigh of relief.

"What about Jean-Louis Chevalier?" I appealed. "He would never make a deal with Connor but he had him. This is about the Horn of Subjugation."

"So what?" asked Connor with an annoyed flick of his hand. "Humans have used similar prisons against our kind since time immemorial. I wasn't the one who snared the wraith. That was done by humans. I intend to free him. A gift, I might add, which Cisco himself never gave."

I grumbled because he was right. Desperation crawled into my voice. "And in the meantime, you subjugate countless other humans to your will. More loopholes."

The shah raised a hand for silence. He pursed his lips and then addressed Connor.

"Service should arise from honor and duty," he said. "As you have agreed to serve us—for another eight hundred years, if we are not mistaken. Forcing others under your thumb with the use of artifacts is callous. Offensive. We would not have you represent us like so."

Connor swallowed and spoke with a hard edge. "The heartstone is Earthly. Same goes for the Horn, and the vampire's compulsions, and the voodoo curses. All these things are not of the Aether."

"But you are suitably representative, are you not? Would you forsake the will of your master?"

Connor showed his teeth. "Our wills differ. It is only our duties which bind us. I am no longer beholden to your oversight so long as I enrich your coffers. *That* is our agreement."

Each of them smiled almost imperceptibly. This was a chess match between two skilled players. Their motivations were complex and layered and, frankly, this entire trial was a conflict of interests.

The shah grabbed his scepter from the air and hugged it to his man-boobs. The throne rotated so its back was to us. A dramatic show of deliberation. It only lasted twenty seconds before the shah spun back around and addressed us.

"Needless interference with the Earthly Steppe is frowned upon. Even worse, subverting jinn law carries heavy penalties." The throne tilted slightly toward Connor. "But we have not heard proof that such interference was needless or subversive. We will not condemn you save to remind you of the responsibility of your post."

Connor bowed deeply. "A wise decision." He held the position and turned his head to sneer at me.

Of course. This had all been bullshit. Not a trial but the appearance of one. Just another rigged game. Connor pulled himself off the hook with nothing more than a silver tongue and a promise of future continued payment.

"At least look into the accusations," I insisted.

"We will not," snapped the shah. "You come before us without proof."

"We didn't come before you. You dragged us here. What proof could we possibly have with us? Give me time and I'll get anything you need."

"We have made our ruling, human. Our courts are not as laborious as you might be accustomed to. Connor's trial is over. Yours will come, but first it is time to address the worst of the offenders. Tyson Roderick, you have shirked your duties in the Aether for ten years."

"By Connor's order," he asserted.

"We will hear no more of Earthly artifacts," overruled the shah. "It is the human desire for treasure that creates them. Let their world suffer for them."

The officiates pulled Tyson to his feet and held him tight.

"You have spoken against a prior master. You have attacked other aspects in the Aether. We are not unjust. Were these Earthly matters, the same leeway Connor employs might also befall you. We might have ruled it outside our jurisdiction and let the two of you deal with it." The shah leaned forward and scowled. "But you came *here*."

"I—"

Tyson's protest halted as the shah waved a grubby hand. The elemental's mouth vanished, smooth rock taking its place. Tyson grunted and pulled against his bindings. His magma flared brightly. Just two soldiers held him, but they were strong.

"We haven't even addressed your worst crime," said the shah. The rough baritone of his words was severe. "Humans are strictly forbidden from the Aether."

Tyson grimaced under the force of the officiates.

The shah's throne floated to me. "You are a predicament. Not subject to jinn law, yet not free to wantonly kill and destroy in our kingdom. Those are the laws of any land, under which you are liable."

"And what of Celestial law?" I asked. All the eyes in the room watched me. And for once, I had to believe. "The angels don't look kindly on those who shirk it. Ask the dragons who hide out in the mountains. Ask yourself if your cities and your power are at stake."

He scoffed at my charges but I could tell they held weight. "The empire is not on trial here." He didn't openly refute my statement, but he did deflect it. "We are weighing your crimes, Cisco Suarez. Whatever you have done in your steppe is irrelevant. We won't bore ourselves further with its details. And we are inclined to overlook your actions here as you were obviously strung along by this battle aspect."

"He destroyed my property," complained Connor. "He killed my man."

"Defended himself, more like," returned the shah.

"Do not kowtow to the Celestials."

"Celestial law does not protect him in the Aether. But we will return him to his world all the same. We judge the human free of charges." The shah's bald head canted toward Connor. "Be gracious we are in a merciful mood today."

The threat implicit, Connor was happy to stay ahead of the game. He bit that silver tongue and nodded acceptance.

"However," proclaimed the shah, "the aspect's crimes are grave indeed. What do you have to say for yourself, Tyson Roderick?"

He grunted uselessly against his sealed mouth.

"That is what we thought," chuckled the shah. "Your judgment will be swift and merciless. For your crimes against the Aether, we condemn you, Tyson Roderick. Eternal servitude. You are hereby returned to your former master, to be dealt with as he chooses." The shah licked his lips. "We are certain his punishment will be duly reformative."

Chapter 29

Connor Hatch laughed. He was liberated, free and clear. And Tyson Roderick was his now.

"Well, Cisco," he said with savor, ever gracious in victory. "It looks like we'll meet again on the streets of Miami."

Connor bowed to the shah a final time and stepped to the door. The two officiates holding Tyson released him. I waited to be released too so I could help him open a can of whoop-ass, napkin math be damned, but Tyson just stood there, his back to Connor.

The ifrit cleared his throat. "Come now, Tyson. Don't make this harder than it has to be. You know you can't fight us."

I tugged an arm but the officiate didn't budge. The mindless golem didn't even seem to notice.

"Come on!" commanded Connor.

The elemental grunted repeatedly.

"At least let him speak," I said.

The shah shrugged and waved a hand. Tyson's mouth reappeared. The shah then scrunched his beady eyes at him. "You must comply, you know. Resistance is impossible."

"I will never serve that man," spat Tyson.

The shah snarled. "Your continued insolence is grating."

Connor laughed and grabbed the elemental's shoulder. "You have no choice."

"No," said the shah. "He does have a choice in the matter. And he has made his."

"What do you mean?" I asked.

"If the aspect refuses to serve, we will comply with his request. We hereby sentence you to oblivion. A summary death, executed forthwith."

The golden scepter waved in the ruler's hand. The door swung open and a jinn holding a forked polearm entered.

"What?" I yelled. "No!"

Despite not being held, Tyson remained firmly rooted in place. He didn't run. He didn't shy away from the jinn with the fork. In fact, he kneeled again. He waited.

"Get up, Tyson!"

I searched for the threads of magic that forced him down and held him in place. If they existed, they were invisible to me. The executioner stopped over the elemental, held the fork high, and turned his head to the shah. I strained against the grainy arms holding me back.

"Tyson," I pleaded, "this isn't about pride anymore. This isn't about revenge. You need to stand up right now. Stand up. Either to obey or to fight."

The volcanic elemental turned to me, a flicker of orange in his red eyes. "Perhaps Kita and I will be reunited," he said softly.

For the first time, I realized Tyson's motives were nothing but pure.

Connor scoffed. The shah lowered his scepter. The executioner thrust the heavy fork down into Tyson's back.

Tyson lurched as the tines plunged through his body and protruded from his chest. Electricity crackled, jumping from metal to metal, frying him.

Tyson Roderick raised his arms and let out a harrying bellow. His rockskin hardened and blackened. Unable to overcome the power of the soldiers, I watched helplessly as my companion crumbled to dust.

The electricity winked out. The room silenced and darkened. A grainy pile of leftovers was all that remained of the elemental. An officiate reached over and began absorbing the remains, sucking them into himself. Was that what the officiates were made of?

"What did you do?" I whispered.

Connor's eyes were wide, his teeth bared. He was in a frenzy at seeing an opponent vanquished. But as the dust cleared away, something startled him.

A spinning token of magic glowed from within the elemental's remains. A golden shard.

I'd seen something like it before. Outside the hunting outpost, the first sign of civilization I'd encountered in the Aether. Three jinns were summoning an elemental in a pyre. One of them inserted a golden sliver into the conjured salamander. It was a magical seal. A remainder of the summoning process.

"A mark?" asked the shah, genuinely startled. "*Your* mark, Connor Hatch."

The ifrit stuttered. His mark, from when he had summoned Tyson long ago. Except it was still there. The elemental had never been properly released. Before his days and nights were done, the heartstone had assumed control.

The seal was a game changer. Connor's malfeasance in

physical form. This was a contingency Tyson must've been aware of. A sacrifice to provide the only proof he had.

"You fool," berated the shah, his meaty head shaking and dripping with sweat. "You forgot to remove your mark. You used your Earthly artifacts but carelessly left behind your signature. And then you bring him here, spin the truth until his mark is made bare, plain to see, offending us with its presence."

"It's just an old—" protested Connor.

"He was no rogue!" boomed the shah. "He was abandoned. Your property, your crimes. He was put to death while bearing your mark. Do you not see what this means?"

"It's not the first time an aspect rebelled against his master."

"You created him. You let him loose in the world. First in your playground, then in ours. Even more vile, you came before us and lied through your teeth." The shah turned to his aide. "It is a good thing we held council privately, else our good name would have been besmirched."

Connor scrambled. "I never would do anything that—"

"Connor Hatch," chided the shah. "Do you believe you are a shah unto yourself? A king of kings, above the law because of a tithe?"

The shah waited. When Connor realized he was supposed to answer, all he said was, "You were waiting for this the whole time."

The shah narrowed his eyes. "You are stripped of your jinn protections," he proclaimed. "Stripped of all service and status for one hundred years."

The ifrit's face paled.

"You are hereby exiled from the Aether. Wander the world as you see fit, but wander here no more."

"But my home."

The shah was ruthless. "Your possessions in the Aether have been assumed by the empire. Live in your Caribbean paradise, or even in the wallows of the Nether you are so fascinated with. We wash our hands of you."

Connor traded glances with the aide, the shah, the officiates. Even me. His mind was reeling from whiplash. He desperately wanted to save himself, but nothing came.

"Connor Hatch," decreed the shah. "Welcome to exile."

The king of kings clapped the scepter between his thick hands and Connor disappeared.

The executioner loitered a moment with an eye on me. The aide waited as well, but dismissed him at the shah's behest. The executioner rested the polearm over his shoulder on his way out. The aide motioned to the officiates as well. They finally released me and exited the room as a group.

My arms were raw, like someone had taken sandpaper to them. I rubbed them gently. The aide receded into a corner, leaving me shivering under the cold glare of the shah. Just me left now. And the spinning golden seal.

The shah sighed deeply and wiped his brow. The trial had taken its toll on him.

"And you," he declared, "are no longer ignorant of the ways of the Aether. We would advise you never to return."

I opened my mouth to say something as the jeweled scepter cut through the air. All sound went out a fraction of a second before the world went white.

Chapter 30

I'd just seen Tyson vaporized. Connor banished. So when it was my turn to go, you'd better believe I was crapping my spiritual Aether pants.

I returned to form. Not my Aether body but real, actual form. Replete with imperfections. The scratch in my throat. The poke of the knife in my belt. That abominable bright-orange Phish shirt. I ran my fingers through the shag rug and remembered where I was. The dank library offshoot of the museum archives. Back in the real world. My world.

My eyes adjusted to the faint light in the room. Relief washed over me. No cops here anymore. The fireplace was dark. The Taíno coffins and artifacts, gone. A strip of yellow police tape snaked over the floor, trampled by movers no doubt. This was a crime scene but the evidence was priceless. No doubt the museum staff would be tasked with restoring the Taíno relics. Still, Connor and his men had murdered a curator and a security guard to get this location. They caused public havoc. This room held potential evidence leading to those perpetrators and would be searched again.

Between an elemental, a jinn, and a dead man, the police were sure to be stumped.

Besides the missing relics, the study appeared to have been straightened up. My eye caught a dark blue globe sitting on a mahogany end table between two leather chairs. Had that been there before? I studied the crystal sculpture and took a few calming breaths to center myself. That whole experience in the Aether now felt like a dream. But the world had certainly turned. I guessed the sum of the experience resulted in a day's passing.

And the death of Tyson Roderick.

I ground my teeth. After the ethereal experience in the sky, the sensation was pleasantly grating. But as my worldly senses sharpened, I detected coarse breathing behind me.

I spun, hoping to see the volcanic elemental intact. No such luck. Of all people, Connor Hatch was on his hands and knees, experiencing taste and touch as if for the first time, just like me. I froze. He blinked and focused on me, confused.

Connor Hatch. Three feet away from me.

I lunged. His features hardened immediately, a good soldier heeding the call to battle. The jinn braced to meet my raised fist. I pooled shadow into the blow and hammered his right cheek.

Nobody was more surprised than me that the punch actually connected.

Connor's head snapped to the side. A tooth jangled to the wood floor past the rug. The jinn bounced after it and slid to a hard stop against an unforgiving bookcase.

We stopped and stared at each other. Connor spat blood and wiped his jaw.

"You're exiled from the Aether," I said slowly. "You can't blink anymore."

The jinn's eyes widened in shock. I could tell he was trying to blink. Once, twice. That confident patience he'd taken for granted had grown from the ability not to lose a tooth like that. I wondered if this had been Tyson's plan all along.

I rose. Connor twitched as he demanded his body to teleport. Failing that, he rolled to the side.

I dove into the shadow and appeared beside him. Connor lifted his hand but I snapped it down. Then I leveled him with a body blow. I gave him a left and a right and a left again, punching opportunistically more than for damage.

His hand flushed with red. I ducked as a lance of fire tore through the ceiling. I rolled to my feet, alert. Connor's eyes narrowed.

His defenses were gone, but his weapons were intact.

The sound of something rocking on wood startled me. I took my eyes off Connor for a split-second and scanned the room. Nothing.

I felt the incoming heat and threw up my shield. Turquoise energy strobed against brilliant flame. My shield held, but I backed away to keep the glancing flames off me. My retreat brought me up against the stone fireplace.

"Perhaps I can't blink," hissed Connor, pressing his magic to me. "But I can still burn."

"Burn this," I growled.

I reached into the darkness of the raised chimney, pulled out my shotgun, and leveled the sawed-off barrel at him. My finger squeezed the trigger. The hammer snapped into the firing pin.

A light mechanical click was my only reward.

Of course. Firearms work best when loaded. I'd emptied the weapon shattering the hotel window. The rest of my ammo and spell tokens had burned up in the inferno.

"Can't a necromancer catch a break?" I complained.

I flung the shotgun through the air like a boomerang. It rocketed right through Connor's flames and hit home, popping against his skull. The fire faltered and dissipated.

Connor went down to a knee, clutching his head. A sliver of blood trickled over his fingers. The sawed off fell back into shadow. Before I could advance, another sound interrupted us.

A click, like glass cracking. My eyes finally located the source: the dark blue globe of blown glass on the end table. A single splintered crevice ran along the prime meridian from one pole to the other.

Suddenly I knew for sure this globe hadn't been here before.

Connor grunted in pain. His expression was harried. Scared, and rightly so. But he wasn't terrified. He wasn't a quivering wreck. And, if he was anything, he was cocky.

"You fool," he spat. "I can bleed, but I'm not human."

His fists tightened and burst into flame. Like his ifrits in the Aether, the fire ran up his arms. It flared brightly, consuming his shoulders, sending sparks into the old books behind him. The crystal globe seemed to shiver against the newfound light.

"No," I shouted. "The fire—"

The glass spiderwebbed. A deep light emanated from within.

Over the course of the last day and a half, I'd seen a lot of strange things. A magic world. A magic elevator. A magic

VW Bus. Now I had even witnessed a magic bomb.

Without wasting a second, I dove into the open fireplace. I shifted into the darkness and snaked up the chimney. I wasn't Mary Poppins. I couldn't slide up on a gentle wind and drift to safety, but I could stuff myself a few feet above the opening in the stone pillar.

The blast was as fast as I was. A shockwave turned the world blue. The opaque light followed me and dissolved the shadow. It ran up the chimney and jerked me back to physical form. My alligator boots scraped for purchase against the rough interior as the whole tower shook with the boom. Scraps of debris flew into me. Pieces of glass. Splinters of obliterated wood. I covered my ears, tucked my head, and braced my boots into the wall as the library literally exploded.

My ears rang. I blinked away the light but I knew I wasn't thinking straight. The shockwave had knocked me senseless. The stone chimney rocked. Dust and mortar rained down from above. Too late I realized the whole damn thing was coming down.

The chimney stack broke away. Thousands of pounds of stone crashed through the roof and walls of the library. Dust blotted out all ambient light. Above me somewhere, the chimney collapsed in on itself, but the thick base I was in held together. Upended but intact. After a frantic bout of crashes, the demolition settled into stillness.

I choked away dust and fled to the shadows again. There were no crevices large enough to escape through, but at least I didn't need to worry about breathing.

"Relax, Cisco," I assuaged myself between coughs. "The upside to being buried alive is that you're still alive."

I didn't want to vocalize the downside.

Chapter 31

I was stuck debating my options for only a minute before I heard sounds around me. Walls being overturned. Wood beams being dragged away. Holy hell, this was a prompt rescue effort.

Light flooded into my tomb and I squinted. It wasn't a fire or flashlight, it was the sun. I cautiously poked my head out of the newly exposed fireplace and saw why. I wasn't inside anymore. Or rather, the entire library was now outside. The ruins of the quaint chamber were nothing more than blackened rubble. No semblance of the room in the vicinity of the bomb remained.

"Cisco!" cried Darcy. "You're alive!"

The teenage telekinetic. That explained the expedient excavation. She hurried to help me climb from the rubble. I accepted her hand and shook my head, still reeling from the blast.

"What the hell happened?" she asked.

We shambled to the grass. Half the building had been leveled, and the other half would never be deemed safe for public use again. Worse, a crowd was beginning to form in the neighboring property. Workers. First responders wouldn't be far behind. We rushed to the curb just in time to see Winthrop's orange-and-white van veering through a tight U-turn and speeding away.

"Berna!" yelled Darcy, half crestfallen and half pissed.

I glanced back over the smoking rubble. Everything was scorched and melted. Much of it was disintegrated. So much for the crime scene. I spat out a dusty loogie and began marching down the sidewalk. So much for Connor Hatch, too. And to hell with these people.

"Cisco," called Darcy, still a little pissed. "What the hell happened?"

I stomped away, no stranger to what she was feeling.

"Hey!" she yelled. Her sneakers rapped the sidewalk until she circled in front of me and leaned her hands against my chest. "What the hell did you do in there?"

My eyes flared. "What did *I* do? What the hell did *you* guys do?"

She scowled. "I don't know what you're talking about."

"Sure you don't. You're just a kid."

She lifted her chin. "I'm old enough to know things."

"Yeah? You know why your friend Berna took off just now?"

Darcy pouted. "I wasn't supposed to help you."

"Yeah, right." I stepped around the teenager and proceeded down the sidewalk. One thing I'd learned about kids was that their eagerness to argue exceeded mine.

Darcy didn't try to stop me again. She was together enough to know we had to clear out of the area. She fell in pace beside me as we turned down the block. Already sirens were blaring to life. That would be the fire department, soon followed by the police.

A block further, I sprinted across Sunset Boulevard and

flagged down a Metrobus. I hopped on and reached into my jeans for cash. When Darcy climbed in behind me, I frowned, peeled an extra bill away, and fed them into the machine. Just like my teenage years, I walked to the very back of the bus where I could lean against the wall and feel the warmth of the engine against my shoulders.

"Look," she said, "I came after you. Against orders. The least you could do is talk to me."

I scoffed. "Cut the bullshit, sweetheart. You guys planned this. You were taxiing me around the city to keep track of me. The Society tipped Tyson off to my location. You knew he'd take me to the Aether on a suicide mission. Kill himself and probably me to get Connor exiled. To strip him of his ability to blink."

"Tyson's dead?" she asked genuinely. "We weren't keeping tabs on you, we were helping you. Keeping an eye on things without interfering, as agreed."

"We never agreed to sacrifice Tyson."

She took a measured breath. "Look, it's true that Winthrop was in contact with him, but Tyson's revenge was his own affair."

"Winthrop used him."

"It's what he wanted."

"Winthrop used *me*," I said.

"Didn't it give you the same opportunity?"

I smiled dryly. "I don't recall asking to be blown up."

"We didn't have anything to do with that."

"Of course you did. The whole plan was to strike Connor through me. My life? Tyson's? Neither mattered as long as you got Connor. That little bomb back there was activated by Connor's presence. The Society's insurance plan in case I didn't finish the job."

"I swear, it wasn't us."

"Pssh. If not you then Berna. Why do you think she didn't wanna stick around and chat?"

The young mage's face darkened. "No way. This had to be Margo. If she knew we were going after Connor—"

"This was Winthrop and you know it. He set me up to take down Connor. At any cost."

"I don't know that."

"Think about it. This was always a suicide mission. The Society doesn't risk going to *South America*. You think they want any piece of the *Aether*? So they sent me. Either I died there or I died here. Either way, I'm expendable."

"You're dedicated," she corrected.

"Same thing."

I shook my head and stared out the window. I'd probably had that kind of idealism once. The passing cars and pedestrians went about their everyday business, ignorant of the destruction we'd left behind. Ignorant of the rampant monsters in the world. The police sirens faded into the passing miles.

"What was that spellcraft?" I asked. "It was like solid blue fire."

Darcy shrugged. "That doesn't sound familiar."

"Fire's not going to kill Connor," I said.

"You said he couldn't blink anymore."

"He's been stripped of his protections but he's still a jinn. An ifrit. He's literally made of fire. Trust me, if I could survive that blast, he could. He was gone before you dug me out."

Darcy worked her lips between frustration and despair.

"This couldn't have been Winthrop. He would have told me."

"Did he tell you to stay away from the building? Did Berna ever have a chance to slip in with the bomb?"

The teenager worked the answer over in quiet concentration. That was for the best. I didn't need to hear the thought process to know how it played out. She would come to the same conclusion I had, eventually.

"It doesn't make sense," insisted Darcy. "Why kill you if he wants you to find the city of gold?"

I shrugged. "He doesn't want me to find it. That's the easy part. He just wants to stop Connor from finding it first."

She crossed her arms and turned away, focusing outside her window. After a minute of silence, she shook her head firmly. "No way. It had to be Margo."

I didn't bother correcting her. It *could've* been Margo. It could've been anyone. But I couldn't afford to concede theoretical possibilities right now. A very likely and straightforward sequence of events led to this road. The only conclusion was a very likely and straightforward punch to Winthrop's mug next time we crossed paths.

Darcy? Hell, we'd butted heads before. And I'd never admit it but she was strong enough that I didn't look forward to tangling with her. But on this count? I figured she was innocent. A good-natured pawn in a dark army. It was possible I could trust her, but I couldn't trust the Society. They were strange and mysterious and had decades of political motivations to satisfy. It's like I had said to the Mother of High Valley: bureaucracies get so complicated they only make sense from the inside. Darcy was too young to comprehend the depths greed and ego drive men to.

"If Winthrop's innocent," I offered in a rare concession, "then he'll talk to me."

"Impossible."

"Well, does he want my help or not?"

She sighed. "He does, but not at the cost of our lives. Listen, if Margo did this, she may already be on to us. Winthrop can't risk exposure... I can't either. I'm sorry, but you're on your own."

She pressed the bell to signal the driver to stop. He pulled to the curb at the next bus bench and flipped the doors open. Darcy stood and waited.

"You're not gonna say anything?" she asked.

I shrugged. "I didn't want your help anyway."

She swallowed silently and nodded. Then she hopped off the bus.

Chapter 32

A series of Metrobus transfers got me back to my hotel on the beach. A combination of light coaxing and elbowing the dashboard got my old pickup started. It was a 1970 F-250 with a missing radio and power nothing. Most of its character had been acquired over time rather than being a stock option. The patina of rust, for example. And the minor poltergeist that haunted the engine compartment. He'd been especially well-behaved lately. Luckily, that streak continued. I was broadcasting my mood loud and clear and even the afterlife didn't want to fuck with me.

I let the glove box fall open. A box of pastel birthday candles. A cheap Farm Stores matchbook. A deceptive amount of cash in small stacks. And a mostly empty box of birdshot. I didn't have my belt pouch anymore so I had no supply of homebrew bullets laced with spark powder. I plucked the vanilla shotgun shells out one by one and stuffed them into my jeans.

Before I shifted into drive I noticed the folded shirt on the back seat. I smiled, changed into the white tank top, and tossed the orange shirt into the trash. Cisco Suarez was back.

I drove north along the barrier islands until I hit

Hallandale Beach again. Connor's yellow house with the fountain. From a distance, it looked just as dead as before. Even more so since the two rental trucks were no longer in the driveway.

I didn't have time for covert sneaking this go around. Public transportation in Miami is laughably bad and I had to be way behind Connor at this point. He couldn't teleport anymore but he had amazing resources at his disposal. If I was gonna catch up, I would need to move fast. I pulled right into the driveway and walked to the front door.

Somewhere in the middle of all that I realized I should've stopped at a local voodoo supply store, but I had to work with what I had.

I kicked the door down, pulled my sawed-off shotgun from the ether, and slid a shell into its breech. A deep, smoky flavor clung to the walls and carpeting, like the cartel had been celebrating Connor's exile by grilling up a whole pig. His own *Nochebuena*. Only it wasn't Christmastime and I wasn't so sure what I smelled was pork.

When I rounded into the living room my fears were confirmed. A charred corpse lay on the sofa. It was Sleeping Beauty, in nearly the same position as when I'd seen him last. Except he'd been decidedly less crispy a day ago. The poor sucker had burned so hot and fast that the couch was barely scorched.

I took a long breath. I never figured Connor for the stereotypically evil movie villain who indiscriminately kills his own people. Flunkies will turn on you real quick if that becomes a habit. Was I finally getting to him?

Movement through the back windows caught my eye. The freaking submarine was at the private dock. I barged through the back door and charged through the patio and the yard. Bubbles of water flooded to the surface. The sub was diving. Connor had returned to his safe house and loaded everyone up and was taking off, just minutes before my arrival.

I ran along the wooden rail of the dock but it was no use. The vessel was submerging and already sailing away. The electric engine was unnaturally quiet. I raised my shotty to fire but held off. Announcing my presence wouldn't help. I checked the shoreline for any other boats but it was clear. The entire inlet was private and the submarine had been the only ship. Connor was gone.

I cursed and stomped inside. The house was empty, as before. Even the coffee-table book about the Taíno was missing now. I slapped my palm over my face and held off a growl. I'd been so close. Any number of things could've gone down differently and I would've been here in time. Skipping the argument with Darcy. The bus delays at the beach. Hell, I could've run a red light or two. Everybody else in Miami did.

I stumbled dejectedly down the stairs and was again overpowered by the smell of roasted human. I looked over the body. The mercenary had probably caught Connor when he was most pissed. Exiled, beaten, nearly blown up. The mercenary must've confessed to Connor that I'd snooped around. Stolen his gun. Found a lead to the museum. So Connor offed the guy as punishment.

Poor Sleeping Beauty. He'd gotten a hell of a poison apple. Or maybe that was Snow White. Point is, the dude was dead.

But then, his loss could be my gain. I could make time

for a quick trip to the voodoo supply store after all.

I jumped in my truck and tracked down what I could, wary of putting myself on the radar of any necromancers who might be hunting me. Voodoo spellcraft requires meticulous preparation. Most of the powders and poisons I employ are mixed from scratch by my own hand. Frankly, I don't trust the stuff you can buy on the street. Chances are you'll get some half-effective salve cut with baby powder. That's if you don't get conned completely. Me? I don't get conned. And I don't work with subpar sacraments. But right now I had to use what the street offered. It wasn't that hard to track down and I didn't need much.

Back in the privacy of the house I got to work. Step one was sprinkling invigorating powders over the fresh body. Old Crispy here didn't look so fresh but he hadn't been dead long. That's what counted. I didn't have intact eyes to see through but his soul wasn't far gone. I rubbed coarse grit into his mouth and ears and eye sockets to prep the vessel.

Next I started the ritual. Most voodoo comes at the mercy of time and circumstance. The more difficult the spellcraft—and this one was a doozy—the more stringent the requirements. My talent could make up for a lot but I wouldn't have gotten anywhere without the ritual. I set birthday candles around the body and lit them in sequence, muttering incantations and compelling the corpse to my will. I poured hot wax on his chest over his heart (trust me, he wouldn't feel it) and glued the last candle in place. Then I lit it.

The final requirement of the ritual came in the moment between the sun going down and the light leaving the atmosphere. Twilight. A period when life and death are married. It was fortunate the evening was lining up with my little party so all I needed to do was wait and hope the voodoo poisons were efficacious.

I wasn't disappointed. The room darkened in the absence of the sun and the candles burned with a mystical glow. Still weak against the sunlit remains of the day, they shone without giving off light.

A sharp intake of breath preceded a rasping cough and, just like that, the spirit had returned.

The charred body convulsed on the couch. I pressed his shoulders and shushed him. The birthday candle on his chest flared and rocked but held firm.

"Who calls me?" came a ghostly voice.

The corpse didn't really have much in the way of lips anymore, but it wasn't physically speaking anyway. The voice came from somewhere within, from a place science has yet to discover. The jaw of the blackened body did move up and down with the speech, but it was much too slow to line up with the words. It was like watching a badly dubbed film.

"Who calls me?" it asked again.

"You don't ask me questions," I said, voice crisp and firm. "This works the other way around. You're dead, get it? You're dead and you can go on your way in a minute, but I need to know where Connor went."

The burnt flesh of the jaw cracked as it stretched open. "Connor Hatch," said the spirit. "He is collecting the Haitians."

"Collecting?" I asked. Then I shook my head. I had to keep things simple. The Haitians meant the various voodoo gangs of Little Haiti. The necromantic core of Miami. Of America, really. And right at the head of that power structure was Jean-Louis Chevalier and the Bone Saints.

The birthday candle popped like oil in water. It was burning unnaturally fast. Already half gone. I grimaced. That's what I got for using cheap sacraments.

"What does Connor need the necromancers for?" I asked.

Teeth rapped against each other as ashes fell away from the mouth. "Connor Hatch needs them to enter the island."

The island. So there was a city of gold. There was an island. Winthrop was right. But what did he need the necromancers for?

"What's on the island?" I asked.

The candle popped again. Chances were, this South American mercenary didn't know a whole lot about spellcraft. He couldn't have been privy to Connor's innermost plans. But the transition to the afterlife can be eye-opening. It was possible this corpse could figure the bigger picture now, in hindsight.

"What's on the island?" I pressed.

The body's head turned sharply to meet my gaze. Sparks from the candle bounced across its face. The blackened corpse's jaw widened and widened until it cracked and fell away, but still the dead man seemed to look inside my soul.

"Death," it rasped. "Death."

Its hand clenched my wrist. I pulled away but its grip was strong. Its head leaned off the cushion towards me.

"DEATH!"

A flare of heat exploded, washing into my chest and slamming me to the floor. The corpse, likewise, was shoved back into the couch. I rolled away and readied my shotgun, but the body was again sleeping in peaceful repose. The birthday candle on his chest was a smoking pile of wax. All the other candles in the circle winked out as one. The ritual was over.

I took a slow breath and nodded. The slumbering corpse was now devoid of all humanity. He'd been a little frisky, but he'd given me enough to work with.

Chapter 33

By the time I reached Little Haiti, the city was dark. I parked under a busted streetlight along the curb. Most of the block was enclosed by a green iron fence. Within was a nondescript complex of apartment buildings. Nothing much at first glance, but for those in the know it was the criminal headquarters for the Bone Saints.

I left the truck and walked away from the grounds, circling into the residential portion of the block and sneaking into a backyard that shared a border with the apartments. I'd used this trick once before. That had been in the middle of the day under the glaring sun. This time I had the night on my side.

One advantage I didn't have this go around was the brand-new pet I'd used to scout ahead. The black cat. He couldn't help me this time. It was stupid but a part of me was sad he wasn't around anymore. It's like we were connected somehow. We more or less started our journey together. It didn't seem right that his ended before mine.

I shut the thought out of my mind and surveyed the scene.

Gangbangers wandered the grounds here and there but the operation was a bit off. The guards were nothing more than armed local kids. That part wasn't all that strange. The recent gang wars had depleted membership of all the voodoo players so the Bone Saints had to rely on new blood. Young blood. So what I saw wasn't so strange. It was what I didn't see.

There were no thralls guarding the buildings. You take a gang of necromancers and one thing's for sure: zombies will be running security. I didn't see that right now. And while lack of security helped me, anything out of the ordinary was a problem. I could chalk it up to the gang wars being over. Or could be that Jean-Louis Chevalier wasn't the leader I thought he was. But no.

The real reason for the disarray was that Jean-Louis Chevalier wasn't Jean-Louis Chevalier anymore.

Look, it's not like we're besties or anything. On any other day I'd avoid strolling right up to his compound stoop. But if it had come to that, *on any other day*, I wouldn't have expected to be attacked on sight. Tonight, all bets were off.

Seeing Jean-Louis at the dumpster the other morning had changed things. The Horn of Subjugation changed things. I could no longer rely on an uneasy alliance with the Haitians.

But if not that, what else did I have? Why was I here?

All I knew was what the charred mercenary back in Hallandale Beach had said. Connor needed the Haitians for something. And I needed Connor. This was where I had to be, plain and simple. If Chevalier had information, I had to get it from him. And if it came to fists instead of words... I'd do what I needed to.

At the fence, I stepped through the shadow and out on

the other side.

I blanketed myself in darkness and crouched low as I made my way forward. The undead might have been harder to fool, depending on how they were attuned. The kids leaning on the outdoor stairwells talking smack? They'd never see me coming.

I slipped through the yard to the building I knew was the command center and made my way up to the second floor porch. The door was open, the inside only lit by the distant city lights. Chevalier was sitting on the sofa alone watching TV. Well, he was watching *the* TV, but it wasn't on. His skull face paint and expression combined to create the image of living death. Not a flinch at my presence. But he was ready. Dressed to the nines. Silver earrings dangling to his shoulders. Silver-fingered gauntlets. His tattoos shone faintly on his bare chest.

"Suarez," he said without turning to me.

I stiffened, pissed that he'd noticed me. Then surprised he had. I hadn't made a sound.

I circled the small table in front of the couch to get a better look at my friend. I stopped right in front of the TV. His eyes were silver and crisp, but he looked exhausted. The sight tore me away from my mission. From the information I wanted. Instead I was hit with the human element in all this dirty business. I felt sorry for my friend.

"When was the last time you slept?" I asked.

His brow furrowed. He heard my voice but it took a moment to compute. Then all he said was, "Sleep."

"You're fighting it, aren't you?" I crouched down to meet his eye on a level. "You're fighting the effects of the Horn."

His expression darkened. "You gave him the Horn, Suarez. You made a deal with the jinn."

"I didn't mean to," I said. "It wasn't the plan." I knew that line of reasoning wouldn't get me anywhere. How could he, of all people, sympathize? He and his men were direct victims of my actions. But in my mind, there had been no other way. It was impossible for me to get to Connor if I had to constantly worry about the safety of my family and friends. Having them squared away was the only way to isolate him. To keep Emily and Fran from becoming another Kita Mariko. And I was almost there.

"I'm gonna get it back, Chevalier. I promise. I'm gonna fix this."

For the first time, the bokor blinked. Several times. It was an overwrought movement. A dream state. When he tried to focus on me again, his right eye partially glazed over.

I ground my jaw. The last few days must've been a constant struggle for him. For the gangs. I let the darkness seep into my eyes so I could examine him. His voodoo tattoos glowed brightly. So did his eye. There was an enchantment on it. No. A curse.

I reached out and tugged on the dog collar. Shadow gathered over the bokor's eye. I wasn't sure what I was doing. I wasn't versed in lifting curses, that's for sure. But I couldn't stay idle. I tried to smother the dark magic with my own blackness.

Chevalier's face began to soften. I couldn't whisk away the spellcraft that clung to him, but perhaps I could provide temporary relief.

We stayed there in the shadows for a moment. The

Intrinsics flowed freely through my body. Left me wired. But my friend leaned back into the cushions. It was working.

"A useless gesture," rasped another old friend. This one had a Spanish accent. I hadn't heard it in a while.

"This is turning into a reunion," I said. My cool voice masked my nervousness.

My old companion appeared in the corner. First just a skull suspended in air, two red hollow eyes cutting through the black. Then the rest of his body appeared. A steel helmet with a feather. A breastplate. Worn fingerless gloves, boots, leggings. A matchlock pistol and a side-sword hanging on a belt. Full conquistador battle dress.

It didn't need to be said, but this was no normal conquistador (if such a thing existed these days). He was a five-hundred-year-old wraith, the spirit bound to the Horn of Subjugation.

He had a new significance now. A distinction he hadn't had before. One that was perhaps inevitable. For the first time in a decade the Spaniard, my companion, was my enemy.

Chapter 34

"I was wondering when we'd run into each other," I muttered, standing to face the wraith.

He didn't draw a weapon or take up a defensive stance. He just idled in the air with eerie stillness.

"So this is your latest project?" I asked. "Enslaving living, breathing humans? I thought you weren't evil."

The fixed teeth of the Spaniard's skull somehow worked into a smile. "I am but a slave myself, my former master."

"Can't you fight it?" I pointed at Chevalier, quiet on the couch. "He's doing his best."

"His best is hardly enough. Neither was mine. The will of eleven Taíno shamans sealed my fate centuries ago. I cannot go against my master."

"Even if it means going against your family? You're my ancestor, for shit's sake."

"Brujo," he said in a patronizing wisp, "ask your dear sister and parents which is more powerful: blood or a blood curse."

My face hardened. The wraith had a point, but it was a low blow.

He drifted toward me. I closed my fist and readied myself, but he didn't come within reach.

"Connor does not wish to destroy you," he said. "He seeks something more profitable than a finale. More powerful than death."

I scowled. "Subjugation."

The Spaniard raised shriveled fingers.

I felt it immediately. The assault on my mind. This was a trick I'd witnessed the wraith perform many times: direct control. He could stop people in their tracks. Make them blind to the reality before them. Make them forget. His power was so absolute and unforgiving that he could even force a man to raise a gun to his own head and pull the trigger.

My jaw twisted under duress. I raised the internal alarm. Drew all my defenses. I'd been a mindless drone for ten years, a zombie hit man under the vampire Tunji Malu. I'd promised myself I would never serve another.

The necromancer's attack was swift. Strikes of lightning to the brain, irregular and multi-pronged. There was nothing to do for the sheer amount of pain it inflicted. I had to concede that much. I had to accept that fending him off might mean sustaining irreparable damage in the process. But I had to do it. Better dead than a slave.

As soon as I let the pain fall out of focus, my mindscape widened. I noticed more insidious threads weaving their way into my subconscious. This was a multifaceted attack. The pain was just a distraction.

The darkness thrummed around me. I beckoned Opiyel to answer and cracked open the floodgates. The physical remnants of shadow outside my body faded. I soaked it inward, fortifying my mind. Bolstering the very idea of my individuality.

A wave of bone-colored magic beset me. It seemed to light up the room, but I knew it was in my mind. My darkness battered it away as the sheets grew stronger. Thicker. The longer I held them off, the more outnumbered I became.

I almost panicked. Instead, I realized I could fortify my magic as well. As I did so, I drilled down and studied his attack.

The ivory threads snaking into me were numerous. They worked together and advanced as one. Woven together and reinforced they were daunting but, just like physical string, they were weak on their own. I fixated deep into their recesses and attacked their roots, ripping away wave after wave. More kept coming. With every success, two more threads struck elsewhere.

This was the wraith's power. He was a master of mind control and manipulation. Yet, despite the horrors I'd witnessed, I'd seen his limitations as well. Animists had a measure of defense against him. I'd even seen a particularly willful Columbian street soldier fend him off. If all it required to beat the wraith was a stubborn personality, I'd win this battle of wills hands down. No contest.

But there was a creeping worry I hadn't accounted for yet. The Spaniard, specifically, held some kind of dominion over necromancers. He could turn them into wights. Bring them to heel. This was a power I had never seen in action until Jean-Louis Chevalier cornered me in the alley.

I turned to the bokor. He sat on the couch and watched with a troubled expression. Whatever this power was, it wasn't immediate. Hell, if Chevalier could fight it off for a few days then there was no way in hell I was gonna let him show me up. I gritted my teeth and doubled down against the Spaniard's assault.

The slow success I'd had thus far bolstered my confidence. It was like a trick. Flipping a water bottle and having it land standing up. You might mess up the first few times but it really isn't that hard. Once you get it, it's easy to look like a seasoned expert. Admittedly, in the grand scheme of things, bottle flipping is a ridiculously useless skill. You can't make the same criticism about fending off mind control.

Each passing moment, with every strike and counterstrike, I grew more efficient. It was a learning process but not particularly complex. What felt like minutes were really seconds, more instinct and willpower than book-smarts. I snipped those threads faster and faster. I learned how to snap those threads from a distance and en masse. Thousands of tiny slivers of darkness working independently in unison, like the Spaniard's own magic.

"I'm not a zombie," I grunted.

Entire sheets of bone collapsed on themselves.

"I'm not a wight."

Multiple fronts of the assault fell away.

I thought of what Malik had said. The defining trait of our kind. Freedom.

"I'm a human being, damn it!"

With the next crashing wave of power, I completely banished the wraith from my head.

His ivory skull snapped back. His red eyes pulsed. In shock, in surprise. In respect. I had so cleanly obliterated his hooks from my mind that he must've wondered if a year's effort could do any better.

The room went dark again. Quiet. We stood for a moment before a heavy, raspy sigh escaped the Spaniard's lips.

"It must be another way then."

I narrowed my eyes. Now I pulled my spellcraft to my physical body. The darkness gloved my fist.

The Spaniard scoffed.

Jean-Louis Chevalier rose from the sofa, both his silver eyes fully glazed over. He wore a sneer and followed my retreating steps with pure hatred.

"No," I said. "Jean-Louis, you can still fight this. You can still break his control."

The bokor raised his fingers to his lips and let out a sharp whistle. Boots stomped up the concrete steps outside.

"What did you do to him?" I demanded.

Several more men stormed in. Not zombies. These were living, breathing men, also under the spell of the wraith. I was surrounded by wights.

Jean-Louis Chevalier had once warned me of the dangers of the Horn. Of the power of the Spaniard. He had told me the magic wouldn't just control them, it would eat them. Absorb them. It was a corrupting force that would slowly leech at their existence until they became something worse than death. Now I was experiencing those consequences firsthand.

The last person up the exterior staircase took his time. He had a light step, without the flurry and alarm that ran through the wights. These were the steps of a man in patient control.

Connor Hatch stepped inside the apartment and laughed.

Chapter 35

"My favorite necromancer," said Connor with a dry smile. "Still alive and kicking. You're like a cockroach."

"I could say the same thing about you, except it looks like the potshots are taking their toll on you."

The jinn stroked his red beard in amusement. His mane was thick, but not thick enough to hide the purple bruise on his cheek where I'd socked him or the lump on his forehead. He favored his side where I'd tenderized him a bit. The most notable change about him, however, was the leather strap over his shoulder. The Horn of Subjugation hung at his side.

"You do keep me on my toes. I'll give you that much." Connor turned to Chevalier. "Get the preparations underway. I want to be gone in five minutes."

The bokor nodded and marched from the room. I was hoping his four flunkies would follow but they stayed behind, all eyes on me.

I snorted. "You can't pencil me in for more than five minutes? After everything we've been through?"

"It's not you, Cisco. It's me. I've grown, and you're still the same sorry excuse for a human as when I first found you."

"You've grown? Is that what you call being exiled from your home?"

He grinned devilishly and addressed the Spaniard. "I think it's time you gave our pathetic friend an attitude adjustment."

The wraith lowered his head. "I can't."

"You will do as I say," demanded the jinn.

"Master, I am... unable."

Connor blinked plainly before taking it in. He turned to me and sucked his teeth.

I tightened my jaw. "Not quite as pathetic as you imagined, huh?"

"But still human."

"That's a point of pride for me. How's it working for you? You've lost your power to blink. You can't return to the Aether. You're more human than ever, I'd say."

Connor Hatch grinned. He wouldn't be outdone. He strolled to the sofa and took a load off, resting an arm over the back. "I admit it, Cisco, I didn't see it at first." He sighed and kicked his feet on the table. "We all take our limitations for granted. Those who grow up without the ability of flight can watch the birds all day without a fretful thought. But if you happen to be, say, an angel stripped of his wings, you can bet your bottom dollar you miss the skies every day."

My eyes narrowed. Besides making sure none of the wights or the Spaniard moved on me, I had to be ready for any tricks Connor had up his sleeve. He'd already mentioned leaving in a few minutes—it was entirely possible he was stalling me. His mention of the Celestials, though, was more than allegorical. What was he getting at?

"So there I was," he continued, "like a mouse on a wheel. I tried bringing the Taíno shamans to me, to join them into my power over the dead." He waved a careless hand in the air. "You were at the library. You saw how that ended up." Connor's eyes flicked to the Spaniard. "Even with the grand power of my loyal servant, that pursuit ended in nothing but failure. After all that public spectacle it was, quite frankly, embarrassing."

Connor's shoes hit the floor and he leaned forward, elbows on knees, steepled fingers. "But I was blind to my limitations, Cisco. I'd taken them in stride. I'd assumed things couldn't be any different. But your little show in the Aether changed everything. Now I can proceed full steam ahead."

His teeth came out again. He was savoring this. I circled the wraith carefully and pulled the blind away from the window. The pickup trucks I'd seen at the Hallandale house were lined up with several others. Scores of Haitians were loading up. Not just wights, but the undead too. They hadn't been guarding the grounds because they'd been corralled, ready for deployment. It was crazy. The entire gang must've been down there.

"What's going on?" I asked. "What are you talking about?"

"We're talking about the grand tragedy that you've played out from the beginning. The life of Cisco Suarez. Acts one and two are over, I'm afraid. This is the part where you realize your pivotal role in my rise."

"You're gonna feel my pivotal foot up your ass."

"Stop it," he chided. "Now you're the one embarrassing yourself. Don't you see that you've done nothing but help me get where I am? I used you to find the Horn. You personally handed it to me. The destruction of the Covey, the hits against my drug empire, even restraining me from access to your family—those were all setbacks, but purely temporal. Don't you see that? If my overriding goal was to raise your little Fran for myself, then I would have lost, yes. But my overriding goal was always to be a master of death." He leaned back.

"Even with the Horn, it has been a humbling few months," he confessed. "Turns out, necromancy takes quite a bit of skill and passion. In all this time, I hadn't been able to take the leap forward that I needed. That eureka moment, that breakthrough, eluded me. That's because I didn't know to question what I didn't see: my own limitations."

He smiled. "And then you wander into the Aether and stumble onto a solution for me."

My face darkened.

Connor's voice took a grating tinge. "You didn't just strip me of my *power*, Cisco. You stripped me of my *limits*. I'm no longer bound by jinn law."

Holy crap did that sound bad. "The Celestials..." I protested weakly.

Connor sprung to his feet. "I defy the Celestials! They're as bound to their archaic dictates as I was. I don't need to deal with them because they don't dare interfere. They don't dare break the rules." He looked inward. "Even more pathetic than you, honestly. At least you put yourself out there. Boots on the ground. You might not realize it, but I admire that."

A car outside honked several times in sequence.

The jinn raised his hands in a shrug. "I guess that's my cue." He turned for the door.

I stepped forward. The Spaniard moved in but I shifted through the shadow past him. When I materialized, the wights were already converging on me. I elbowed one in the side and spun past the other. I dove into the darkness again and closed on Connor. He spun to find me already on him. I cracked him in the temple and he fell over. I'd split that purple lump open again.

He swept his leg weakly. I absorbed the blow and held my ground, only to notice at the last second it was a feint. His real attack came in a flash of fire, aimed at my chest. I dove under the blast and pounded him with a few body blows. I struck his sore side and he cried in pain. We rolled on the floor until I started taking some blows of my own.

The wights. They piled over us, punching and kicking, beating their way at me. Sometimes hitting each other in the process. It was relentless and brutal. I couldn't retreat into the shadow because there were too many hands on me. I had no choice to but spin around and face them. Their strikes glanced off my Nordic tattoo, but they came from too many angles.

The jinn scrambled away in the chaos. I didn't bother reaching for him. I had bigger problems. My bloodlust had blinded me to the weaker opponents in the room. Still bokors. Still formidable. As if to punctuate my mistake, Connor flipped on the light switch and sucked away most of my shadow.

The mind-controlled Bone Saints didn't stop at holding me down. They thrashed with fists and feet.

"Time to turn the potshots on you," snarled Connor.

They beat me some more before pulling me to my knees and holding me down. I was dizzy and tender and tired.

Connor stood over me, bleeding and laughing deliriously. He *really* wasn't taking this mortality thing well.

"You must be wondering," he said, getting control of himself. "I now have influence over all the necromancers in Miami. You, Cisco, are my enemy, but you're also a necromancer. And although you do channel the voodoo High Baron, your primary patron is Opiyel, the Taíno guide dog." He waggled his finger in the air. "And the Taíno are the ones who bound the Spaniard to the Horn in the first place. Their gold wraps him tight. You might think it protects you from his influence."

I spat blood on the floor. I didn't feel protected.

"It was kind of you to find Dr. Trinidad for me," he said. "Just like you, I've been researching the pictographs etched in the Horn. The copper alloy tumbaga, 'stiff but malleable' as the good doctor would say. I've been experimenting with altering the pictographs, attempting to remove the built-in protections. Fear not, Cisco, because when that happens you'll be underhand once again. Instead of being Tunji Malu's pet, you'll be mine."

"Over my dead body," I muttered.

"That," he said, "can be arranged." He headed outside and growled, "Take him."

The wights pulled me to my feet.

Chapter 36

For the record, I wasn't really worried. (I mean, a guy has a reputation to maintain, am I right?) Yes, several stronger-than-they-looked gang members who were slowly being sucked dry of their magic escorted me downstairs, but I'd been in worse binds.

The wights were abominations, but they weren't all-powerful. They weren't Aether officiates, for one. In a straight fight I'd kicked their asses before, so I didn't feel especially threatened even if I was kinda technically their captive.

The problem was that the wights were people. Or they had been. I had to believe they could still be returned to their normal selves if I could steal the Horn from Connor Hatch. So the last thing I wanted to do was start blowing holes in the Bone Saints.

The main gate to the compound was open and the trucks were revving their engines. So many wights and zombies and boxes were loaded into each vehicle that their suspensions sat low. Connor took the lead truck. The Spaniard drifted past me.

"Put him in chains," he ordered.

They shoved me face down in the dirt and pulled my

arms behind my back. I grimaced and watched the wraith join Connor in the lead truck before they rolled out. One by one the other trucks followed.

Chevalier's eyes flashed as he hopped into the back of the pickup in front of us. His cold eyes watched me. I wondered if he remembered me. If there was any humanity left in him.

"Take the knife," he said.

Crap. He remembered that.

The zip tie clamped around my wrists. The wights rolled me over and pulled the blade from my belt. I didn't have any spell tokens but they found the shotgun shells in my pockets and tossed them on the ground. Once disarmed, the wights picked me up and threw me in the bed of the last truck. Then the pickup shifted into gear and rumbled over the gravel road until we hit the street. The gate to the Bone Saints' compound hung wide open. No one was left inside.

I pushed up to my knees to check the road. The convoy of trucks snaked around the block. Ahead, the lead truck turned east onto 54th Street. Connor had to be going to the water. He'd come from the sub and he was loading it up again. No question about it. And the bad guys were taking me along for the ride.

I was just getting ready to relax when my parked pickup started by itself and rolled into the street just ahead of us. It was a sudden lurch that took our driver by surprise. The two trucks collided. Everybody in the bed heaved forward. The wights who'd been standing up launched onto the asphalt.

What the? My truck was empty. The weak poltergeist that had taken up residence in the engine compartment must've finally decided to go rogue. Maybe it had gathered power over the months. Maybe it was given life in the deathly presence of the wights and the wraith. I wasn't sure, but I knew it wasn't trying to help me.

My rusty pickup flew into reverse and backed up just enough to pick up speed and hit us again. I braced against the impact.

Normally I'd applaud the little haunt for saving me, but in this case I'd actually *wanted* the bad guys to take me to their secret lair. Connor had made a career out of slipping from my grasp—this was the one time I was actually guaranteed to stick with him.

The wight who was driving tried to circle around the obstruction but my truck crashed into us again. Our radiator cracked and spewed steam. I watched Chevalier's truck disappear down 54th Street and growled. If you wanted something done right...

In the confusion, the wights had understandably lost track of me. I used the opportunity to hop out of the back of the pickup. The zip tie binding my hands was no problem, either. The brainless wights hadn't taken the Spaniard's word "chains" literally, but they should have. Iron can keep me rooted in this world. Living hands, too. Plastic? Not so much. In midair, I shifted into the shadows and displaced my position by a foot, leaving the tie behind. Then I phased back to solid as my alligator boots clunked onto the street.

The rest of the getaway was bound to be more difficult.

For starters, I was surrounded by a truck full of wights. No zombies, though. And no serious players. Since our truck was the last in line, it was mostly composed of the leftovers and rejects. Like Connor Hatch had been picking his all-star football team and we were riding the bench. (What did that say about me?)

This was good and bad. It was no trouble to knock these guys around 'cause they were just kids. The driver was the only one of the bunch who could pass for twenty. The last thing I wanted to do was cut their lives tragically short.

The Haitians came at me, clouded eyes creased in unmollified anger. I batted one kid to the side. Grabbed another by the arms and swung him in a circle around me, keeping the others at bay. For a minute there it was laughable. Twisted reality TV: one man against an army of third graders. But I had to give these kids more credit than that. It wasn't long before the voodoo came out.

The driver circled the front of the truck and threw a handful of feathers my way. Dude must've plucked a whole bird. They weren't crow feathers. Not dove feathers. Just your garden variety Miami pigeon. The initial thrust of his hands spread them in the air. The Intrinsics took over and each individual feather reared and fired at me like a quill, aiming to stick me with the pointy end. It was a good bet they'd been dipped in some nasty toxin, too.

Rather than risk the spellcraft catching me in my shadow form, I raised my barrier shield. It was meant for small projectiles of little mass. Feathers were the perfect candidates. They popped like firecrackers as they hit the energy field. The hardest part was keeping them all off at once so I erected a shadow wall to slow them down.

Two wights charged my flank. I sidestepped one, grabbed the other, and spun to use him to block the last incoming feather. It struck his shoulder. I threw him to the street and he fell over, coughing.

Two more wights came. I forced my shadow wall into them like a large unstoppable bowling ball. It couldn't squish them (or make that cool sound when you bowl a strike) but it sure as shit shoved them out of my way.

Just when I was starting to have too much fun, a fist connected with the back of my head. I fell forward, mostly to deflect the force of the hit. In the same motion I reached into the ground and pulled out my shotgun. I flipped it in my hand, caught it by the barrel, and whacked the kid behind me over the head with the stock.

The initiate with the feather wound was shaking his head on the ground, looking more confused than wounded. Don't get me wrong, he was slightly foaming at the mouth from the poison, but his eyes were clear. The poison was countering the effects of the wraith's magic. Pulling him back into the realm of human. I knew then the Bone Saints could be saved. The kid reached for some powder at his waist and applied it to his wound.

The driver came at me again. This time he pulled a knife. At first I thought he'd lost his imagination, but the little dagger danced like a cobra. That definitely scored points for originality.

I fended the other kids away with my shotgun-turned-club and stepped into the driver's personal space. I easily deflected his swipe with my left forearm. The arrow tattoo flared brilliantly as the snake attempted (and failed) to bite into my flesh. My right hand softened the bokor's stomach like a meat pounder. He dropped the knife. It bounced on the street like any other metal. Then I ripped a pouch of voodoo poison from his waist and flung it at the converging crowd.

"Stay away and I won't hurt you!" I warned.

I'd caught some of the kids with the powder, but this was a pretty standard voodoo trick. Many of them saw the attack coming and knew to close their eyes, avoid inhaling, and flee the area. I'd say a good two or three got the full treatment and had to call off the attack. I could only hope they'd be knocked out of their trances as well.

That had cleared some space for myself. The wights were relentless, though. They came at me again.

Headlights blinded me. An engine roared. I sank into the shadow just in time to avoid being leveled by my own pickup. The truck barreled over me, skipped the curb, and crashed into the wrought-iron fence surrounding the empty compound.

That had been close. I took a heavy breath and ran my eyes over the scene behind me. A few others hadn't been so lucky. The driver and two kids rolled on the ground in pain. One tried to get up and immediately collapsed.

The rusty pickup shifted into reverse.

"You son of a bitch," I spat.

As it backed up, I ran alongside it and opened the driver's door. I heaved on the steering wheel before I was fully inside. The pickup spun and avoided the Bone Saints on the return trip. The back bumper slammed into the other truck, which was a good deal more busted up than my 1970s behemoth. They don't make 'em like they used to.

"You're really starting to piss me off," I said to the ghost, climbing in and shifting to park. I slammed the door shut and pounded the dashboard. The interior and exterior lights blinked on and off. The horn sounded. The wipers scraped back and forth on the dry windshield. The poltergeist was doing everything in its power to tell me it was pissed off too.

I clawed under the seats, hoping I'd left some spare spell tokens around. Nothing doing. No balloons. No mirror. All I had was a birthday candle, a used book of matches, and a single stray shotgun shell. Oh, and I had a spare tank top down there too. Not exactly top-notch exorcism material. I stuffed everything but the shirt in my pocket.

Wights pounded on the windows and doors. I was surprised the glass held. I laid on the horn (which probably didn't do much since it was intermittently going off anyway) and gassed the truck, steering around the hobbled Bone Saints in the street. Best thing I could do for these kids was leave them far away from danger. If it's one thing I'd learned, poltergeists are unpredictable.

I shot down the street, flooring the gas pedal and trying to catch up to Connor's crew before they disappeared again. The pickup unexpectedly swerved into oncoming traffic. I slammed the brakes and spun out, narrowly avoiding another collision.

Great. You know those bumper stickers that say "God is my copilot?" Well, this was kinda like that except my copilot was the ghost of a dead gangbanger and he was suicidal.

I gunned it again, but with a bit more care. The wheel kept trying to steer me into the nearest obstacle, and I kept doing whatever it took to survive. The sum total was I could (mostly) stay in my lane, but it took all my effort and slowed me down a bunch.

Metal crunched against metal. My neck jerked as I got into another accident. This time, I'd been hit from behind. The other pickup had taken to the street again. The radiator leak wouldn't sideline it immediately and the wights gave no shits about long-term damage to the car (that's kids for you). A quick glance showed someone behind the wheel who wasn't old enough to drive and three more wights in the truck bed.

All of a sudden this was a good old-fashioned car chase.

Chapter 37

We sped through Little Haiti, fortunate the road was mostly clear. I tried to fake my pursuers out with a hard turn onto 54th, but my poltergeist passenger made it difficult to pull off last-second maneuvers. It resulted in me telegraphing all my moves. I might as well have used a blinker.

The steering wheel fought for its own control the whole time. With the other truck still behind me and none of the others in sight ahead, I had no choice but to move onward and hope for the best.

The other truck was faster. It gained on my left and tried to force me off the road. I rolled my window down, extended my sawed-off shotgun, and blasted the right front tire. The rubber exploded and shredded off the wheel. Sparks flew above our heads and the other truck skidded into mine. The kid overcorrected the slide to the left and drove into a light post across the street.

So much for the good old-fashioned car chase.

I dropped my empty shotgun into the shadow and chuckled, pleased with how well that had worked out. The wight exited the truck and stood around, unsure how to proceed. His friend standing in the truck bed had no ideas.

Wait a minute. There were supposed to be three of them in that truck bed.

A knife punched through the ceiling above me. I jerked my head away. That was *my* knife. Those fuckers were in my truck now. One of them pounded on the back window and the other was draped over my roof, stabbing holes through the metal. As the pickup swerved his legs swept over my windshield. He scrambled for purchase and snapped off one of the wiper blades with his foot.

"This day is turning out just dandy," I said.

The wight in the back got smart and reached in through my open window. His forearm smothered my mouth and pressed my head against the back window. (These tanks didn't have luxuries like headrests.) At first I didn't think the wight had much of a strategy, but his right fist began pounding said window. It's a good thing he wasn't a boxer but I could feel the blows through the glass.

The real crux of the problem came when the knife punched through the roof again. The blade slashed across my temple. Warm blood trickled down the side of my face.

Did I say *that* was the real crux of the problem? Sorry, that was a bit of a downer, for sure, but the flashing red lights ahead of me were the real doozy.

Two black-and-white metal arms swung down to block access to Biscayne Boulevard. A freaking railroad crossing, flashing and dinging and doing its darn best to warn off the living and dead alike.

I hit the brakes. Nothing happened. In my head I formed the image of the poltergeist—a Bone Saint himself but one I'd killed a long time ago as a zombie hit man—smiling in glee as his revenge was finally upon him.

With less than a block to go, I tried to turn the wheel but the damned ghost had found his backbone. It was locked up tight. The knife in the roof pulled up and out, readying for another stab. I let go of the wheel and put both hands to work against the wight's arm, peeling it from my face and ducking away from the knife as it once again punched down.

A train horn blared. Not in warning anymore—in alarm. The engineer kept the noise on and applied the brakes, for whatever good that did. Nothing was stopping that thing in time. I clenched my jaw (and my butt cheeks) as the pickup bore on a collision course with the metal juggernaut. I pumped the brakes a few more times in a last ditch hope of escape, but there was no response.

The train chugged forward. The truck ran the red light. And I realized I had a single chance.

My boot pounded the gas pedal all the way down to the metal. The pickup lurched out of its controlled cruise and crashed through the barrier arms blocking the road. The wheels skipped over the tracks hard and the entire truck caught air for a split second.

Then we landed safely past the tracks right as the train sped past. Sparks rained into the sky as the train raked against my rear bumper.

The pickup hopped up and down on the other side as I fought for control. The wights hung on for dear life. And I spied a little Cuban kid tagging the back side of a gas station.

That did it. I shifted to neutral, pulled the parking brake, and leaned my whole body into the wheel, fishtailing the truck to a stop. The two wights took flight and landed hard in the street ahead. I jumped out and yanked my knife from the roof. Then I stomped toward the kid with the spray can.

He was just finishing up an artsy letter A when I snatched the can from his hand. He spun around defiantly but saw the blood on my face and the two wights on the asphalt. He turned and bolted.

"Smart kid."

I marched back to my truck. It was still in neutral, slowly rolling backward in the street with the door open. I hopped on the front bumper, shaking the paint can up and down. Then I drew a giant pentagram on my rusty hood and rubbed some of my blood into the center for good measure. It wouldn't banish the poltergeist but it ought to contain him for a while.

The light on Biscayne turned green. I hustled back into the truck and tossed the spray paint on the passenger seat. Then I bypassed the recovering wights and drove down the road, looking for signs of the other trucks.

Connor wasn't in sight, but it was a good thing they were going east. The truth is, there's only so far you can go east before you're in the Atlantic Ocean. We were practically swimming already. I rolled ahead into the breezy neighborhood of Morningside.

A gatehouse administered access to the district. It announced you were now on the *right* side of the tracks. Little Haiti may have been a minute away, but now you were entering a *nice* neighborhood. The gatehouses were meant to dissuade unsavory types. The street was still public, of course, but minimum wage security guards would take down license plates and keep up a good pretense.

Two things told me that Morningside would have a spike in crime tonight. The arm blocking access down the road was broken, meaning someone had driven through just as I had at the train tracks. The other thing was, there was no security guard at his post. As I passed the gate I saw the man slumped unconscious over his stool.

So Connor was here.

I drove past the large Mediterranean Revival homes. It was a scenic neighborhood, all right. A nice place to go on jogs or walk the dog. Normal stuff that I could never do.

My beat-up rusty pickup with the spray-painted pentagram started thumping and grinding and smoking as I drove down the quiet road. The damn tire was flat and the engine would need looking at. I cursed and pulled over. I'd jinxed myself with that comment about this being a nice neighborhood for a walk. I abandoned the pickup and hoofed it.

No worry here, though. A healthy sprint got me in sight of the water in no time. Morningside Park spanned the coast. A nice green field with a beautiful bayfront view, even at night. The type of place to rent sailboats and kayaks, to play tennis and basketball, to go fishing or swimming in the public pool. This park really had it all.

Including a decommissioned Soviet submarine illegally docked in the Bay.

Connor's men were busy loading up the vessel. Two mercenaries with guns oversaw the dock. Luckily, the park grounds were clear. I sprinted ahead, eager to catch up before they were gone. My initial plan was just to up and announce myself. Get recaptured and go for a ride. But at the last second I was struck with an idea.

The Bone Saints were mostly loaded up already. A few thralls straggled behind—the last workhorses, carrying the heavy stuff from the trucks to the sub. Connor and the wraith weren't in sight. It was Chevalier who was left to the final preparations. He directed the zombies in their loading duties while the mercenaries waved their guns at him to hurry. The bokor complained to them as I hurried to get within earshot.

A mercenary pulled a radio to his mouth. "The last truck didn't make it," he reported.

The reply was muffled and scratchy. The mercenary told Chevalier to finish and load up. He did so, leaving only four thralls to the work.

If Connor was writing me off he must've been serious about keeping his schedule.

I scanned the scene, running out of time. There were only two oblong boxes left in a truck. I wondered what Connor was transporting. More Taíno artifacts? A pair of zombies hefted either end of a crate and carried it to the sub, leaving the last box to the other two. Those zombies were just leaving the dock now, giving me a short window to beat them to it. I rushed ahead and reached the crate, trying to pry the top open before I was seen.

The damned thing was nailed shut. I grabbed the wood and ripped upward. A foot-and-a-half plank snapped off in my hand. A pungent smell washed through the small opening. It was unmistakable and immediately informed me as to the contents of the crate: death.

So the Little Haiti undead weren't enough. Connor was bringing fresh bodies with him too. Making sure he had an ample supply. Those necromancers on the boat were gonna be busy.

The two zombie workers were almost on me. While the

top of the crate wasn't open per se, I had enough of a window to squeeze through. Even if it wouldn't be pleasant.

I dove through the shadow and into the crate, bracing for a tight fit.

Chapter 38

Let's face it: Coffins aren't built for two.

You get one of those high-end numbers the mortician upsells on you—you know, that whole speech about how the dead deserve dignity and it's your lucky day because dignity comes with a four-thousand-dollar price tag? Anyway, the dead don't appreciate a box with a shiny finish or memory foam insert, but one of those coffins would probably be a comfortable enough fit for two people at once.

What I currently found myself inside wasn't one of those souped-up dealies. It wasn't one of those Wild West barely-fits-one hack jobs either. This was a storage crate somewhere in between the two ideas, not meant for a body but remarkably suited for one. Still, two was pushing it.

On top of the tight fit was the unfortunate luck that the recently expired occupant was of the pudgier nature. Soft and ample, like a bloated Stretch Armstrong left out in the sun. I wasn't claustrophobic but this was plenty uncomfortable. My only plan? To wait.

The two zombies lifted the box with little trouble. Surprisingly, their strength and inability for laziness meant they treated the cargo better than your average UPS driver. We were carried at an even keel. Shoes traipsed over the dock. The coffin turned upright as we went up the ladder and down the hatch.

I'd never ridden a submarine before. I just hoped this wasn't a one-way trip.

The small opening I'd ripped from the top let a bit of light inside the box. It was at my feet, though, so I couldn't do much in the way of peeking. Not that it mattered. I couldn't act until everything was quiet. Within a few minutes, my wish was granted. The box was shoved into a corner. Someone gave orders about stowing the cargo and some restacking and strapping down happened. At one point, another coffin was placed on top of mine, blocking out what little light I had.

I waited for the sounds of shuffling to die down. The submarine powered into motion and dove. The diesel engine cut out when we went full electric, and I knew we were submerged and on our way.

To the lost city of gold, then.

When I was sure I was alone (corpses notwithstanding), I shifted into the darkness and slipped out of the crate. At least, that was the way I had pictured it working out. What actually happened was more of a bump against a wall. I rematerialized still stuck inside the box.

"You've got to be kidding me," I muttered.

I felt at the opening in the lid with the heel of my boot and found I was sealed in by the crate stacked above. You might think it an easy thing to slink around the shadows like some kind of unstoppable mist, but it really doesn't work like that. I can't move as freely as vapor. I'm not a ghost in the fog like in some John Carpenter movie. I need a good couple inches of clearance to slip past obstacles. Right now,

I was flat-out stuck.

I sighed and rested my face on the soft pudginess of my roommate. I reached into my pocket and drew out the bent matchbook. It took some gymnastics but I managed to bend my arm at the elbow and bring my hands to my face. I propped my back against the lid of the box and struck the match.

Berna's face stared back at me, frozen in a horrific scream. I yelped and dropped the match. The flame went out and left us in the blackness but I could still see her contorted face. It spoke of unassailable pain and anguish.

Jeez, I'd expected a corpse. I hadn't expected a familiar face.

Then again, was I really bothered? Berna had sold me out. She'd set me up to die with that glass bomb. Maybe I hadn't been the primary target, but she'd considered me acceptable collateral damage.

Her presence in this box meant Connor had been likewise offended by her attack. The jinn had been busy, not only figuring out who'd left that bomb but responding to the threat. I wondered if this changed things. By all accounts Connor had just openly declared war on the Society. For all I knew, Winthrop was lying in the box on top of us.

Crap. Darcy was just a stupid kid in a lot of ways, but she didn't deserve a fate like this. So help me, if she was in one of these boxes Connor was going to pay.

Knowing what was staring back at me now, I lit another match. Berna was dead all right. A Society assassin getting her comeuppance. As I considered her, I realized my head was resting on her boob. I jerked away.

"Sorry about that," I said. I chewed my lip and slid her eyes closed. Dignity in death. It's a lie.

The match went out again. I was almost done with them. I realized I could get as much light using my cell phone and made the switch. Now that one problem was solved, I focused on getting out of here.

My position was no good. I could roll over and force my hands and knees against the lid, but Berna was too shaky a base to provide stable traction and she was too big to give me decent leverage.

"I hope you like spooning," I muttered, squeezing by her and rolling her to her side.

This position was much better. We were both on the bottom of the crate, though I couldn't square my shoulders flatly. The extra vertical space allowed me to get decent pressure against the lid. I wasn't sure if it was enough to lift the nails from the wood, though. I took a deep breath and heaved again before realizing what my problem was: the box or boxes piled on top of us.

Okay, time for spellcraft. I was a fair hand at knocking things around with shadow. I let the cell phone screen go out and braced the darkness against the top and bottom of the box. The wood boards creaked. I could feel the weight above us rocking slightly but it still didn't give.

Man, sometimes being a shadow charmer was a real downer. The problem this time was that Berna and I were in the box. We ate up a lot of the space and thus a lot of the shadow. On top of that, any overt pressure I applied against the lid would return in equal and opposite form back down on us. There simply wasn't anywhere else for the pressure to escape.

Think about it like dropping a live grenade in here. Opening the box wasn't the problem at that point. It was getting out in one piece. Back to the drawing board.

Barring some kind of Iron Man armor or Luke Cage strength, I was in a tight spot. And then it dawned on me: Who said I didn't have Luke Cage strength?

I went to work immediately. I wasn't in a position to use my full suite of voodoo paraphernalia, but I had my belt buckle fetish, the good old skull and pentacle. That gave me sufficient access to the High Baron. The rest of my voodoo was a cocktail of shadow. Opiyel whispered through me and woke the flesh. The process was a little time consuming but eventually my roommate was a little less dead.

"Berna," I said. The light of my cell phone illuminated the side of her face.

"Hunhh," she answered. It was more than she usually said.

I crawled back on top of her so she could lie flat on her shoulders. "You wanna do the honors?"

The ex-animist-turned-zombie slapped her large mitts against the lid of the box and flexed. She grunted as wood shredded and nails bent out of the frame. With a final heave, the lid, the two crates on top of us, and the strap holding us all together snapped and tumbled to the side. The stale air of the coffin gave way to the stale air of the submerged submarine.

"I could kiss you," I chuckled.

On second thought, that was gross. And illegal. And... Berna.

I crawled out and stretched my back. One of my shoulders was sore from the exertion of trying to force my way out. Berna stood without complaint.

We found ourselves in a small hold. Six coffins total and a closed hatch. I considered raising more undead but hours had already been wasted and I wasn't sure how much time I had. But I couldn't ignore them completely.

One by one I cracked the other crates open, dreading the sight of the flashy red bob of Darcy's hair. After checking the last body, I sighed in relief. No dead teenagers. Or senior citizens, for that matter. Winthrop had apparently escaped retribution as well.

Just me and Berna then.

We were stuck in a larger coffin of sorts now. Buried deep underwater and trapped with South American mercs, enthralled Bone Saints, and zombie servants. Even given that I could get past all of them, there was still the Spaniard and Connor Hatch to deal with.

My best strategy was to recover the Horn of Subjugation. Turn one of my enemies back into an ally. Hell, with the wraith beside me I could turn half the crew back to my side.

For now, though, it was just me and Berna. I opened the hatch and creeped ahead. My companion's zombie steps were a bit less furtive.

Chapter 39

The submarine passageway was compact, accommodating only the minimum amount of space for two crew members to squeeze past going opposite directions. The grate on the deck was metal, the bulkhead and deckhead were metal. I was getting a real serious tin can vibe. Still, after my alone time with Berna, I couldn't slam the leg room.

The passageway was somewhat rounded. Pipes ran along the tunnels, a combination of form meeting function. Dotting the bulkheads every so often were random gauges and valves. It was all very technical, to be sure. Very comforting. I put my complete faith in Soviet-era technology and ignored the unbelievable amount of water pressure the hull must've been under.

I didn't really know where to go, of course. I'd had the pleasure of stepping aboard this sub before while it was docked, but that tour only took me down a single corridor. I was somewhere else altogether now, without a clue about how deep I was or how many levels I needed to traverse.

The bridge, right? That's where Connor would be, sitting in his Captain Picard chair with the Spaniard playing Commander Riker sans beard. (Sans face, really.) I had a better than fifty-fifty guess as to which way to go so I started walking.

Boots echoed on the grate ahead of us. I yanked Berna into a side passage and ducked behind some kind of electrical box. I whisked my shotgun from the nether and cracked it in half. Empty. The mercenaries spoke Spanish in hushed tones before they were in view.

"This new blood is creeping me out, bro. They're like animals or something."

"Animals?" scoffed the other. "They're slaves. Notice how they never make eye contact? The boss must've made a deal with the Haitians. Think about it. They can smuggle whoever they want from that piece-of-shit country and force them into work."

I found the single shell of birdshot in my pocket and slid it into the shotgun's breech. Two mercs and one bullet. Perfect. The men were so close I didn't close the shotgun for fear they'd hear the click.

They walked by us and the other guy hissed. "That's fucked up, bro. But it's more than that. They don't talk. They don't complain. They don't eat. It's like they're lobotomized. I'm telling you, this isn't worth what they're paying."

The voices faded into the distance. The South Americans were the veterans. The regular *Agua Fuego* muscle. Now the jinn's priorities were shifting and they were spooked. I waited until the boot steps were gone to snap my shotgun closed. We continued down the hall.

Ahead, I saw what must've spurred the previous conversation. A single thrall was standing guard at a choke point. No gun. No relaxed posture, crossed arms, or comfortable lean. The Haitian thrall just stood straight and watched the passageway.

It was a good zombie job. A fresh corpse. The spellcraft masked the stench and decay. No reason for the average person to conclude it was a zombie. But it was tough to fool a necromancer in these matters.

I had Berna march forward to draw its attention. I was curious what the zombie's response would be. Surprisingly, he didn't do anything except follow her movement. The zombies must've been programmed to ignore their fellow dead. I wondered if they'd ignore the entire crew as well.

When the guard turned to watch Berna, I stepped out and approached. I had a good look. Got pretty close too, but there's only so much you can muffle cowboy boots on steel. The thrall heard me and spun around and...

Only watched me. He was a creeper too. One eye open wider than the other in some sort of prison-yard scowl. It was a tough visage but not one followed by an equally tough corrective action.

In other words, a lapse in security.

I walked right up to the guard and smiled. He watched without a mind for suspicion or trickery. Connor must've trusted the whole crew. And why not? They had no idea I was on board.

I curled my fingers around my belt buckle and grabbed the forehead of the zombie. Kinda like you might do to a younger sibling to keep them from punching you. I didn't have the reach advantage to do that with the zombie, but I only needed a few seconds. I looked into his head, spied the connection between him and his necromancer master, and severed it.

Properly raising new zombies from corpses was a lot of

work and took time. With my skill level and the current situational proximity, making an existing one switch teams was a much more efficient process.

The downside, of course, was that any good necromancer would sense their control being ripped away. If they'd had a fix on their pet beforehand, they could even pinpoint my location. That's the great thing about zombie security. Disabling them sends up alarms anyway. But I wasn't dealing with normal, coherent necromancers. Chevalier had probably stared at that blank TV screen for hours. They were mostly wights now, thralls themselves in a sense. I was banking on them not running on all four cylinders.

After a minute without yelling or stomping or flashing red lights and air sirens, I figured I'd stolen the zombie with no strings attached. So Creeper and Berna and I strolled down the hall, emboldened in our mission.

Okay, we weren't exactly Seal Team Six, but we could take care of business.

We came upon a ladder. I sent the thralls down first, then grabbed the rails, set my boots on the sides, and slid to the bottom. I clapped my hands together, impressed with myself. Then I turned around right in the face of two slack-jawed South Americans. They didn't have guns in their hands but one of them reached for a radio.

Too slow. At my mental command, Berna and Creeper hefted them headfirst into the wall. Bones cracked. Their cries of panic abruptly ended. We carried them to the nearest doorway—crew quarters—and dumped them inside. I was surprised how little space was inside. Their bunks were like little metal coffins. It seemed fitting.

Killing mercenaries was no problem for me. They weren't thralls like the Bone Saints. The only thing enslaving them was money. They'd have me killed in a heartbeat if it meant another zero on their paycheck. They were well trained too. Arguably my biggest threat now. Drug runners with guns, sure, but the radios they carried could blow the whole operation. I had to make sure none of them raised the alarm before I had the Horn.

The room was sparse but I found a machine pistol under one bunk. Nothing else was useful besides the radio. I grabbed it too, lowered the speaker volume, and clipped it to my belt.

As we stepped out, another crew marched down the hall. I shoved the zombies back inside and closed the hatch all but a peep. Bone Saints traveled past in a long line, barking short orders in English and Creole. Even though they must've seen us duck inside, the Bone Saints seemed to be leaving the mercenaries alone. A clear pecking order was emerging on this cursed submarine: Connor, the wraith, the cartel mercs, the wights, and the zombies. Strange company indeed.

You can add Cisco Suarez to the very end of that list. But hey, at least I had Berna and Creeper to boss around.

"We must be ready soon," came Chevalier's voice. "Work on the stock below and meet at the unloading deck. No bokor without a body."

The other wights laughed with a kind of eerie groupthink. The combination of subject matter and gleeful hoots was unsettling. It was clear Connor needed a vast stock of undead for something. The necromancers alone weren't enough. Between the Bone Saints and the wraith, I was looking at a small army. No way could I dink and dunk them one at a time. That's why the Horn was so important.

I waited until the crowd dispersed, unwilling to shred the Haitians with automatic rounds. Every Bone Saint on board was being mobilized and moved out. That meant it was only a matter of time before they discovered Berna's empty coffin. On the plus side, they were heading away from my destination. With any luck the wights would be out of my hair for a while. In a morbid way, that simplified things.

After they'd been gone a few minutes, Connor's voice crackled over the radio.

"Herrera, Gomez, I need you two in the control room."

A moment of static before a hesitant voice answered. "Uh, sure. Right now?"

"Of course, now," snapped Connor. "You want to make it up to me? Be prompt."

The radio cut out. I could picture Herrera and Gomez whispering about the order. They must've been in Connor's doghouse for some reason and understandably creeped out by recent events. That's the problem with a crew of mercenaries. Money can only motivate so far. Cash doesn't have the same pull as heart.

A hatch opened down the hall.

"Let's just go," said a voice. "Leave it."

"But Carter hasn't gotten back yet."

"Screw Carter. Let's go up before we piss the boss off even more."

The two men mumbled and hurried toward the ladder. Herrera and Gomez, heading to the control room.

"Do you," started one of the men, disappearing to the next level, "ever get the feeling this ship is haunted?"

I couldn't hear the reply, but it didn't matter. I already knew the answer.

I took my two sidekicks down the passageway after them. Herrera and Gomez were gonna lead me straight to Connor Hatch and the Horn of Subjugation.

Chapter 40

It turned out we didn't have much further to walk and I could've skipped the detour to the crew's quarters completely. Live and learn, but this was a happy accident. The Bone Saints were out of the way and the mercenaries would be a distraction. Herrera and Gomez were too worried about their destination to notice us following them.

On the way, we passed one more zombie checkpoint. This dead Haitian was old but stout. I named him Baldie and pulled him into my ranks. The four of us were quite the sight if anyone had cared to notice. I held a machine pistol in my left hand and a loaded shotgun in my right. One wrong turn, one wrong encounter with a wight or crew member could've sent it all to hell, but things were finally starting to come up Cisco. Ahead, Herrera and Gomez disappeared into what I figured to be the control room. We'd made it.

I was reasonably certain I could barge in guns blazing, zombies tearing, and make something happen. I had half a mind to do just that. But as long as we were still ghosts on this ship, I wanted to keep out of sight. At least until I knew for sure what was going on.

"Ah," called out Connor's pleased voice, "the prodigal

sons arrive."

We crept forward as the two mercs muttered something in response. Other voices filled the background. Russian. I peeked around the hatch wall and saw the Russian crew sitting at the consoles. It made sense. This was a Soviet vessel. Connor had probably enlisted their services when he'd purchased the sub.

I released a slow breath of relief. So far, not a Bone Saint in sight.

The crew coordinated with each other, ignoring Connor and Herrera and Gomez and sticking to their control panels. Sonar. Navigation. To be honest, I couldn't guess what half the instruments were. And the crew members were just redshirts, waiting to be taken down in a hail of gunfire.

I inched forward and spotted the backs of the two South American mercs. Connor faced us, attention on them.

"I'd promised you sights unseen," said Connor. He paced around the men in a circle, disappointment in his words. "I asked for nothing but dedication."

As he rounded their back, both men swiveled their heads to keep an eye on him. One of them nearly shook in terror. I focused on the Horn of Subjugation on a strap around Connor's neck. It hung low at his side like a messenger bag.

After a full lap, the jinn paused in front of them. "I pay you enough, do I not?"

They nodded, hesitantly at first but then arduously, as if the whole situation was resolved and agreed upon and they'd be able to turn around and walk out of here.

Connor clicked his lips. "If I do indeed pay you enough, then my end of the bargain is upheld. Your shirking of duties means you owe me."

"Boss," said one of the men. "We thought—"

"Do not think!" boomed Connor. The redness of his face held long enough to stymie any confidence the mercenaries had left. They lowered their heads and Connor released all the tension in his face and body language. His demeanor went cool again.

"Service is an underrated asset," he noted. "Perhaps I've been too hard on you. Gotten too used to working with mindless drones."

The two men traded a silent glance.

Connor snapped his fingers. An idea had just come to him. "Maybe what the two of you need is positive reinforcement. Not punishment, but reward." Connor got very excited and circled the men again. Their eyes still watched him.

"It must be the sights unseen," he continued. "I will show you what very few of my *Agua Fuego* cartel men have laid eyes on." Connor snapped again and the Spaniard appeared. Skull, armor, glowing red eyes.

"*Ay dios mío!*" The men recoiled but dared not break away from Connor. The Russian crew members fixed their eyes on their instruments. They'd no doubt seen the wraith before and preferred not to do so again.

"Do not fear," laughed Connor. "You two are in esteemed company." Connor circled them again. This time the men didn't watch the jinn. Their eyes were glued to the conquistador spirit. They trembled and cried and began to beg for their lives.

Before they could form a coherent sentence, Connor placed an index finger at the base of each of their heads. A small needle of flame lanced through their skulls and into their brains. They folded to the metal deck.

"Now," said Connor with a growl, "you will truly see things most men do not."

Instruments beeped. The crew muttered and twisted knobs. The wraith was the only one on the bridge watching the show. If anybody was supposed to applaud, it didn't happen. Connor sighed as whatever pleasure he'd derived from the show faded.

"I take it these will suit you?" he asked.

The Spaniard nodded. "Very well, Master."

I winced at the title.

The jinn moved to a console and pulled a radio to his mouth. "Jean-Louis, I need you in the control room."

I don't know why, but I shot a worried glance at Berna. It was an empty gesture. Zombies can't share feelings like real sidekicks. The worry was that I had to do something before Chevalier came this way.

"Sir," alerted one of the Russians, "we have a fix on the coordinates."

Connor's eyes lit up. "Sonar?"

"Nothing yet, sir."

He watched the screen over the navigator's shoulder and stroked his beard.

The city of gold? I could see the map from my vantage. We had to be in the middle of the Caribbean. So there was an island. But if the crew was searching for it on sonar...

That explained it. Winthrop had been scouring the Atlantic with satellite imagery and getting nowhere. That didn't mean the island didn't exist. That meant Connor's destination was a *sunken* island. That's what this submarine was for. That's why his white whale wasn't on a modern map.

"This is it," said Connor, half hopeful, half hungry.

The Spaniard moved in behind him, pleased. "The Sea of the Antilles."

Their fortune was my fortune. My chance. Both their backs were turned. Once again I considered charging ahead, but Connor and the wraith were too dangerous for that. It was safer if they never saw me coming. Unfortunately, that meant Berna, Creeper, and Baldie had to stay behind. Their boots on the grating would alert Connor immediately.

It was a good thing Cisco Suarez had a lighter step.

I slipped off my alligator boots and moved into the room, phasing through a spot of shadow. The control room, unfortunately, was the best lit room on the vessel. I worked with what I could but most of my approach was good old-fashioned sneaking. A thief in Dungeons & Dragons, rolling a one on my ability check. (This is 2nd Edition. A one's good.)

Halfway into the room, line of sight was a problem. The Russian crew were used to keeping their attention on the consoles, but there were too many of them at too many angles not to notice an intruder strolling around. I hurried. One man stood up from behind a terminal and hefted an assault rifle to his shoulder. It was literally out of nowhere.

And that was the end of quiet time.

I emptied a load of birdshot into his face. My machine pistol whirled to cover Connor and the wraith. The Spaniard vanished.

Before I could pull the trigger, incoming fire came from my left side. The damn redshirts were battle-hardened mercs themselves. I'd mixed it up with the Russians before and knew how vicious they could be. I should've accounted for that.

I opened my hands and released both guns. The empty shotgun disappeared into the shadow. My right hand swung left and snatched up the falling machine pistol. My left hand thrust out to my side and raised my Nordic shield. Bullets pounded against the barrier as I dove ahead into Connor. I spun in the air and locked my gun on my attacker and unloaded into him.

The collision with Connor took us both to the floor. The rest of the crew was on their feet now. There were a few guns in the room, but they couldn't fire. Not with Connor and I locked up.

He snarled and raised a fist of fire. I batted it to the side, grabbed the Horn tight with both hands, and landed a foot in his face.

A miscalculation of sorts on my part. You see, I'd forgotten I wasn't wearing my cowboy boots. It doesn't need to be said that a yellowed sock with a big toe sticking out doesn't do as much damage as a boot heel. But it still got the job done. Connor was shoved away from me. I somersaulted backward to my knees. The Horn was cradled in my arms.

The Russians readied their weapons. That's when my zombie brigade bowled them over from behind. Gunfire erupted in the chaos. Bullets sparked and ricocheted off the deckhead and consoles.

"Watch the instruments!" shouted Connor.

I liked that thought. Berna and the others had the Russians well in hand, so I pointed my machine pistol at the navigational computer and ventilated it.

Just then, Chevalier stormed onto the bridge. Both his eyes were fully glazed over. He was alarmed by the gunfire, but not scared of it. You had to be sentient to feel fear. He wasn't human enough to draw emotion from the cacophony, just alert enough to react.

"Put a stop to this now!" screamed Connor.

The Spaniard reappeared. He raised a hand, bony fingers spread wide. Berna, Creeper, and Baldie froze.

I checked the Horn in my hands. "What are you doing?" I snapped. "Let them go."

The wraith turned to me, eyes burning coldly.

The crew members pulled away from the thralls and recovered their weapons. Half of them didn't get up but there were still enough to be trouble.

Chevalier's dead gaze zeroed in on me. He stomped ahead.

"Not a chance," I said. "Let him go, Spaniard. Free him from your grasp. I command it."

The wraith didn't respond. Connor Hatch cracked a smile. My zombie crack team stood idle, inactive, and Chevalier continued at me.

I studied the Horn in my hands. Ivory length. Brown tip. Metal caps at both ends, sealed in gold. This was the freaking Horn of Subjugation. I was sure of it. I was sure of something else too. It didn't thrum with the unholy power I was accustomed to.

Connor's fist caught me right in the gut. I doubled over. He grabbed at the Horn but I yanked it away.

Chevalier covered my mouth and nose with his hand. I tried to slink into the shadows. Too late. When I struggled to breathe, I found myself sucking in green powder. Not a handful—just a dab. It was enough to send me reeling.

Pestilence.

Connor tugged the Horn from my feeble grasp and his chuckle turned into a laugh. Chevalier kicked me in the face. I fell backward and scrambled to get up. Instead, strong hands clamped onto me and lifted me to my feet. Berna and Creeper each held a shoulder.

I coughed and gagged. Connor watched me expectantly. Jean-Louis stared at me with empty, foggy eyes.

"Et tu, Berna?" I choked out. "I thought there was a spark there."

Connor bellowed loudly and long. He simply couldn't contain it anymore. The turnaround of me showing up on his sub, taking control, and losing it all in a matter of seconds was too much. Even I saw the tragic irony of it.

"The class clown," mocked Connor. "It's always the weakest person who tells the loudest jokes." Connor admired the Horn of Subjugation in his grip. "This is the real punch line."

I coughed and heaved, just barely keeping my lunch down and spitting out the word. "How?"

Connor went to the navigational panel. "Helm," he called. He searched the room.

"He's dead, boss," came a lone reply.

Connor's lips peeled away from his teeth. "Well, who the fuck knows how to read this?"

The same Russian came forward and leaned into the machine. He flicked some switches and rapped the screen. "It's dead, boss."

I fought through the nausea. Looked around for

something to help. This was giving me serious Aether vibes. A flashback to being pinned down by the officiates. These weren't gangbangers holding me anymore but durable zombies. All through it, the conquistador skull was fixed on me. Emotionless. Steady.

"How?" I asked with more vigor.

Connor tore himself away from the instrument panel. "I told you I'd been experimenting with the pictographs, Cisco." He stomped up and held the Horn to my face. I saw the fresh scratches in the tumbaga surface. The shiny new gold exposed below. "The Horn used to obey the bearer. Imagine that. All this power, *control of a sentient being*, based on what was in your hands. It was no more than a weapon. A sword, a gun." He cocked his head. "A very powerful weapon, granted, but one that could be stolen. As ridiculous as the president keeping the nuclear codes on a Post-it."

The jinn pulled the artifact away and reattached it to his shoulder strap. "I changed the marking to obey its master based on word, not property. You can't steal the wraith from me unless I agree to it, spoken from my own lips." He leaned forward. "And trust me, Cisco, that isn't likely to happen anytime soon."

"Hey, Vlad," said one of the Russians. "Check it out."

A few crew members laughed as one of them slipped on my red alligator boots. Connor almost barked at the men but saw the anger on my face. Anything that pissed me off got a pass.

Chevalier noticed Herrera and Gomez lying on the floor. He took in the other dead Russians. "Shall I prepare the bodies for arrival?" he asked.

"There's no more time," said Connor. "Our instruments

are down. We're in location now. We have to make do with what we have."

"Master," objected the wraith, "it's almost sunup."

"That's perfect," said Connor. "The transition requires twilight, does it not?"

"Yes, but when the sun rises, the Taíno dead flee this world and return to their home. The plan was to gain a foothold before they returned. If we enter the underworld now, there will be an army waiting for us."

He scoffed. "That's what I have you for, isn't it? We go now. Make the preparations."

"The underworld?" I asked. "The city of gold is in the underworld?"

Connor snorted. "City of gold? So it was Winthrop who sent you. I'm afraid you've been sadly misinformed. Americans all think they're Indiana Jones. Winthrop's a greedy fool. I didn't think he'd have the balls to go after me, nor the sense to work with you, but he has less idea what's going on than you do. As soon as I find that old hippie I'm going to wring his neck."

"You'd be doing me a favor."

I blinked through watery eyes. It was difficult to focus past the sickness coursing through my blood. I could only concentrate on one thing at a time. So I forgot about the city of gold and Winthrop and the Society's relationship with Connor. I focused on the one thing that mattered right now.

"The underworld?"

My brain was overclocked trying to work it out. The Taíno corpses. The burned Opiyel statue. The Spaniard, the contingent of wights and undead—all utilized to gain entrance into the underworld.

"Get it done," ordered Connor.

The wraith drew his side-sword and sliced open the bodies of Herrera and Gomez. He ordered Chevalier to assist and they drew Taíno pictographs on the bodies in blood.

"Coaybay," I whispered. "You're not just searching for a buried island. You're searching for Coaybay, the Taíno land of the dead. That's what you wanted the Horn for."

"Too right," said Connor with a devilish grin. "And, unfortunately for the natives, I've made another modification to their pictographs. The Horn still binds the wraith, for sure. But the wraith is no longer cowed by the spellcraft of Taíno shamans. We're gonna walk right in there and own the place."

My eyes widened. Connor had been busier than I'd imagined. He was bringing his own army of the dead into the Taíno underworld, where no mortal may tread. That's why the jinn had surrounded himself with thralls. He was never looking for a real place on Earth. An island, perhaps, but one in another steppe. The Spaniard completed the spell that opened an underwater rabbit hole into the Nether. The entire sub listed under the pull of a giant whirlpool.

"Turn off the engines!" ordered Connor into the radio. "Brace yourselves!"

Coaybay, the mythical island of the Taíno people, unreachable by boat or bird's wings, was about to be invaded. Because it was a real place in the Nether, a land of water and earth.

The worst part? I had made this all possible. Jinns are

traditionally unable to enter the Nether. Jinn law forbids it. That's why Connor's initial plan was to bring the Taíno dead to him. To raise them. A feat he'd been unable to accomplish.

Now that I'd gotten Connor exiled from the Aether, he was free to roam the various worlds as he pleased. Game, set, and match.

Between the overbearing strength of the zombies and the pestilence threatening to overtake me, there wasn't much I could do as Connor's submarine circled in the ocean depths.

"Now," announced Connor, returning to me. "The only loose thread left is figuring out what to do with you. Ideally, you would've joined my side, willingly or not. And you can't say I haven't tried." Connor Hatch inhaled slowly in thought. He held his breath and, upon reaching a decision, released it with a sigh. "But it's clear you have a stubborn fixation on bringing me down no matter what."

I shrugged. "Hey, you gotta live for something."

The submarine twisted as it accelerated in the whirlpool. The control room leaned sharply to the side. The hull of the ship groaned under the pressure.

Connor Hatch regarded me with a twisted scowl. "Funny till the end. You think your life is a comedy, Cisco, but it's not. It's a tragedy."

The jinn yanked the knife from my belt and slid the bronze blade cleanly across my throat. My enchanted skin kept the swipe from opening up half my neck, but warm blood rushed over my skin nonetheless. I opened my mouth to scream but the gurgle only forced out more blood.

The lights winked out and returned with a red tint.

Backup power. The submarine hull flexed loudly and screeched. Pipes burst. Alarms went off as the hull was breached. Crewmen screamed. Water rushed in from the bulkheads. The control room devolved into wild rocking and chaos.

And I melted to the deck, clutching the life spilling from my throat.

Chapter 41

Damp soaked my being. It washed right through my flesh and bone, flooded my skull, and breached the depths of my subconscious. Somewhere, there, I was one with the ocean. With the afterlife.

Cisco Suarez was dead. (I think that makes it three times, but who's counting?)

My head twitched. Trickles of water glazed my hair. I was absolutely soaked, lying in a warm bath of Caribbean water with my head on the sand.

Distant gunfire pierced the vast swells of sleep that layered my brain. Screaming. Fighting. It was madness and peace, all at once. Dead people weren't supposed to be disturbed. I blinked lazily, letting the world fall into focus.

I was on a beach, prostrate in gently lapping waves. I pushed up to my hands and knees. My head cleared. My body ached from being knocked around, but it was dulled by the otherworldly nature of this place. The pestilence that had invaded my bloodstream was gone completely.

I shook the water out of my ears and crawled to dry land. I stood and stumbled. The coolness of the sand penetrated my socks. This was sand untouched by the sun.

My fingers ran along my throat. The skin was smooth,

without a wound. Half buried by my feet was the ceremonial bronze knife. I plucked it from the sand and wiped the blood away.

The Nether wasn't a place of spirit like the Aether, but this was very different. I'd been to the Nether before. It's a complex and political landscape of half humans and warring kingdoms. But this wasn't *that* Nether. This was a revered underworld. A place for the dead.

Had I died and gone to Coaybay? Or had the spell worked?

More screaming tore through the dark serenity. It seemed so far away. Easy to ignore. Instead I took in the vast ocean. The troubled sea and black sky merged seamlessly into an endless horizon. Impossible to separate. Impossible to escape.

A quarter mile down the coast was Connor's submarine. It was beached and cracked in half. Bodies of crew members lay scattered, thrown from the wreckage. Black, brown, white—there was no pecking order in death.

I scanned the beach in the distance. It was barren. The coastline sand quickly gave way to a dense jungle. Somewhere within, soldiers hollered in panic.

I carefully made my way toward the sub wreckage. I wasn't tired or cold. In fact, I wasn't even wet anymore. Maybe this was a spiritual place, after all. I could feel the shadows bolstering me.

Halfway to the sub I knew I wouldn't find anyone on board. Not alive anyway. A wide swath of footprints trampled through the sand and into the tree line. Connor and his men. It looked like the Spanish conquistador was going on one last expedition.

Two red boots protruded from the sand on upside-down feet. A hunk of a giant propeller had flattened the rest of the Russian into the beach. I tugged my boots off the corpse, shook the sand out of them, and slipped them on.

As I did, the cries of hundreds of bats consumed the sky. The spirits of the Taíno dead were returning to their underworld for the night. The entire colony rushed straight over my head and disappeared past the dense canopy. I sensed my destination would match theirs. Cisco Suarez was going jungling.

If the coastline was barren the tropical jungle was anything but. Iguanas scurried up trees. Birds fluttered in alarm. Small mammals gave each other chirps of warning. I was surrounded by life of sorts. And more.

Strange things. Black wisps that snaked and twirled through the air like streamers. I could spot them in my peripheral vision, but when I zeroed in on them they vanished. And now, I realized, I wasn't just surrounded by life, but by death as well.

It was an odd feeling. Exotic, yet somehow familiar. I wasn't quite sure what to expect but I was comfortable taking it in. Maybe it was the eternal darkness blanketing this world. A shadow charmer could never complain about that.

Distressed footfalls tore through the foliage. I lowered to my haunches on instinct, darting my eyes to the source. A mercenary, muttering and crashing through branches. Coming right at me. He stepped into my clearing and his eyes widened. He raised his automatic weapon and fired.

I didn't move. I fell into the darkness, becoming a presence on the jungle floor, visible but impalpable. The

barrage of lead shredded the thick leaves behind me until
the gun clicked empty.

I hardened my eyes and stood. "Where's Connor?"

The merc threw the gun to the floor and drew a combat
knife. He advanced slowly but sloppily. He was panicked. In
a rush. He slashed at me. I sidestepped. He spun to come at
me again. I wrapped the shadow around his neck and
yanked him toward me. At the same time, I batted my open
hands into his knife arm. His own blade dug deep into his
chest. I tossed the man to the ground.

Fresh blood painted my hands. Living, breathing
humans in Coaybay. That meant I wasn't dead. That all but
guaranteed Connor wasn't either.

I hunched over the dying mercenary. His breaths came
heavily. He'd been running from something, and it wasn't
his own people. I considered interrogating him but his eyes
glazed over. I frowned and opened the small sack over his
shoulder. Ripe green guava fruits spilled to the ground.

I pulled my own knife. The voodoo instrument. I cut a
guava in half. Rich juice flowed over my fingers. Part of me
figured these were just rations for the expedition, but
another part suspected more.

Guava was associated with death in Taíno culture. The
ghosts of the dead transform to bats and leave Coaybay
every night to feast on the Caribbean fruit. Hell, the god of
Coaybay, Maquetaurie Guayaba, was named after it. The
Lord Without Life gives the spirits his blessing to leave
every night, so long as they return. With that kind of
cultural significance, guava was probably a sacrament of
some sort. A spell token burnt up in the acquisition of
magic.

Strange. I looked around the jungle and didn't see a lot of guava. The fruits I did see were withered and yellow. These must have come from the ship. From topside. As I scanned the trees, what I saw looking back at me froze me solid.

A giant, flightless owl stood on the jungle floor. It was absolutely prehistoric. Long, scaled legs ending in curved claws. A large brown body. Its head was ashy-faced; a bowl of white against the brown, with two orbs of black carefully studying me.

In my crouch, the terrifying thing was taller than I was. At first I didn't move, but then I slowly rose to my feet, letting the knife hang limply in my hand.

The owl let out a stern hoot, turned, and sped off along the ground.

I breathed a sigh of relief. Something about the bird's face struck me as familiar, but I was happy to see it go nevertheless. I didn't feel safe hiding in the trees anymore. I pushed ahead through the dense growth.

The path the excursion had taken was easy to follow. A wide tunnel of chopped branches and vines. A large contingent. Even though much of the crew had perished in the shipwreck, there were still far too many to take on alone. Of course, none of that mattered if they were far ahead of me. I had to catch up to them first if I had any hope of stopping the jinn.

After some light hiking, the jungle cleared as quickly as it had begun. Its tree line ran along the inner portion of the island, a wall to a hidden sanctuary. Wide slopes of wild grasses and ponds gave way to more arduous terrain in the distance. On the plains in between, a sight of horror played out before me.

Men as black and featureless as shadow streamed through the sky on leathery wings. The wings weren't dragon-like. Different from the feathers I imagined Malik sported. These were mammalian wings. Bat wings.

The beings streamed through the air, brushing the sky with dark lines. They swooped down on the mercenaries below. Russians. South Americans. Caribs. The men rained spurts of gunfire upward but the dark residents of Coaybay were unaffected. Fight turned to flight. Resolve turned to fear. Blood painted the fields. The *Agua Fuego* cartel was being obliterated. Mowed down by the arbiters of the underworld like white blood cells fending off foreign invaders.

A strange thing happened to the mercenaries when they fell. As arbiters attended to the bodies, blue pillars of light broke through the sky and dissolved their essences. The soldiers vanished, ascended to the heavens. This was an underworld, sure, but it was a holy place for the Taíno. The mercs didn't belong here. They couldn't remain.

I watched from the edge of the jungle as shadows gathered around me. Three arbiters converged, standing upright on the ground. Up close I could see they weren't really featureless. Within the magic that cloaked them were Taíno men and women. Soldiers with painted lines of red over their faces and chests. Defenders wielding spears and stone hatchets.

Their empty white eyes considered me a moment. Then their faces softened. The arbiters faded back into their magic and took to the air, searching for more intruders.

As with the owl, this unsettled me. I was technically an

intruder as well. A living man. A descendant of a conquistador, no less.

But in spite of all that, the humid air seemed to warm me. To welcome me.

It was a strange feeling.

The comfortable familiarity I had with this place. The approval of the arbiters. This feeling wasn't just a feeling. I had been here before.

Ten years ago, when I had been dying at the hands of Tunji Malu and the Covey, I'd cast a powerful spell on myself. A last-second gambit. The Wings of Night. Instead of letting death take me, I embraced it. My soul sprouted ethereal bat wings and fled to Coaybay. In the meantime I had abandoned my body. It was abused and used as a mindless hit man.

The Wings of Night was a spell I shouldn't have known. One I had never been taught. One I shouldn't have had the power to cast. Even now. But it had been real. I'd been dead and my soul had been in exile for ten long years.

This was the living proof of where I'd been hiding. The Taíno underworld, Coaybay.

I scanned the emptying fields. Men scrambled into the jungle, looking for escape. I ignored them and made my way into the open, along the main path of footprints. Despite the appearance of the arbiters, most of Connor's men had been able to forge ahead. Their tracks didn't lie. I followed the trampled grass as it skirted the hill, taking the path of least resistance.

I still wasn't sure what Connor was doing, but I was getting closer to finding out.

Chapter 42

I pursued the expedition, hoping it didn't have more than an hour's head start. Probably half that, given the presence of panicking mercs. Even as I sprinted past them, a Russian tumbled to the floor and swiped at an arbiter with his knife.

I didn't help. I didn't slow. I didn't bother. I sprinted ahead, slowly rounding the hill.

The expansive plains sluggishly rotated into view. More expanse. More grass. After a solid ten minutes of chase, I had to slow to catch my breath. Imagine that, a spirit underworld and I still needed to breathe.

I hooked my hands on my hips and took in the landscape ahead and behind. The area was unnaturally quiet. No more *Agua Fuego* soldiers getting slaughtered. I was worried I'd taken a wrong turn.

I slowed my breathing. Calmed my heart. Then I closed my eyes and listened.

Some screaming and gunfire came from the jungle. I tuned that out and listened more deeply. There was something else. The clanking of metal, I thought, echoing over the hills. With my eyes shut, I tried to pinpoint the location. It was difficult because the landscape bounced and muffled the sounds. I rotated my body in place until I was sure I was facing the source. Then I opened my eyes.

I was staring straight up the slope. Just a gentle hill before me, but the terrain quickly grew steeper and rockier. I could chase the expedition the long way around the hill, the way they had traveled, or I could take the mountain pass and cut them off.

I charged up the slope. It quickly grew arduous, but I used the shadow to assist my climb. Little dashes sprinkled between bouts of running and jumping did wonders. The higher I scaled, the wider I realized the base of the mountain was, the more time I knew I was gaining.

I finally made the summit and crossed over. There they were in the distance. A band of explorers pushed through the hills. The head of the contingent was already over the slope and out of sight so I couldn't get a full count of the men. Fifty at least. What I saw them doing was more worrying.

Arbiters gathered around the enemy force but were unwilling to close on them. The Taíno defenders grouped together in frustrated restraint. Every once in a while, leathery wings would take flight. An arbiter would strafe and attempt a quick strike, but the Haitian wights parried the blows with machetes.

These men were protected somehow. The arbiters were aware of some threat, left confused and unsure. Even the few that took action were rebuffed.

It was because of the Spaniard. The arbiters didn't recognize the zombies. The dead. And the necromancers were half dead themselves. Wights, not in full possession of their human faculties. They held some sway in this underworld.

That had been Connor's second modification to the Horn of Subjugation. He'd empowered the Spaniard against the Taíno. Against the very arbiters who were meant to defend Coaybay.

I raced down the mountain side, skipping and slipping and phasing through the darkness. This was what I had long avoided. Fighting my friends. Fighting others under the control of Connor. That had been me once. I'd killed innocents. Even after that, once my mind was clear, I'd stabbed and killed Kita Mariko, herself just a thrall.

I clenched my jaw till my teeth hurt. I couldn't just kill indiscriminately anymore. I wouldn't return to that ever again.

My descent sped up until I caught the tail end of the excursion party. A single wight spied me and broke away, bringing two zombies with her. A lone arbiter saw the confrontation and hovered nearby, unable to take action.

I tried to invade the bokor's connection with the thralls. It was easy to visualize in Coaybay. Easy to see the workings of the dead. But the necromancers were strong here, too. I could see the guiding spellcraft but couldn't break it or seize it for myself.

As the zombies bore down on me, I abandoned that plan.

A tether of shadow snagged one thrall's leg. The other came at me unchecked. He swung. I ducked around him and forced my knife into the back of its neck. In and out and in and out. A series of quick punctures.

The zombie batted me away. The little blade wouldn't do enough damage. Not for a magically animated thing of death. And in the presence of the necromancer, breaking her hold wasn't working. Without my bag of tricks or some cemetery dirt, the zombie would keep coming after me.

Wait a minute. What is a cemetery if not grounds for the dead? The Nether was water and earth. The soil beneath me was real enough.

I sliced open my palm and grabbed a handful of dirt. When the thrall came at me, I shifted past his blow and kicked the back of his knee. He tumbled to his back and I jumped on his chest. I used my knife to pry open his teeth and shoved a fistful of bloody grave dirt into his mouth.

"Shh," I said.

And the thing went to sleep forever.

The wight boiled with rage at the affront. With her other thrall unable to free himself of my shadow, she came at me herself.

I didn't see the clouded eyes or the penetrating rage. I ignored the machete. Instead I saw a young woman in her twenties, thick dreads running to the small of her back, delicate fingers and smooth skin. She could've been a beach model or a surfer or a volleyball player. She was a real person, damn it.

Her large blade came down and I couldn't ignore it any further. I blocked the strike with my forearm and rolled my back into her. My intention was to disarm her but her arm slipped through my hands. She also bit into the back of my neck. I cursed and shoved her off.

Then the arbiter moved in.

Something about the combat or the zombie going down must've triggered his defense mechanism. The shadowy arbiter had been hovering idly, but he finally spotted the danger. He swiped at the wight but she rolled away. Again he struck, but she parried his spear. The woman lurched forward beyond his defense and thrust the machete through the arbiter's chest.

The shadow wailed and stretched until it was nothing more than a black curl. Then it winked out.

Before she could reengage me, I rapped the back of the wight's head with the butt of my shotgun. She fell to the ground, unconscious. Out of immediate danger, I stared wordlessly at where the arbiter had been. He was there no longer.

The gravity of this expedition was dawning on me. This was Connor Hatch, not only bolstering himself against the spirits, but defeating them. Oppressing them. Conquering the Taíno all over again.

Everything I knew about the Spaniard was that he deplored forced service. When my sister had been taken by a soul catcher, the wraith spat at the mention of the santero who'd been robbing souls from graves.

But how much did I really know about the Spaniard? How much could I really trust? Subjugation had been his cruelty. He was cursed with it now. Maybe forever.

The last zombie growled at me, dumbly tugging against a shadow he could never break. I packed more dirt into my hand and dispelled him as well, leaving me alone on the hillside.

I walked listlessly over the next peak. I crouched and wiped the sweat from my brow as I watched the full force of Connor's men marching toward the center of Coaybay. There must've been a hundred of them. Chevalier and his Bone Saints and their dead. Haitians and former crew, South American and Carib zombies. Some of the cartel were still alive even. They huddled toward the center of the pack with their useless automatic weapons, using the rest of the force to shield themselves from the native threats.

Connor and the Spaniard marched at the head of the expeditionary force, bold and unafraid. Almost all powerful in this place.

Look at them all. Many of them were innocents. Even ignoring that, there were too many. Too damn many. The arbiters themselves could do little more than watch. And yes, the few who grew too brave were viciously put down.

I buried my face in my hands for a moment. Then I hissed and took to my feet. I wouldn't wallow in hopelessness now. The truth was: there was nothing I could do. No way I could overcome such a superior force. But that didn't mean I had to accept it either. Even if death was the outcome, I could fight.

All I needed was an opening. A plan.

I followed after them, adrenaline wiring my nerves. My mind raced. I was desperate and I didn't care.

On the lower ground, where the soil was damp from pond water, I saw more proof of life in Coaybay. Feline footprints lightly pressed into the ground. Small. Domesticated. The trail led away from the expedition and into a nearby swamp.

"It can't be," I said.

I reluctantly broke off my chase and followed the animal prints. Another patch of jungle rose before me. Wet mangroves and swamp brush. Under the tangle of aboveground roots, a black cat with green eyes gazed my way.

And he wasn't even burned up a little.

Chapter 43

"You're not dead," I said to the cat.

He spun on his paws and dashed into the brush.

I rolled my eyes. "Good to see you too, little buddy."

I traipsed after him, knowing he'd wait until I caught up before leading me further. The cat was flighty and cautious and mysterious as hell, but I believed he held no ill will toward me. He was a guide of sorts. Random. Haphazard. I wondered if there was any meaning to it whatsoever, but I knew he wouldn't hurt me.

The trees grew taller. They bent and twisted over my head. The already dark landscape became more bleak and suffocating. My alligator boots splashed in deepening water. A black lagoon stretched before me. The shoreline was infested with roots. It was difficult to traverse yet still, every now and then, I caught a glimpse of the stray cat. And I followed.

The darkness grew into a smothering black haze. There were no swamp creatures in these parts. No life splashing in the water. No chirping insects in earshot. The blackness grew too dense even for me, your accomplished shadow charmer. I had trouble walking against it. I was afraid to phase into it for fear of being forever trapped.

When I had pressed as far as I could go, in the center of a small submerged glen, I paused. The leaves were still. The water a flat mirror. Even for an underworld this place was surreal. It was more than a feeling. It was a presence.

From out of the trees emerged a giant dog's head. It was all black, with a body that disappeared into the brush behind. Despite the massive size, the features of the face were compact. A small nose on a medium snout. A tidy mouth that hid the teeth. Piercing black eyes under a somewhat shiny coat. Most striking were the large alert ears standing at attention, each almost the size of the head itself.

The dog showed itself without any aggression, but it commanded my absolute attention. It was a force of nature. And then that force of nature spoke.

"Shadow walker," came the voice. Rather than carry through the air it reverberated in my skull. Both a whisper and a bellow, it hit my being like a geyser. I buckled to my knees and craned my neck away from the being.

I knew exactly who he was. Opiyelguobiran, the Shadow Dog.

My patron.

"Long has your road been to arrive here."

I gritted my teeth under the great weight of his words. I couldn't believe it. Opiyel was a real, sentient being. A patron. A source of magic. A venerable, powerful thing.

And here he was, talking to little ol' me.

"A dog spirit in a cat," I said dumbly. "That was you."

"The only way to guide the living," he returned.

I recalled the day the taxi hit the stray cat on Biscayne Boulevard. It had just been random happenstance. An opportunity for the god to intervene.

"You have been welcomed into Coaybay before. You are needed again."

Welcomed. He said welcomed but I knew he meant invited. I raised my eyes to him. "The Wings of Night were a gift from you," I reasoned.

"Yes," he said. When the Shadow Dog spoke, his mouth didn't move. His face was a near statue except for his liquid eyes and the occasional twitch of an ear.

"Why?"

He snorted. *"Any question so broad will have an equally meaningless answer."*

"I mean why me? Why am I so important? Does this really just come down to the actions of a Spanish necromancer five hundred years ago?"

The Shadow Dog blinked patiently. *"The Spaniard was the father of your line. You thrum with his power. But Taíno power flows matrilineally. The mother of your line was a Taíno woman. Your power stems from them both. And from me. And from others, including yourself."*

Whoa. This was getting deep. My lineage was a bridge between worlds, just as Earth is between the Aether and Nether, just as the Intrinsics are between human and spirit. All my power, all my spellcraft, was based on the opposition of forces produced by a long-distant father and mother. That would make a hell of an episode of *Family Feud*.

"You speak for the Taíno," said Opiyel, *"but you inherited the protections of the Spaniard. He cannot contain you."*

"And you?" I countered. "Why can't you do anything? You and Maque are pretty much gods here."

"Maquetaurie was stripped of his power by the Christians. He is nothing more than a watcher now. An owl. Patron to none."

"And what about you?" I pressed.

Opiyel seemed to smile. *"No one can capture the shadow."*

I thought of the patron's legend. The Shadow Dog. The One Who Cannot Be Bound. He was said to have vanished upon the arrival of the conquistadors. That was why so little was known about him.

"No offense, Opiyel, but if you're still free, why don't you take care of the rogue jinn yourself?"

The Shadow Dog did not waver. *"In life the Spaniard learned a great many talents. Notably how to block Taíno power."*

"But he couldn't overcome the Horn."

"His prison is formidable. The only alternative for an enemy to whom death means not defeat. Eleven shamans constructed the artifact to inhibit his will, but it can be released by the will of the bearer."

"He's a slave," I spat. "He wouldn't be here otherwise. He's been compelled against his will, precisely *because* of what the Taíno did to him."

The black dog's eyes shimmered as he regarded me. *"Then perhaps it is time to rectify that."*

An image flooded my brain. The sealing of the Horn. Gold and copper melted together under fire. Cooled and polished to a sheen. Fire and water. Sharp instruments scrawling symbols of power. The familiar pictographs played across my eyes.

But that was only the preparation of the ritual. A new vision of fire and water rushed through my mind. The image of a screaming man, bound to a stake, burning alive. I knew only a hint of that feeling. What I witnessed now was pure immolation.

When the Spaniard's flesh was blacker than ash, the

shamans carried over a large pot of water steeped with leaves. The entire stake was upturned into the vat. Steam erupted into the sky. The charred corpse was doused in the brew before the vision ended in a flash.

I panted as I recollected my senses. Visions from gods didn't go down easy. Why had Opiyel shown me that? Why was he speaking to me now?

"What was in the water?" I asked. It was the only coherent question I could think of.

The patron nodded his large head upward. I followed his gaze. Bulbous yellow fruit hung above my head on a low branch. I didn't remember seeing hog plums before, but somehow I knew what they were and how they tasted.

"Take it," insisted the god.

I looked at him strangely but rose to my feet. I grabbed the yellow husk and pulled. A branch broke off in my hand. Two hog plums and several long green jobo leaves. The same leaves the Taíno had steeped the Spaniard in.

"Tributes for the coming trial."

The voice put me on my knees again.

"You may eat one."

I only hesitated a second. At some point, you need to pick sides and trust somebody. I knew who my friends were in the real world. Now I was making a choice in the underworld. I sliced open a hog plum and tasted the pulp.

"It's sour," I said.

"All the fruit in Coaybay is. That is why the dead fly to your world at night. They partake of the sweet guava, just as the living must take in the sustenance of the hog plum if they are to survive in the land of the dead. The fruits are a bridge between life and death."

"A bridge between life and death," I repeated.

"Two worlds: one sweet, one sour. Life and death are in everything. Maquetaurie Guayaba knows this. The guava ripens and falls from the tree. It decays and grows rotten. Yet the seeds gestate and begin life anew."

The Shadow Dog paused, lending significance to his next words. *"Death is inseparable from life. You must trade one for the other."*

I bit into the fruit and took in his words. They made a sort of esoteric sense, but I couldn't tell if they were just poetry.

"What about Connor? He controls the Horn now, whether he holds it or not."

"You must stop the ritual."

"What ritual? I still don't know what Connor's truly getting at."

The Shadow Dog turned his head as if watching far-off events unfold. Maybe he was. *"The jinn seeks the same as ever. Service."*

"Subjugation," I countered. "But Coaybay? A jinn in the Nether. It doesn't make sense."

Opiyel turned to me again. The sudden attention was difficult to bear. *"Human spellcraft is a gift from the spirits. Impossible without channeling the Intrinsics. Coaybay is a wellspring of such power. Such spirits. Vast and potent, all under the subjugation of one will."*

Holy shit. Connor was seeking to channel human magic. The reserves of loyal spirits, long dead. Except he was doing it by enslaving the entire Taíno underworld. Vast and potent was right.

I growled. (I think the dog appreciated that.) "He has to

be stopped."

"This is what you are meant to do, shadow walker. This is your purpose."

"And yours? Will you fight with me?"

Opiyel sighed. *"That is not my purpose. That is for the arbiters, as you call them."*

"The arbiters are getting the unholy shit kicked out of them," I pointed out. "They can't intervene. In case you haven't noticed, I can't do a whole lot by myself either."

His answer resounded in my head. *"That is where you are wrong."*

My back seized up for a second. Then (I shit you not) real, no-joke bat wings sprouted from my back. The shadows extended and folded over my shoulders. Clothes grew and cloaked me like armor. I watched as ashen lines ran up along the back of my arms and fingers. A surge of power like I'd never felt before rushed into me.

"The Wings of Night," I said in reverence. "You're gifting them to me again."

A snort escaped Opiyel's snout, more a laugh than anything else. *"Once you have the black wings, shadow walker, you never lose them."*

The Shadow Dog pulled back into the trees. The darkness closed around him so completely he was gone within a second.

"Wait," I cried, shooting to my feet.

The jolt of power storming through my muscles propelled me into the air. I crashed through the branches and overhead canopy. I launched straight up into the sky. High above Opiyel's lagoon. Overlooking the island below. At the apex of my ascent, shadowy wings snapped to full extension with the sound of a hundred cracking whips.

Cisco Suarez was fucking flying.

Chapter 44

I scanned all of Coaybay with heightened senses. It wasn't just my vantage in the sky. There was a distinct sense of touch involved. I could almost feel the anguish of the island's inhabitants. Like the arbiters themselves, I felt the great coming threat.

An ominous wind buffeted my wings. A storm was moving in, bringing choppy water and dark clouds thick with moisture. Waves crashed ashore. The jungle walls swayed. A deep rumbling echoed from somewhere distant.

I turned my attention downward. I still held the spare hog plum branch. I kept it and glided above the landscape, over the hillside Connor had marched through. Over to the far side of the island. According to legend, this was where the dead congregated. They were Connor's endgame.

As I rounded the highest mountain, the invading army came into view. My extra-sensory sight zoomed impossibly close to the main attraction. A cave nestled into the base of the mountain. Clear shallows ran from the open mouth in a wide circle like a lake. The army stood in formation around the cave, the water barely at their knees.

Undead soldiers marched the inhabitants outside. Taíno locals, dead themselves. Unlike the arbiters, the souls of the dead appeared flesh and bone—strapping muscles, black tattoos—except for an unmistakable difference. Their faces were so blurry as to be indefinable. It was like they had no faces at all.

The zombies forced the captives to kneel in rows in the shallow water. Chevalier mindlessly barked orders and organized the affair. Already there must've been a hundred Taíno on their knees.

Connor Hatch chuckled at the sight before him. Service. This was the heartstone times a thousand. Was it possible to actually harness all that power?

The Spaniard drifted at the jinn's side, shining armor and all. A few human mercenaries followed them with leather sacks. The Bone Saints encircled the entire scene, many staying out of the water entirely. They kept eyes of warning on the neutralized arbiters at the outskirts.

The clouds gathered around me as the sky itself grew angry.

"Just like old times," said Connor to the conquistador. "Except instead of providing gold and cotton, this is a tribute of raw, unbridled power."

The Spaniard's eyes flared. Connor nodded to one of his men. The mercenary dragged over a sack, reached in, and handed Connor a guava. The jinn snickered and smashed it to a pulp in his hand. He approached the first Coaybay resident and traced a symbol on his chest. He then placed a burning palm over the symbol. The native yelped. When the ifrit pulled his hand away, the mark was seared into the man's flesh.

Connor stepped to the next subject, held out his hand, and accepted another fruit. One by one, Connor was subjugating the helpless spirits, and the only one on the entire island who could do anything about it was me.

I set my wings and roared through the sky. The speed and sound created in my vacuum were that of a jet. Hundreds of heads below turned up to see me streak through the smoky sky. I landed in the center of the shallow lake on my hands and knees, wings outstretched above me.

The entire island shook. The force sent the water away from me in a ring. It knocked some people over. It washed over Connor's open palm and put out the fire. It even crashed into the ranks of wights on dry land.

That wasn't all of it. The ground continued to shake and shift. Everyone still on two feet widened their stance and braced themselves. The earthquake rent the land for a good seven seconds before calming.

Slowly, I pushed to my feet. Thunder rumbled in the distance. The Wings of Night folded around me. The earth settled. The waves returned my way, gentler and shallower than before.

"Connor Hatch," I pronounced loudly, "I demand your full, undivided attention."

His eyes burned. Such a brazen show of force enraged him, but it did something else too. A chord of fear echoed through his hand. Just a tremor. A jinn known for his reserve was losing his temper.

"Tear him apart!" he screamed at the top of his lungs.

The *Agua Fuego* mercs were the only soldiers of sound mind and body. They were the first to act. Not only did they immediately take offensive positions, but they were armed with automatic weapons. Assault rifles, machine pistols, and cannons with slower firing rates but heavier loads.

The rush of power flowing through my blood was intoxicating. I had so much confidence that all I did was walk straight at the unit of gunmen.

They opened fire.

Soft-noses. Hollow-points. Armor-piercing. Buckshot. A military-grade barrage of metal came at me like a hurricane, and I smiled.

The projectiles shredded the water around me. Jets of liquid shot into the air. The rock floor of the lake shattered and clouded the water. Bullet after bullet tore right through my shadow armor like I wasn't even there.

Of course it did. What else would you expect of shadow armor?

I didn't even need to phase out of my physical form. I advanced on the mercenaries as their fire kept coming and I laughed. And then I broke into a sprint.

The men couldn't believe it as I broke their ranks. I jutted an Uzi upward and made a South American blow his own head apart. I spun with the weapon and took down several Russians. When my mag ran dry I snatched a Kalashnikov from the water and fired it wet, mowing through the Carib drug runners. I cycled through their own weapons, man after man, and filled the lake with red.

Of course, there was a lot more going on.

The wights rushed in from the perimeter, coming at me from all sides. Leading the charge were their pets. Zombies. They might've been dead, but they sure as hell didn't belong here.

In my heightened state, I could feel that now. Somehow, the water at my feet rippled out to them. Through them. I sensed strains of the Spaniard's magic, the same that infected the wights. The zombies weren't directly controlled by the wraith—they just had the scent of him.

It was time to wash away that veil.

A shadow burst at the feet of the nearest zombie. The water rolled up with it, taking hold of her. The dead woman fought against the bloody water, but it clutched her tight. My spellcraft weaved through rotten flesh. Rather than attack the voodoo that animated her, I struck the curse that veiled her presence. With a single splash, the zombie was announced to all of Coaybay as an interloper. The arbiters narrowed their white eyes and swooped in. Several passes chunked the zombie into inert body parts that sizzled and dissolved in the lake.

The attack stunned the wights. Suddenly the arbiters had teeth. The Bone Saints weren't in immediate danger from them, but they had to consider the new battlefront.

Amidst the confusion, drops of rain began dotting the lake with ripples.

I raised both hands and drew in the darkness, sucking it into my every fiber, drawing it from the sky and the ground and the Nether itself. I reached through the falling water that soaked everything in sight. Then I flashed my palms out and ten shadows burst from the water and lanced as many zombies. They, too, were washed bare. More arbiters took to the air with raised hatchets.

And so it went. Thrall after thrall fell before getting near me. The damage I inflicted stymied the advance of the Bone Saints themselves, but whenever a bold wight neared, I erected a wall of shadow and forced them backward out of the lake. My omnipotence was so realized it felt like playing

Doom in god mode. I shoved and froze incoming threats at will, letting the arbiters clean up the scraps.

Every single corpse, previously living or dead, was attended by the ghostly protectors of Coaybay. I'd seen it before but, up close and surrounded by it, it was awesome. A single strike rended a hole in the sky where a blue column of light ate away the physical remnants of the intruders.

I punched. I shoved. I bowled through the battlefield. During the chaos, the earth rumbled again. It was an aftershock and a light show to go along with the most brutal Armageddon mosh pit ever.

My bloodlust abated as the scene cleared. The Taíno were still on their knees in neat rows. Connor held the bag of guavas himself now. The entire battle, he'd been enlisting more subjects to his cause, like he could just cut and run and keep whoever he'd marked. But his army was in tatters now. The mercs were shredded. The undead, dead. The Bone Saints were the only group unscathed. I'd shoved them away in lieu of killing, and the arbiters still had trouble breaking their defenses. I was happy with that stalemate. It kept them out of my hair.

The rain was beating down now. Streams of water rolled across the outskirts and joined the shallows. A coming flood. I leaned forward and skidded across the surface of the water. A wake fired up on either side as I passed. I was my own personal Jet Ski. Connor spun around in time for me to catch him in the chest. I took him down hard under the surface.

I wanted to end this. To bury him right here and now. He rolled and bucked against my strength, but it was more than just my strength now. I was a defender of Coaybay, cloaked and anointed. Even a jinn couldn't shrug that off. His arms beat against me as I held him below the surface.

"The great Connor Hatch," I mocked, "drowned in a foot of water."

A single explosion capped off at my side. Black powder, unlike any I'd heard before. The puzzle teased my overclocked mind for milliseconds before I felt the ball pierce the shadow armor and enter my gut. I attempted to dive away but I'd already been hit. I tumbled to my side in a splash. Connor resurfaced and gasped for air.

The Spaniard stood firm with one arm extended, a worn glove wrapped tight around his matchlock pistol. My hand, at my side, came away with warm blood.

Chapter 45

The rain battered the three of us in the center of the valley.

"I can't let you do that, brujo," said the wraith. Fresh smoke curled around the barrel of his pistol.

I put pressure on the wound and regained my feet. My alligator boots sloshed in the shallows. Connor coughed for air and crawled away. I had to ignore him for now. I flanked away from him and toward the wraith, keeping my eyes on him, readying my shield.

"We both know you don't have time to reload that," I groaned between clenched teeth.

"True enough," he conceded. The Spaniard hitched the weapon back to his belt and drew his side-sword. It was a straight blade. A workmanlike predecessor of the rapier. Not as thin or ornamental, but with a similarly rounded handguard. The conquistador swiped the air twice, getting the feel for the weapon again.

I'd seen the Spaniard duel with that blade only once before. In my brief visit to the Murk, a land of spirits that mirrors our world. A poltergeist had dogged me for days, growing more and more powerful by the hour. The Spaniard had cut him down with a single swipe.

"It doesn't have to come to this," I urged. "We were

allies once."

"That ended the moment you laid the Horn at Connor's feet."

"I'm here to get it back. I'm here to free you."

The Spaniard raised his sword to my face. "That is not the will of my master."

He swiped across my neck. I jolted backward with heightened speed. The maneuver was easy, actually, but the Spaniard wasn't rebuffed. He dashed forward with me, slashing several times in quick succession. I dodged each one but the last. A well-timed blow came down hard toward my head at the end of my stride. I held up my left forearm and the side-sword struck the tattoo. The marking flared to life and the clang of metal echoed through the valley.

But the wraith, ever familiar with my technique, slid the blade down my arm and caught the end of my shoulder. His spiritual sword cut into a black wing before I could pull away. Pain shot through me. The wound threatened to dislodge my magic. The Spaniard was attempting to clip my wings.

As I had done in the Aether, I folded the darkness into a blade that extended from my hand. Purple and black energy throbbed into my own shimmering sword. I brought the point into the air and held it firm against my opponent. If the Spaniard's barren skull had eyelids, they'd have been wide open right now. We measured each other for a long moment.

He feinted to one side and then spun away and attacked the other. My shadow blade deflected his strike. I pulled him to the side, using his momentum to draw him off balance. The maneuver was executed well enough, but it was difficult to unseat ghostly apparitions who had no need to stand on the ground.

For my part, I had reflexes like never before. Slash, thrust, parry—I matched the Spaniard in a well-choreographed bout. Our weapons clashed and scraped in beautiful staccato. All the while, I kept watchful attention on Connor Hatch.

He listed on his hands and knees as he surveyed the battleground. His cartel was decimated, the zombies torn asunder. The arbiters strafed and struck at the Bone Saints, but the wights still possessed the power of the Spaniard. Their curses weren't so easy to wash away. They fended off the natives with ease.

And then there were the Taíno. Without the army bending them to mercy, some scrambled to their feet and made for the safety of their cave. Jean-Louis Chevalier rounded up some unfortunates and herded them back in place, but they were slipping through the cracks.

Connor was witnessing his power shaken.

Then there was me going toe to toe with his secret weapon. Swords clashed in the rain, each deflection a reminder of my own power.

The jinn started laughing like a madman.

"You think all my planning undone?" he raved. "You think I care for the human lives you destroy?" Connor pulled himself out of the water and balled his hands into fists. The moisture steamed off him as he burst into flames. The sudden fire reminded me of the vision of the Spaniard being burned at the stake.

Except, I knew, ifrits couldn't burn.

Connor screamed and yelled as the flames grew around

him. Not just up his arms but down his whole body. The water boiled. His hair and beard pulsed with energy. He was going full Super Saiyan.

"Let them all die," he screamed. His voice raked through his throat. "Let them all burn in this Taíno hell. I can buy a new boat. I can hire new help and find new necromancers." Connor paused, madness in his eyes. "And I can kill you as many times as it takes, Cisco Suarez."

Fire pulsed in his hands. A sword of his own extended, this one pure flames. It was a large two-handed number. It looked like a holy weapon from the crusades bathed in hellfire. A beautiful paradox.

I batted the Spaniard's side-sword away and rolled to meet Connor's incoming blow. The heavy overhead strike attempted to cleave me in two, but shadow met fire in full force. The entire valley flashed.

As we held our blades together, the wraith advanced on me. I erected a wall of darkness but he passed through it with barely a hand wave.

I clenched my jaw and sapped more of Opiyel's power. Here, in his world, it was plentiful. My sword grew another blade, downward, like a staff with blades on either end. I kicked Connor in the stomach to buy some room and spun the weapon horizontally around me to keep them both at bay.

The two of them organized and fought me as partners. Their first strategy was standing at opposite sides of me and closing in unison. I blocked the jinn's claymore with my arm and jutted my staff at the wraith. He knocked the end away. I spun and faced him, swiping him with the far blade. It glanced off the side of his breastplate, leaving a deep scar.

When Connor recovered his slow weapon, I pulled my staff straight back past me and forced him away.

My new power was a temporary advantage, but both my enemies were tacticians. They protected themselves first and foremost and had the endurance to match mine. Their attacks grew more coordinated. Each time we traded strikes, they advanced closer past my guard.

I was mostly afraid of Connor's heavy weapon so I made sure to keep away from it. That framed their next strategy. The Spaniard became a quick study at guessing where and how I would dodge Connor's blows. The trade-off for not receiving a back-breaking strike was allowing several cuts and slashes into my armored wings. The shadow armor, the arbiters, even Opiyel—none of us could easily shrug off the jinn and the wraith. Alone they were strong. Together they were... winning.

Despite being an open valley, the battlefield quickly grew claustrophobic. I ducked the wraith's sword and spun my staff in an arc. At the end of my twirl, I feinted at Connor with a thrust. Instead of going for a stab, I pulled back and swiped the strap around his neck. The Horn leaped through the air and into my hands. Then I spread my wings tall and wide and shot into the sky.

"It will do you no good, Cisco!" yelled the jinn, staring up at me. The distance between us grew. A jinn, stripped from the sky. It was like he'd said. He must've hated not being able to fly.

The wraith was a different story. He ascended after me, leading with his side-sword.

"This isn't you!" I called after him. "You hate forcing souls into service. That's against everything you learned in your prison."

"What do you know?" he snapped.

Our blades clashed. Thunder cracked in unison. The roiling clouds all around us lit up with electricity.

"The soul catcher. You hated what he did. What he represented. Connor seeks to steal power the same way. Instead of a glass jar, he's entrapping the entire island."

The Spaniard alternated strikes. High, low. Left, right. "You forget, brujo. I have no choice but to comply."

"Only as long as you lack free will."

I batted the wraith's sword to the side and kicked my boots off his breastplate, creating distance between us. Then I gripped the gold plating that sealed the Horn's end caps. The Spaniard's ashes were inside the artifact. All I had to do was get them out. I clawed at the seal with shadow, but the Taíno gold was impervious.

The Spaniard closed the distance between us and slashed. I dove below and swooped around him at breakneck speed. He could take to the sky, perhaps, but I was the only one that could fly.

Below, Connor growled and let his claymore disintegrate to sparks. "Give me your magic!" he screamed to the marked Taíno shamans.

Connor held his arms outstretched and the fire roared around him. It tinted a harsh red. An unnatural hue. A foreign sun. Hellfire. The jinn's feet lifted from the water as he drew slowly skyward, like his shah master.

"Yes!" he growled. "Give it all to me!"

I worriedly parried another of the Spaniard's strikes. As our swords pushed past our faces, I washed my hand through the blood in my gut and caught the wraith's throat.

His skull snapped back and his eyes flickered. My blood sizzled as I tightened my grip around the Spaniard's neck bone.

"Ahh!" he rasped.

My knee shot up, bolstered by shadow. It dented the bottom of his breastplate. The wraith doubled over in the sky. I dissipated the bottom half of my weapon so I could spin my sword around quickly and swipe it upward. The shadow tore through the conquistador's leather gauntlet. He released his side-sword. The blade fell through the sky and embedded itself into the rocky lake floor.

With my opponent still reeling, I rolled the sword in my hand and brought the tip to the center of his breastplate. The Spaniard's red eyes grew full and bright.

I held the pose for a long second.

I released his throat and decked him with my sword hand. The wraith flew backward through the growing mist.

"Cisco!" bellowed Connor.

I spun and saw him below me, floating ten feet off the ground. He was glowing crimson now. Channeling Taíno magic, joining it to his. The powered-up jinn was so hot the raindrops sizzled before they touched him.

"It's time you witnessed the power you helped me get," he said.

He clapped his hands together and a supernova exploded from his palms.

All my hairs stood on end. I immediately dismissed the shadow sword and positioned a barrier of darkness between us. I fired up my shield of brilliant turquoise. I even folded my wings around my body and face.

A red beam of light, eight-feet in diameter, struck me. It

was a laser, touching his hands and the clouds all at once.

The hell beam completely engulfed me. It obliterated my defenses. Raw Intrinsics bowled through me like a freight train riding a shockwave. My shadow wall evaporated. My shield sparked out uselessly. And my Wings of Night burned.

I, too, fell from the sky. A comet, beaten and battered from traveling millions of miles through space and time, worn out from collision after collision, burnt up by the atmosphere, and flailing, my last seconds of life spinning and out of control, my last act of note forming a crater in the ground.

This time when I landed, I shook with the earth.

Chapter 46

Tossed under the encroaching waves, I would've been swept away if not for the embedded side-sword protruding from the surface. I clutched the hilt for stability.

My wings rested at my sides, frayed and smoking, the water a comforting reprieve. I shook my head, feeling the shadow slip in and out of my grasp. Dazed and down.

That had been a hell of a blast.

Connor Hatch laughed and floated above me. "Get them ready," he ordered Chevalier. Some wights had managed to break away from the arbiters. The Taíno were forced into place again. Silently, the Spaniard drifted back to his master's side.

I looked down at my hands, no longer gripping a shadow sword but holding something much more powerful. The Horn of Subjugation.

"It's no matter," said Connor. "You may hold the Horn, but I own its undeniable power." His hands glowed crimson again as he readied another debilitating strike.

I didn't raise my defenses this time. Instead I held the Horn up to shield my body. "Would you risk destroying the source of such power?"

The jinn paused. He realized his predicament. If he

immolated me, scorched me from existence, I would take the Horn with me. Without the Spaniard, without control of the wights and protection from the arbiters, he would lose his hold here. He already had twenty shamans in his service, but many more potential subjects surrounded him.

Even if Connor could cut and run, make it out alive and take those twenty with him, was he willing to limit his potential by destroying the Horn early?

The jinn laughed. "Well played, Cisco. But you hold an impotent piece." He signaled for the bag of guavas. Chevalier scooped it from the water. "The Horn can never be taken from me now." He turned to the Spaniard. "Dispatch him."

The wraith drifted my way.

I panted in the water, all but defeated. The rain stung against my face. A single branch drifted by on the rushing current. The hog plum washed into my lap. Several jobo leaves swayed in the water.

Opiyel's vision came to me again. I imagined the other great powers I'd encountered. The ashy-faced owl in the jungle. The black cat in the Aether. The dragons and the Celestials. Malik had shown me what I needed to see. Not just the greater picture, but the symbol for victory.

As the wraith drew closer, a tropical storm brewed around us.

"You're wrong," I spat back at the jinn. "You showed me how."

Connor's eyes darted to the knife in my hands. No more shadow. No more spellcraft. I held the small bronze blade, useful only for ceremony. I located the pictograph cluster Dr. Trinidad had translated for me. A sun, a man, a bat. A man trapped between life and death. The wraith.

I took the knife to the soft metal and made a scratch across the symbol of man. I shredded the jobo leaves and steeped them in the water with a fistful of blood. A bridge between life and death. I painted the symbol with the magical tribute and pried at the seal.

This time, the gold bent away and the cap opened.

"No!" screamed the jinn.

The Spaniard came upon me and effortlessly pulled his side-sword from the rock with a thunderous scrape. He lifted it above his head in preparation of a lethal blow.

I upturned the powder horn. Chunky ash poured out and was swept into the strengthening wind. We watched the ashes of the Spaniard spread into the sky. They drifted over the hills. They flew into the swirling clouds. They fell into the lake and dispersed.

The wraith paused, sword in hand. He stretched his jaw and locked eyes on me. "Freedom," he said dumbly, confused.

I washed the Horn in the current, making sure no traces of ash remained within. "I keep my promises," I said.

The Spaniard, still stunned, looked down at an open hand. The wind buffeted his tattered rags and he faded into nothing. His armor, his weapons—they all simply vanished.

"No!" yelled Connor again.

The earth rumbled. Rain battered our skin. The wights clutched their temples and fell to their knees. Connor's red fire blazed. He contorted in anger.

In pain.

He'd lost the Spaniard's protection from the underworld. His newfound power, the hellfire—it was burning him alive.

The jinn convulsed and lost his place in the sky. Like a lead weight, he hit the water and landed unceremoniously on his ass. The skin on his face peeled as he twisted in overbearing agony.

"Now you know how it feels," I said, rising to shaky legs. "I wouldn't wish it on any man. Or any jinn. Not even you."

I tucked the Horn into the small of my back and approached Connor, a hog plum branch in one hand and a knife in the other. The ifrit swiped at his face and arms, desperate to free himself from the smothering flames.

"Fire, then water," I said, stopping above Connor. "That's the ritual. Immolation, then dousing."

I curled my fingers into his mane of red hair and forced his head underwater. I submerged his whole body. He shook and struggled against me. The thrashing water kicked up blood and ground jobo leaves.

I stabbed my knife into his back. Bright red blood washed over my fingers. I released the jinn and plucked the hog plum from the branch. I bathed it in Connor's blood and mashed it to pulp in my hands. Connor resurfaced and gasped. He lifted a weak hand and flames sputtered to life in defiance.

"You can't kill me," he rasped.

"Maybe you're right," I admitted. "You don't drown. You don't immolate. Like you said, you're made of magic. You don't have a physical body so I need to give you an analog. An effigy."

I thought of what Opiyel had taught me. I needed death for life. The Spaniard had been death. The jinn was life, forever and everlasting, at least from the perspective of a human.

"You were smart to utilize the guava here. It's an important symbol to the Taíno. Its sweetness is desired by the dead. It represents death. But the hog plum is sour and represents life. Think of this fruit as your body. Eternal life, trapped for all time."

I clutched Connor's burning hand to mine. The hog plum within our grasp charred before I lowered it into the water. The mashed fruit was a paste now, made up of soot and blood and pulp and seeds. Close enough to ashes, I figured. I stuffed the concoction into the Horn and drew shadow magic into it.

The earth rumbled again. We rocked from side to side with another aftershock. The rain bit into us sideways. The wights, ignoring the rising weather, had ceased their struggle and calmed themselves.

"You forget," gloated Connor above the din of the storm. "The Horn is meant to trap a man. I may be exiled, but I'm still a jinn. I'm immune to the artifact's snare."

I smiled coldly and showed Connor my new marking. A human with a line drawn to connect his two legs into a triangle. I hadn't just scratched out the symbol, I'd modified it. Changed it from one meaning to another. It was the same symbol Malik had shown me in the Aether tea house. The same symbol I'd seen on the warning sign in High Valley, banning jinnkind. I'd changed the symbol from a man to a jinn.

The Horn of Subjugation was now a cage for Connor Hatch.

I folded the cap closed. I set the gold wrapping in place and forced it into Connor's still fiery hand. The heat melted and finalized the seal. When I cooled the artifact in the water, the jinn's eyes widened in sudden surprise.

The heavy rumbling in the distance roared closer. A towering flood crashed over the hillside. A tidal wave, caused by the recent seismic activity. The entire valley of the dead was invaded by an avalanche of water. With all our power, we were nothing more than ants against it. Every single person in Coaybay—the Taíno, the arbiters, the Bone Saints, Connor, and myself—were heaved off our feet by the deluge.

I spun and tumbled, losing hold of the world. Losing perspective and place. I gripped the Horn tightly, determined not to lose it, not to leave my business undone. I twisted and rocked and rolled to the ground. The flood was, thankfully, only momentary. The water drained, leaving me on the edge of the hill. The outskirts of the valley. The Horn was nestled in my hand. Connor wasn't in sight.

A hand reached down to assist me. A Taíno inhabitant with a blurry face. His chest carried Connor's brand. The water had washed the fire away. There was only a dull mark now. Like the man's face, it was indistinct.

"Thank you," I said.

The native spoke words I didn't understand. Our languages were foreign. The sentiment wasn't. We understood each other just fine.

I turned and looked over the valley. The rain slowed and sputtered out. The water receded to normal levels in minutes. The clouds rolled away, the rumbling subsided. Everywhere, Bone Saints were rising to unsteady feet. Surveying the land as if for the first time. A line of Taíno regrouped and headed back into their holy cave. No zombies or mercs had been left standing.

I stumbled down the hillside, feeling the anger of the underworld settle. A Haitian man keeled over and choked out water. I grabbed him and pulled him to face me. He had a scar above his eyebrow. His actual eyes were what I needed to see. He wiped the water from them and opened them weakly against the strange world. Clear brown. Not a trace of the Spaniard's fog remained.

It was done. Coaybay was peaceful. Safe. No more threats to the Taíno underworld remained.

The arbiters gathered in formation encircling the valley. Their glowing white eyes contrasted starkly against their shadowy forms. Their attention locked on the Bone Saints. The arbiters raised their spears and hatchets, spread their wings, and launched into the air.

"No!" I shouted, running to stand between the opposing parties.

The arbiters were too fast now. And I too sluggish. They sped high above me. I didn't have my wings anymore. The shadow warriors swooped down on the defenseless men and women, piercing their hearts. Blue columns of light enveloped the Bone Saints.

"Don't kill them!" I yelled. "They weren't in control! They're human again!"

In the distance, Chevalier turned to me. The look of shock and surprise on my friend's face turned to panicked alarm. Arbiters closed around him. Instead of raising a weapon, he raised his palms in defense.

I raced toward him. In my frantic pursuit down the hill, I tripped and rolled. My elbows and knees scraped against rock but I shot to my feet again.

The arbiters struck like snakes. Their weapons bit into Chevalier and the heavens opened above him.

"Shadow walker," boomed a resonant voice in my head.

I folded to the ground under the unstoppable force. I turned to face the Shadow Dog, towering behind me. It was difficult to see his entire form against his words.

"It is done," was all he said.

Then a wave of darkness exploded outward from his being and consumed everything.

Chapter 47

For like the fifteenth time that day, I regained consciousness in a foreign place. Warm water nudged me to and fro, dragging me over sand.

I was still in Coaybay. Dead for good, then. My work complete, I could finally rest.

Rough shaking tore me from my bliss. A muffled voice. I cracked open my eyelids and was assaulted by blinding sunlight. I spasmed in shock.

Not the underworld then. It was daytime. I was back in the Earthly Steppe. Back home.

"Suarez," repeated the voice.

I squinted up at Chevalier. We were on a morning beach. He was kneeling over me, checking my vitals. I pushed his hands away.

"Beached again," I muttered. "It's a pirate's life for me."

"You would make an awful pirate, Suarez. Too many promises to keep."

I rose to my haunches and took in the coast. Twisting mangroves over wild sands. Boats and high rises in the distance. We were in Florida. Probably a natural park along the coast. Secluded but within sight of civilization.

A scene from an apocalypse surrounded us. Dead thralls

and mercenaries rocked in the waves and hugged the coast. All the intruders from Coaybay had been cast out, living and dead. The angelic blue light had expelled us all from the Nether.

There was good in that news, though. The beach was populated by clusters of Bone Saints. They huddled around each other and tended to their wounded. The arbiters hadn't killed them.

I turned to my friend. Checked his silver eyes for signs of fog. I knew I wouldn't find any.

"I remember it only in pieces," he said. "Less at the end. The wraith had nearly drained us."

"But you'll live," I countered. I swallowed dryly. "I'm sorry for putting you and your people through that."

"Some of 'my people' want to kill you."

I curled my lip. "And you?"

"I think you'll get yourself killed soon enough without help from me." We traded a grim stare. "You are a dangerous man, Cisco Suarez."

"Says the head of a Little Haiti street gang."

I studied the Horn of Subjugation in my hands. Its thrum of power was gone. Or different. I couldn't be sure.

"What will you do with it?" asked the bokor.

"It's not a threat to us anymore."

"No," he agreed. "The only threat is you."

Chevalier trudged off to his men. He was bitter, and I could see why. His gang was in tatters. I'd played a dangerous game to protect my family and defeat Connor. I'd opened the Bone Saints up to utter domination.

But it was a threat that had always been there, even without my involvement. I hadn't created the Horn. It was a five-hundred-year-old time bomb just waiting to go off. It was me, after all that time, that put a stop to it. In the long run, the Bone Saints might see that. Chevalier would come around. I couldn't say the same for the rest of the Miami necromantic community.

I watched my friend in the distance, relieved it was over for them. My gaze trailed off to the thick mangroves behind. A pair of red eyes watched me from the shadows.

My face darkened.

The Spaniard wasn't dead, he was loose.

I fought off a shiver and gave him a nod. The barren skull acknowledged me with a dip. Before I could do anything else, the wraith vanished. That was kind of his thing.

It was a new day. A bright morning. I had high hopes things would finally be back to normal, but I wasn't quite there yet. My work wasn't yet finished. I watched the clear sky over the horizon and felt an echo of the rumbling from Coaybay.

Maybe it was just me.

Chapter 48

The passage was long and dark and winding. Dirt walls joined over my head in a tangle of roots. I was in the Nether again, but this place wasn't nearly as exotic or mysterious as Coaybay.

I knew of several rabbit holes in Miami, ones that didn't require elaborate rituals to enter. I'd taken one down to this steppe to wander. I was in the margins, the edges of the world that weren't ruled by silvan circles or other factions. These twisting halls were a wild, convoluted maze. Free of politics if not danger.

Little scourgelings skittered at my presence. Chitinous mandibles sniffed the air. They knew I was here. It aggravated the numerous beasts. Normally they'd trail me at a safe distance until they congregated in overwhelming numbers. Then they would strike and feast on my flesh.

But not today. Netherlings were deeply terrified of primal beings and I had one in my pocket. Like Connor had said, he may have been exiled, but he was still a jinn. The underground halls seemed to empty before me. The creatures scattered and begged me to move on.

I walked and walked until the passages grew smaller and more remote. I made my way through the unending darkness. Eventually, I found the perfect spot.

A chunk of limestone bridged the corner of the wall and the floor. Too massive to displace, it had been left as part of the narrowing corridor. I tugged at the powerful shadows to shift the dirt and heft the gargantuan rock out of place. Then I pulled the Horn of Subjugation from my belt.

"Not the Nether," insisted Connor. He stood beside me, minorly bruised and cut up, but not too worse for wear. His flowing red hair and beard seemed too bright for this place. "This subterranean hell is dank and depressing."

I chuckled. "Not a sun or open sky in sight. Imagine that. You might actually get homesick here."

"And what will you do?" he returned. "Abandon me for good?"

"Like a genie in a lamp," I said.

I dug a small hole in the space behind the rock and wrapped a cloth around the artifact. I nestled it snugly in place and covered it with dirt.

This would be Connor's new home now. Isolated and lost. Except finders wouldn't be keepers. Because of Connor's modification to the pictographs, any new bearer of the Horn wouldn't inherit its power. That still came down to my word.

It was a safeguard that wouldn't be necessary. This earthen passage was barren and ill-traveled. Any Netherlings that did come this way would sense a disturbance. They'd avoid this cursed tunnel at all costs.

No, Connor Hatch would be left alone for quite a while.

I finished packing the dirt and considered the spot grimly. "You once told me jinns live interminably long."

Connor's hardened face could do nothing but grimace.

His eyes simmered with inner heat, but his power was contained.

"Think of this as your own private hell," I told him. "A chance to ponder your mistakes for the rest of your miserable life."

A tendril of shadow heaved the limestone back into place. I did my best to make the area appear undisturbed. I turned and marched down the tunnel the way I'd come.

"You'll be back," called Connor, but his voice was weak. Uncertain. "You'll need my power one day and you'll come back to get me."

I let myself smile, finally. An expression of relief as much as joy. I was eager to get out of here.

"Don't count on it," I said and disappeared into the shadows.

-Finn

Acknowledgments

This has been (and still is) a great series to write, and I simply couldn't have done it without my amazing production team who've stuck with me the whole way. Thanks to my editor, Philip Newey, for continually improving my work. Thanks to James Egan for making every cover a work of art. Neil Hellegers deserves high praise for his gritty rendition of Cisco and the cast. Thanks to City of Miami Police Captain Dan Kerr, who I ping from time to time with hard-hitting questions (although he gives me funny looks whenever I ask about jinn politics). Of course, thanks to my wife for putting up with my restless nights scribbling story notes in the dark (she doesn't notice).

Finally, I'd be remiss if I forgot to thank the legion of fans in my reader group. These books are for you. As long as you keep reading, I'll keep writing.

-*Domino Finn*

About the Author

I'm Domino Finn: hardened urban fantasy author, media rebel, and guava paste lover. (Pro Tip: Smear it on Cuban crackers with cream cheese.)

Don't believe the hype. *Black Magic Outlaw* will be back. Join my reader group at DominoFinn.com to get the first word on sequels and cover reveals. And, hey, you can see what else I'm up to.

If you appreciated *Fire Water*, know that your kind words are vital to my success. Really. Please leave a review where you purchased the book, even if it's only a line or two. A few clicks from you go a long way.

Finally, don't forget to keep in touch. You can contact me, connect on social media, and see my complete book catalog at DominoFinn.com.

Made in the USA
San Bernardino, CA
30 April 2017